Copyright © Chris Coppel (2025)

The right of Chris Coppel to be identified as author of this work has been asserted by them in accordance with section 77 and 78 of the Copyright, Designs and Patents Act 1988.

All rights reserved. No part of this publication may be reproduced, stored in a retrieval system, or transmitted in any form or by any means, electronic, mechanical, photocopying, recording, or otherwise, without the prior permission of the publishers.

Any person who commits any unauthorised act in relation to this publication may be liable to criminal prosecution and civil claims for damages.

This book is a work of fiction. Names, characters, places and incidents are either products of the author's imagination or are used fictitiously. Any resemblance to actual events or locales or persons, living or dead, is entirely coincidental.

First published by Cranthorpe Millner Publishers (2025)

ISBN 978-1-80378-283-6 (Paperback)

www.cranthorpemillner.com

Cranthorpe Millner Publishers

Printed and bound by CPI Group (UK) Ltd
Croydon, CR0 4YY

'What would an ocean be without a monster lurking in the dark? It would be like sleep without dreams.'

Werner Herzog

CHAPTER ONE

1940

The residents of the seaside town of Deal had ensured that the laws pertaining to the nightly blackout were closely followed. They hoped that by doing so, it would make it harder for the German bombers to target them. Though not a strategic target as such, the Luftwaffe were known to drop any remaining ordinance that had not successfully been released onto their primary targets over the coastal regions of England, before their return flight to Germany. If they could destroy a rail line or gasworks while doing so, all the better.

Despite all windows being covered and no streetlights having been lit, the villainous moon had chosen to rise full and bright, bathing the south-eastern coast in a pale blue glow.

As the townsfolk huddled within their homes, they could do nothing but pray that any remaining explosives did not find their way down atop their humble little town. Though their fear of the German bombs was, on that night, at the forefront of their thoughts, there was also a new fear that had crept into Deal like a winter fog stealthily enshrouding the coast as the air temperature and dew points converged.

Starting three weeks earlier, something had entered the town.

Something unseen.

Something deadly.

So far it had taken six lives. The police were baffled. All six victims had been found alone in their homes. All six had been viciously attacked by something claw-bearing and of a size that could take down even a strong man. The most horrific aspect of the killings was that the victims had all been disembowelled and their bodies partially consumed.

There was no trace of a break-in at any of the residences and all victims appeared to have been assaulted as they sat or lay, seemingly taken by surprise.

After the first murder, the townsfolk not only blackened their windows at night as required by law, but also took extra measures to lock and barricade themselves within the hoped-for safety of their homes.

Despite the extra caution, whatever it was seemed able to gain access anyway.

*

It waited until it sensed that the town was still – that its occupants were at rest and at their most vulnerable. It moved through the old underground system created by the smugglers of earlier times and stopped at each branch of the rough-hewn tunnel and sniffed at the stale air, hoping to pick up the scent of something alive – something suitable to feed upon.

Halfway under what to the residents was known as Middle Street, it stopped. A smell drifted down from a set of ancient stone steps that led up to a small access doorway. It climbed until its head was only inches from the old timber and sniffed again.

There it was. The tang of human sweat and heat. By its reckoning there was only one human beyond the access door and, judging by the back odour of stale hops and grain, it knew its prey to be incapacitated by the dark, sour-smelling liquid that so many forced themselves to consume.

It had learned early on that it had the ability to change its form from its natural appearance to that of a human male. It had found that by entering a dwelling in the latter cloak, the prey was a little less startled by the intrusion. At the point when it reverted back to its natural self, there was not enough time for the human to even cry out.

As it gently manipulated the old smugglers' door out of the way, it felt the earth above tremble as a dull thud reverberated within the tunnel. It had felt the same thing a few times before, when flying machines high in the night sky seemed to release something from above that caused great shaking, a cacophony of sound, and ultimately, fire.

It was not concerned. Whatever was happening above ground had little effect on the hunt.

The dwelling was in partial darkness. Only the light from an ebbing coal fire allowed it to see the details within the small room. Even had there been no light at all, it would still have been able to locate its prey just by the body heat and human odours.

The male was sitting in an upright chair and appeared to be asleep. As it approached, it could sense that the human was not simply in slumber, but rather, was in a semi-conscious state, probably brought on by the foul liquid.

It determined that in this instance there was no need to maintain the human guise. This made things much easier considering that it couldn't feed properly until it had returned to its canine-like form with its razor-sharp teeth held in multiple rows within its long bristly snout.

The man momentarily stirred as he scratched his nose then slumped in complete stillness as before.

It was mildly disappointed that the human would not be able to show fear before dying as that always made the killing more enjoyable. Still, these night sorties were not for enjoyment.

They were for food.

It slowly rose onto its hind legs until its face was only inches from the human. As it sunk its teeth into the flabby flesh that covered the male's neck, the metallic taste of fresh blood flooded its senses.

It moved down to the man's bloated belly and had just taken its first bite when a high-pitched whistling filled the room. It heard and felt something strike the house only milliseconds before an explosion brought down the upper two floors of the structure. For a moment it felt itself being struck from above, then it felt nothing at all.

*

There was no shortage of volunteers in Deal during an air raid. When 197 Middle Street was hit by the bomb, help arrived within minutes. The fire department managed to put out the flames in record time permitting others to frantically search the rubble for any sign of life. Hooded flashlights were cautiously used to ensure that little of the illumination could be seen by the enemy above.

"Oi!" Sam Little, the town's greengrocer, called out from atop one particular pile of wooden beams and shattered brick. "I think I've found Ben."

Others gathered and immediately helped remove enough rubble so that they could see what was underneath. The men stood in shocked silence. It was obvious that Ben was dead, but what had so startled the volunteers was that his injuries looked unlikely to have come from the bomb blast. His throat and stomach seemed to have been torn open and quite obviously been gnawed by some sort of animal.

It wasn't until they moved more debris aside that they found another body. This one was not human, as could be determined by its elongated snout and a muzzle filled with long, blood-drenched fangs. The most troubling part of the find was that, hanging from the creature's jaws, was a sizeable piece of raw meat tangled up in some sort of material. It wasn't until one of the men recognised the fabric as being from old Ben's favourite sweater that they realised that the lump of raw meat was actually a part of Ben himself.

As they stared at the creature, it started to move. Sam was closest and immediately hit it over the head with what remained of a floor joist.

One of the men began to blow his volunteer's whistle to alert the police, while another headed off towards the marine barracks to see what help they could offer. It was obvious that whatever had been trying to eat their friend was doubtless the cause of the other recent deaths within the small town.

Within minutes the creature started to reawaken. Even before Sam could raise the piece of wood to subdue it for a second time, it launched itself upwards and ripped out the man's throat before disembowelling three other volunteers then charging off into the night.

During the war, the local police constabulary was little more than a few retirees; however, the Royal Marine Corps' non-commissioned officers training operation had moved into the Deal Marine Barracks less than half a mile down the road. Heavily armed and with a lust for vengeance against the Germans, they were more than happy to hunt down the creature in lieu of battlefield action.

Despite an extensive search, they found no trace of the beast that night. But, by the light of the weak morning sun, a trail of blood, assumed to have been the result of its head wound, was found on Middle Street. Using hunting dogs, they were able to track the creature to a small, abandoned farm building on the outskirts of town.

Attempts to gain entry resulted in numerous casualties. Even after they discharged their weapons into the wooden structure and heard the screams from within, the creature – though obviously wounded – lashed out at anyone who tried to break into the premises.

Finally, it was decided that the only course of action was to burn the building to the ground. The old timbers went up in spectacular fashion and the Royal Marines and townspeople watched as the building burned to the ground. After dousing the remnants with seawater, they sifted through the ash and found the charred remains of the creature.

"What do you think it is?" one of the observers asked the others.

"No bloody idea," the nearest man replied. "It looks like a huge dog, but it just seems too big for a dog or even a wolf."

The men decided that the best thing they could do was drag the remains from the burned building and find somewhere safe to store it.

They ended up transporting the corpse in the back of a military ambulance to the town's veterinarian. Doctor Balmer was used to dealing with a wide array of large farm animals and was fascinated by what the men carried into his practice just off Alfred Square.

"Maybe some kind of wolf?" one of them theorised.

"This is not the carcass of anything I've ever seen before. It's got some canine attributes, but at the same time, there appears to be some human similarities as well. This is going to take some research. Why don't you men leave it here and check in with me tomorrow. I would hope to know more after I consult my reference books."

As the hours passed and Balmer's attention remained focused on pictorial refences of large dog-like examples, he didn't immediately notice that the cadaver on the examination table was no longer curled in a foetal position as it had been when it was brought to his surgery.

It was now lying on its side with its front limbs pointed straight out as if it were trying to reach some invisible object.

When Balmer glanced down to compare the shape to one he'd found in his book, he immediately noticed another change. As he stood, riveted, the carcass started twitching. Worse still, a grey-green ooze began to leach from burned, putrid flesh. It only took the doctor a few moments to realise that the creature appeared to be somehow reanimating itself. Too shocked to initially move, he could only look on as the beast started to take shape from the inside out.

It wasn't until it was almost completely re-formed and had fixed its yellow eyes on his that Doctor Balmer finally acted.

When he had gone out earlier that day to put an ailing horse down, he had taken two syringes of phenobarbital with him. One was more than enough to kill just about any four-legged creature, but he had been trained to always carry a spare 'just in case'.

As the creature started to right itself, Balmer plunged the needle into its side and emptied the entire syringe into the monster. It let out a horrific scream and tried to lunge at the human, but the poison was too strong and its effect almost immediate.

The creature fell back onto the table and its living flesh began to putrefy. Gagging and terrified, Doctor Balmer ran screaming out into the square.

CHAPTER TWO

Present Day

Celebrations were in full swing in Deal, a seaside town tucked away in the far south-east of Kent County.

It had been a month since the wreckage of the iconic, tri-masted schooner, the *Lady Lovibond*, was discovered protruding from the Goodwin Sands eight miles off the coast. According to legend, the ship foundered on 13 February, 1748. It was said that the first mate had intentionally grounded the vessel on the Sands during a raging storm, killing all on board. The supposed reason was that the captain had brought his new wife onto the vessel for the journey, a woman that the first mate had secretly been in love with for years. In a fit of jealousy, the first mate decided that if he couldn't have her, nobody would.

What made the legend even more salacious was that since the sinking, the ship had been sighted in the Channel every fifty years, under full sail and emitting an eerie spectral glow.

The accepted reason for the wreckage suddenly appearing on the Sands was that a once-in-a-thousand-year hurricane had rampaged through the English Channel only a few days earlier. As the tide had been low, the top surface of the exposed barrier was swept away revealing layers that had not been seen in centuries.

On the morning after the great storm blew itself out, a resident of Deal, who had just happened to be looking at the Goodwin Sands though a pair of high-powered binoculars, clearly saw something jutting into the air. He exchanged his binoculars for his iPhone and managed to take a couple of half-decent photos that he posted on every social media site he could think of.

Within hours, a small armada of boats headed to sea to check out the mysterious object. The RNLI launched lifeboats from Ramsgate, Deal and Dover to investigate the sighting, but also to keep some sort of control over the hordes who had little understanding of just how dangerous the sandbank could be. Perhaps if they had known that over two thousand vessels had been wrecked upon it, they might have been a tad more respectful of its lethal history.

The tide probably did the most to save the wreck from pilferage. By the time the boats made it to where the remains were protruding from the sand, the tide had begun to turn. The lifeboats spent the following hour using their loud hailers to warn the various small craft that stepping ashore during a flood tide would doubtless result in loss of life. Because the bank became completely submerged at high tide, even the RNLI would not be in a position to help if anyone got in trouble.

Once all the small craft headed back towards shore, one of the ribbed lifeboats was able to bump up onto the sand allowing two members of the crew to approach the wreckage.

What had been visible from the shore turned out to be the remains of a wooden ship's bowsprit, forepeak and figurehead. Though they had been badly eroded, little water damage was evident. The officer in charge of the lifeboat ordered the team to return to their vessel, but just as they started back, one of them noticed something shiny sticking out of the sand. Even as the waves began to lap higher and higher, the crewman managed to extract the object before dashing back to the boat.

The man had found the ship's bell. Though the engraving had also been heavily eroded, it was still legible enough for them to see the name of the vessel: the *Lady Lovibond*.

The wreck attracted global attention. There was something about the boat's age, the mysterious spectral sightings and the doomed, romantic backstory that forced its discovery to the forefront of the public zeitgeist.

Deal became the centre of the media universe as small parts of the ship were carefully transferred back to land. Everyone was holding their breath for the big day when the hull itself would be brought ashore after a mammoth dredging and securing operation.

Apart from the mere size of the venture, it was the danger that kept the salvage team on their toes. Having to work on a wreck that sinks below the surface twice a day during high tide was a nightmare.

The promenade that ran the length of the Deal coast was clogged with video crews from across the globe. Large, chartered media barges lay two miles off the Sands trying to capture anything and everything that was happening on the barrier as the ebb tide began and the newly exposed hull came back into view.

The atmosphere in Deal was one of unhinged jubilance. It was as if everyone had simultaneously decided that the bringing ashore of the *Lady Lovibond* hull was an excuse to turn the town into one wild, seemingly never-ending, party.

In an odd stroke of luck, another event was taking place on the same day – one without the funds for any serious media promotion. At the north-west end of the town, a new tourist attraction was about to have a ribbon cutting to mark its formal opening. Shaft number 57 of the old Betteshanger Mine was being reopened, this time to the public. It had taken three years to dig down from an approved site within the town limits so they could secure the old tunnel. A modern 'touristy' version of the miner's lift had been built and, at noon, guests and visitors would get the chance to travel down over twelve hundred feet so they could partake in a controlled sampling of what the old-time miners had to endure.

The mayor and council had expected a crowd in the low hundreds with media coverage from local radio and, maybe, BBC Kent if they were lucky.

Thanks to the media mass that had gathered in town, they were able to reap the benefits of the serendipitous *Lovibond* event. With the wreck not going to be lifted until high tide at 1:00 p.m., the media that were stuck on shore had little else to do, so had latched onto the mine re-opening story to fill the time.

*

Harry Zain stood at the bow of the massive dredger waiting for the tide change. As engineer in charge of the operation, he knew the risks of trying to dislodge a two-hundred-and-fifty-year-old wreck from a sandy tomb. Harry had, in a previous life, been lead engineer with the Royal Navy's Tactical Submarine Emergency Response Team. He'd seen what creeping sand could do to a submerged hull when a training exercise went badly wrong, or what happened when an Astute Class sub inadvertently nudged a sandbank off the Azores and brought down the better part of an undersea cliff. While the current project was hardly a life-or-death situation (in the case of the sub in the Azores, no lives were ultimately lost), Harry still gave the task the full brunt of his experience and engineering prowess.

The job had been made slightly easier by the Corps of Royal Engineers that had, soon after the first sighting of the *Lovibond*, managed to erect a twelve-foot sea barrier into and onto the sand that surrounded the wreck. This allowed some prep work to be undertaken even at high tide.

The barrier was scheduled to be removed the moment the tide was at its lowest, at which point the process to remove the ship's hull would commence. The plan was to physically float the wreck off the sand using inflated collars lashed to heavy-duty waterproof webbing, which had already been fixed beneath the old ship. The idea was that as the tide reached its highest point, four tugs would keep the floating collar and the webbing in place and the old schooner would rise off the Goodwin Sands for the first time in over two and a half centuries. The webbed platform holding the wreck would then be towed slowly to Dover Harbour where it could be craned gently onto shore.

Harry watched as the water level slowly rose on the Sands. As the sea began lapping only inches below the exposed wreck, he signalled for the four tugboats to take up the slack on the recovery harness cables.

A hush settled on the open water. Even the usually vocal seagulls were quiet as everyone waited for the ocean level to reach its tidal high point.

With agonising slowness, the seawater rose. Harry closed his eyes, briefly praying to a god he no longer believed in that all the planning had not been for naught. He only opened them again when he heard the distinct sound of wood rending, engines over-throttling and people shouting.

It took him a moment to realise what he was seeing. The wreck appeared to be floating on the mesh pad as planned; however the tugs seemed to be having trouble keeping the platform on the surface of the water.

"What the hell's going on?" Harry shouted into his headset.

"Something's snarled up with the wreck. Probably an anchor," his number two replied from his better vantage point on a ribbed boat only a hundred metres from the wreck.

"I thought we found the *Lovibond*'s anchor!"

"That's the problem, Harry. It's not *her* anchor."

"What does that mean?"

"It means that the *Lovibond* has somehow become ensnared with the anchor from another vessel."

"Cut the anchor chain," Harry instructed. "It's got to be older than sin. I'm amazed it hasn't broken under the strain."

There was no immediate response.

"Matt, did you hear me?"

"I heard you it's just that... the anchor in question isn't that old. I can read the markings. It was made in Sheffield in 1938."

"It's not that unheard of for one wreck to get snarled up in another ship's anchor. I bet the one that lost it must have had some explaining to do."

There was again silence from Matt.

"Matt?"

"That's the thing. The crew thinks the anchor is still attached."

"To the sand?"

"No. To the boat that it belongs to."

Harry took one of the dredger's ribbed dinghies and, ignoring the growing chop, opened the twin throttles all the way.

By the time he reached the floating platform, a team of two naval engineers was close to severing one of the links of the rust-covered anchor chain. He could see that they were running out of time. The tension on the wreck where the anchor was snarled was causing the platform to list at one end as the tide rose.

"Before you finish that, let's attach some line and a buoy

to the end so we can find out what it belongs to after we've saved this old girl." He gestured to the hull of the schooner.

Minutes later the chain was cut and instantly pulled into the water by its own weight and that of whatever was on the other end. A coil of heavy gauge rope whizzed over the flotation devices, followed an instant later by a marker buoy the size of a small car.

"Right," Harry said. "That's enough fucking around for one day. How about we finish up what we came here for?"

CHAPTER THREE

Moments earlier, Jay Sallinger was standing fuming to himself on the fantail of the research vessel, *Deep Knowledge*. As the senior researcher at the Marine Archaeology Trust, he had been given the sought-after assignment of examining and studying the wreck of the *Lady Lovibond*. He had spent the past three weeks studying up on the ship and preparing himself and his team for the task.

He'd woken up in a positive and excited frame of mind. It was the long-awaited day when the wreck would be eased off the Goodwin Sands and floated to shore, at which point his assignment would begin in earnest.

At thirty-nine, he was the youngest full researcher at the Trust and knew full well that the publicity from this assignment was likely to cement his reputation. The fact that he was to be the only senior researcher on site only made the project that much more tantalising.

Then, only three hours earlier, a research vessel flying the French flag had joined the flotilla. Jay knew for a fact that nobody had mentioned there being any French interest in the wreck. He had texted Sir Michael Walling, the director of the Trust, hoping to rile the old man into some sort of deterring action. Instead, Walling had responded that, only a few hours earlier, he had been advised by the Home Office that the French were sending their own marine archaeologist to the site and that it had been agreed that Jay was to work with the foreign researcher and share their results.

Jay could smell a political rat somewhere in the equation and also knew that shared research between countries would do little to further his career. In fact, if they'd sent who he assumed they had, the distraction would hinder every stage of the work. He tried telling himself that they couldn't possibly justify having the lead professor of Maritime Archaeology at Aix-Marseille University drop everything and spend the next weeks or months doing the preliminary study of the *Lady Lovibond*.

Jay had almost convinced himself that the French were far more likely to assign someone from the Ministry of Culture rather than a classroom, when he heard a distinctive megaphone-enhanced voice calling to him from across the water.

*

Emma Tramis Looked over at the other research vessel and waited to see if the man at the fantail would acknowledge her hail.

This would be the first time in five years that the two had spoken, if he did, indeed, choose to even respond to his exwife. She tried to tell herself that the feeling of excitement and slight nausea was due mainly to the auspiciousness of the occasion, not the fact that she was about to spend some considerable time with Jay.

Though their separation and subsequent divorce had been filled with hatred and venomous rhetoric, there was something about Jay that still sent a shiver through her system whenever she saw him. Even though they hadn't talked in years, they had spied each other from a distance at numerous conferences and scholarly events.

When both were starting their careers, they had met at a student symposium in Athens. She had at first been put off by his long hair and penchant for rolling and smoking his own cigarettes while downing countless espresso coffees.

Jay, even back then, had been his own person. Unlike the other students at the gathering, he didn't even seem to be listening to the various speakers and instead would sit and draw schematics for test equipment improvements. It wasn't until the Q and A sessions after each lecture that it became clear to Emma that Jay had not only been listening, but had absorbed so much of the detail of what was said, he was able to not just question the lecturers but successfully argue some of their findings.

Ironically, it was those very characteristics that she had initially found so attractive that ended up being the cause of their breakup. As an only child of narcissistic parents who were too worried about what everyone else thought of them to ever consider focussing their love and concerns on their son, Jay grew up with some serious intimacy issues.

Emma's parents had been the exact opposite and, if anything, smothered and over-protected their daughter at every turn. She had thought of Jay as emotionally wounded and believed that she could help him attain happiness through affection and nurturing.

Somehow, the pair had stayed together for a full three years of relative harmony before their overstuffed baggage began to unpack itself with growing frequency. The result was Jay's inner child pulling him away from possible future rejection while Emma's drove her to overcompensate with almost doting attention.

As Emma looked across the water at her ex, she couldn't help wondering, as she often did, whether, if they'd found a way to ride out the stormy seas within that stage of their marriage and perhaps even learned to actually talk to each other, things could have turned out differently.

Finally, Jay gave her a wave and gestured to his cell phone. Emma was about to blast her phone number out of the megaphone when one of her team stepped up to her and handed her a piece of folded paper.

She felt like a fool. Partially because it was now apparent that everyone on her ship must have heard her initial call across the water to her ex-husband, but also because the piece of paper was the contact list for all the key players involved in the recovery operation. Emma had seen it earlier that morning in a text and had even checked if Jay's name was on the list, together with his cell number and address in Deal.

Emma retrieved her phone from her windbreaker and dialled Jay's number. She watched as he reacted to the ring and lifted his to his ear.

"Hi, Jay," she said, keeping her voice as upbeat as possible.

"So, they did send you," Jay replied flatly.

"You sound pleased."

"How would you feel? I was lead researcher up until I got the email this morning telling me that there was now a shared interest in the *Lovibond*."

"What were you most upset about? The fact that you have to share or that you have to share with me?"

Before Jay could respond, alarms began to sound across the water. The floating platform appeared to be snagged on something and was listing badly.

"You're closer," Emma stated. "What's going on?"

"It looks like it's got snarled up in some old anchor chain?"

"Its own?" she asked.

"I don't think so. It looks newer. I think..."

Emma could see Jay lift his walkie talkie to his face as he, at the same time, muted the call to her. Less than a minute later he unmuted the call.

"It's not just some chain, there's an actual anchor hung up on the *Lovibond*'s bowsprit. They're about to use an acetylene torch to cut the chain and free up the wreck."

Even as he spoke the fierce heat from the torch severed one of the old links of the chain sending the bulk of it back under the water and onto the sand.

"I can see the platform stabilising," Jay advised.

Before Emma could reply, the alarms suddenly quietened. They could both then see the platform begin to move away from the discovery zone.

"We'd better follow it in," Emma suggested.

"It's going to take most of the afternoon getting it into Dover harbour, then most of tomorrow to get it ashore and into the security area. I'm going to stay out here for a while. I'm curious about what that anchor belonged to."

"I thought you were here for the *Lady Lovibond*?"

"I am, but there shouldn't be any other wrecks on this site and the anchor that snagged the *Lovibond* is dated hundreds of years later. I think it's worth investigating where it came from."

"Still the rebel, I see," Emma voiced.

"Not a rebel. Just curious, which, as far as I am concerned, should be the driving force of any good researcher, otherwise they might as well hang up their tools and do something safe like teaching."

Before Emma could respond to his 'teaching' slight, Jay disconnected the call.

CHAPTER FOUR

Harry Zain stood on the deck of the dredger for the entire six-hour trip into Dover harbour. As the flotilla rounded the breakwater, all manned vessels sounded their horns as a welcome back to port for the *Lady Lovibond*. Something she had not managed to do for over two hundred and fifty years.

Dover was a tricky port to enter at the best of times, and all ferry traffic had been halted for close to an hour as the platform, now only being towed by one tug, reached the assigned jetty. A gaggle of media and technicians waited anxiously as a second tugboat gently nudged the floating wreck until it could be securely tied to the freight dock.

Harry spent the rest of the day supervising the two cranes that were to be used to hoist the platform out of the water and gently lower it to the concrete loading area where anxious researchers and technicians stood salivating in anticipation of what was to come.

*

Once the area around the Goodwin Sand's wreck site had been cleared of almost all vessels, Jay Sallinger and two other members of his research crew climbed into the *Deep Knowledge*'s ribbed shore boat and made their way to the exact coordinates of the *Lovibond* wreck. It was an ebb tide and, though the Goodwin Sands were still covered by water, the team could see some of it only a few feet below the surface.

Jay lowered a fibre-optic waterproof camera, a device for which he held four key patents, into the water. The three looked at a Garmin multi-screen array mounted in the control console of the boat, and within seconds could see the sand as clearly as if the Channel water wasn't even there.

Helena Malins, who was American and the youngest of his team, pointed excitedly. "The chain goes right into the sand."

"The question is," Jay remarked, "how far down does it go and what's at the other end? Just because the anchor was found amidst the wreckage, doesn't mean it's still attached to a vessel."

"Hopefully we will have a name in the next hour or so," Brian Leonard, the last member of the team, commented. "Lloyds promised to check all wreck data as well as missing vessels from 1938, when the anchor was manufactured, up to present day."

"I'm not sure you had to make the parameters that broad," Jay replied.

Brian looked over at Jay like a disappointed father. He was Jay's senior by over twenty years and, though he reported to the younger man, was always trying to rein in Jay's enthusiasm and creative shortcuts.

"I know what you're thinking," Brian said with a patient smile. "For there to be a wreck under the *Lovibond*, it has to have been here in the shifting sands for decades at least. I just want to have all the info so that we determine what's down there before we decide what to do."

"What do you mean before we decide what to do? If there's another wreck down there, we need to get to it."

"What if it's not a wreck as such? It could well be a barge or even a towed target from when the Royal Navy was practising in the lead up to WW2."

"I don't think anything other than a manned seagoing vessel would have an anchor of that size," Jay tossed back.

"Well, the tide will be low enough for us to walk out on the Sands in a few hours so, with a little luck we may get a better idea of what's on the other end of that chain."

Helena brushed a strand of blond hair away from her eyes. At twenty-one, she had managed to be selected for the apprenticeship over eighteen other applicants, seventeen of whom had been older and male. A bystander might be fooled into thinking that she got the job because of her tomboy good looks. Those in the know were well aware that it was her double master's and PhD that had got her the position.

"Can I ask a stupid question?"

"May I?" Brian corrected her.

Helena rolled her eyes. "Okay... may I?"

"There are no stupid questions just stupid people who don't bother asking them in the first place."

"Why do you think there's a ship down there at all? I mean, doesn't it make more sense for it just to be some chain that was lost overboard?"

"Firstly, it isn't just a chain – it is a chain *and* anchor," Jay explained. "Secondly, ships don't just routinely cut off their anchor, and thirdly, that chain was stopping the platform and four tugs from moving; in fact, at one point the tugs were being pulled backwards because of the rising tide. There's definitely something big down there and we're going to find out what it is."

"If there is, in fact, something there that's more current than the *Lovibond*, how did it get buried below it?" Helena continued.

"People think of these sands as stationary, but they're not. Once submerged they are at the mercy of fierce tidal forces. Even when the top is visible, the visible sand can be assaulted by ferocious wind and waves, while the undersea portion is hit with entirely different forces. Imagine it like a very slow-revolving drum in a washing machine. Material at the bottom can, over time, move to the top. The Goodwin Sands has a history of bringing old wreckage to the surface. It wasn't that long ago that a World War Two bomber, thought to be lost forever, suddenly appeared."

Helena nodded though her eyes clearly mirrored the fact that she wasn't entirely buying what Jay was selling.

After checking for any other clues visible on the surface, they moved their boat to a safe distance and shared a thermos of coffee, while the tide lowered and the Goodwin Sands began to appear off the starboard side of their small craft. After less than an hour they could see the sandbank stretching out for miles. Jay eased the dinghy's bow up onto the nearest bit of sand and the team stepped ashore with some basic equipment and test instruments. Once the tide had dropped, the anchor chain and the attached ocean buoy were plainly visible on the surface of the sand.

"Try the GPR first," Jay suggested to Helena, who was the one holding the black waterproof case for the ground penetrating radar unit. Normally Jay would have been the only one managing the equipment, but Helena, even at her young age, had somehow accrued almost double the hours on the same model.

The young research intern unpacked the commercial-level unit and fired it up. Even a complete novice could have seen that the instrument was not the type you'd buy off Amazon so you could look for coins on a beach.

The OKM eXp 6000 cost over forty thousand pounds and was not only more powerful than just about anything else on the market, but was also able to display its findings in 3D.

Helena expanded the telescopic probe to its full width and joined the other two at the point where the chain vanished into the sand. She set the parameters to the maximum range, then activated Jay's own software upgrade that allowed the sensor to be programmed to focus on a specific material – in this case, steel.

"Be prepared not to find anything. Even this unit has its limits beyond a certain depth. Add to that the geological make-up of sand and we'll be lucky to find anything without having to take a top layer off the area."

Helena nodded and activated the search mode on the GPR. She slid the probe across the area nearest the chain entry point and the built-in LED screen lit up like a Christmas tree.

"That's just the chain," Jay advised as he studied the screen of his iPad that he'd linked to the unit. "Try and follow it."

Helena took a step forward and the signal lost intensity. She tried again, this time ninety degrees to her right. The signal strength increased. She took a full step forward and could see the distinct outline of the chain beneath the sand on the screen.

"Look at the depth reader," Helena said excitedly. "It's definitely heading downwards."

"That's to be expected," Brian pointed out. "Though it doesn't mean there's anything at the other end."

"I still say we should have attached the chain to the *Deep Knowledge*'s crane and see if we could lift it up," Helena said as she took two more steps."

"That would certainly give us a quick answer," Jay replied. "It could also damage whatever is down there or even snap the chain far enough down that getting to it again would be a very costly mistake."

"What if there is a boat and it's not that far down?" Helena asked.

"Then it would be a first for me. These embedded wrecks are always under way more silt or soil than what we've estimated."

Helena took another step and checked that the unit was still reading the chain. It was. The depth was now seven feet and was still descending.

"What if we tried—" Helena's words were cut off as a loud beeping began emanating from the control unit. Her mouth dropped open as the screen filled with a white image."

Jay leaned across and disabled the alarm and switched on the 3D mode. Ideally, he would have preferred to keep the software active all the time, but the power needed used up the battery pack in minutes rather than hours. He therefore made it a rule to only switch it on when there was something interesting to see.

"Keep going," he said to Helena. "Stay in the centre of the mass."

After she had walked twenty feet further, she turned back to the others.

"This doesn't look like the right shape for a boat hull."

"Sure, it does," Brian replied, grinning. "You're imagining it lying flat on its keel. What we're seeing is the starboard side of its stern. Any minute now and we should see some superstructure."

Less than a minute later the shape began enlarging on one side of the screen. Only moments after that the 3D modelling kicked in and they could clearly see the vessel below them. It was in almost perfect profile as it nestled within its cocoon of sand.

"Am I going mad or does it look as if it's in pretty good shape?" Brian asked.

"You're the sanest person I know," Jay replied. "And, yes, it looks fully intact. If I had to guess, I'd say it's a World War Two naval trawler. Let's get some screen shots and send it up to the office and to the Admiralty. I haven't heard of a trawler sunk on or near the Goodwin Sands that isn't already recorded. Hopefully someone will recognise it and can tell us more about this vessel."

"Are we going to try and raise her?" Helena asked, her eyes transfixed on the screen.

"No, I don't think so," Jay replied with a shrug. "I was just curious what was down there."

"You're kidding," Helena blurted out before she could stop herself.

Jay looked over at Brian and gave his long-time colleague a knowing wink before returning his gaze to the young apprentice. He managed to keep his expression dour for as long as possible before he broke into a smile.

"Of course, we are going to see if we can raise her. She's a piece of our history and, by the looks of her, the sand has managed to wear away whatever rust tried to form. This might be one of the most intact World War Two ships I've seen. That being said, we have no idea what the other side looks like. There could be a hole the size of a Fiat in her. The first step is to get rid of the top layer of sand."

"What's the second step?" Helena asked, wide-eyed.

"Going on board!"

CHAPTER FIVE

Work to remove a layer of the sandbank above the wreck started immediately, thanks to the fully equipped dredger that was still on standby. With its industrial dredging scoop, it was basically able to shift the top six feet and deposit it further along the barrier. What made the task far more daunting was that they were working against the clock as the tide would submerge the area in a matter of hours.

Once dusk began to fall and the sandbank again vanished beneath the English Channel, Jay and Helena donned wetsuits and used the research vessel's industrial suction hose to shift the remaining sand from atop the wreck.

Standing waist deep on a shifting surface eight miles from shore was not something to be attempted by the faint of heart. The cold darkness and the solitude was almost overpowering. They worked through the night taking shifts with other members of the dredger's crew. By the time the tide fell to its next low, the top of the wreck was visible.

By 3:00 a.m., enough of it was exposed for Jay and Helena to dive down and see if they could access the interior of the ship. They made one try, but with the minimal light provided by their Tac torches and a strong tide that was whipping up the loose sand making it almost impossible to see, they decided to wait until the sun rose before giving it another try.

When they made their second dive, the tide was slack, the wind had eased, and the sun had yet to climb high enough to be visible. Unbeknown to Jay, by the time they found access into the vessel through a partially open hatchway leading off the stern deck, they would no longer be alone out on the Sands. The French research ship had emerged from the morning haze and dropped anchor only a few hundred metres from the dredger.

Before the dive, Jay's biggest concerns were that the wreck's hull might have been crushed by the shifting sands and the interior of the trawler could, over time, have filled with that same sand, making it impossible to get inside.

Jay guessed that the ship was around forty to fifty metres long and had probably been designed as a minesweeper and may well have been coming or going from Dover harbour when she sank. The big question was whether the sinking was storm-related or the result of an unexpected encounter with the German Kriegsmarine.

"You ready?" Jay asked via their com link.

"If you are, then I am," Helena replied trying to keep the growing sense of panic out of her voice.

Helena had dived on numerous wrecks before joining the Marine Archaeology Trust, but those had all been at approved holiday dive sites where the environment had been deemed safe and the wreck condition monitored. Entering an, as yet, unexplored wreck with all its inherent dangers was an entirely different kettle of fish.

Jay gave her a thumbs up then glided through the opening and became the first human to enter the vessel in over eighty years. Helena followed close behind as they turned left and pulled themselves along what had once been a stairway leading to a lower deck. Now, with it laid on its side, it was a confusingly claustrophobic corridor of sorts. They reached what would have been the lower deck and made their way along a narrow passageway. Because of the ship's current orientation, they were forced to navigate the narrow space between what was left of the port and starboard walls. There was surprisingly little sand, which was a good thing, but that had given the salt water the chance to eat away at the bulkhead walls forcing the pair to dodge countless stalactite-like rusticles that dangled down from exposed iron wall braces.

"This looks bad," Helena said over the com link as she ducked and weaved around a particularly large rusticle.

"We're not that interested in the condition on the superstructure. It's the hull that will dictate if it's worthwhile trying to get the wreck ashore."

Jay reached the end of the corridor and squeezed through a half open watertight door that appeared to have rusted in that position. Once through, he emerged into what he assumed had been the ship's dining area judging by the dimensions of the space.

Helena swam alongside him and peered down towards the port side of the ship.

"Now, that's not good," Jay said as he saw that sand that

had filled the lower few feet of the space.

He swam down and studied three massive claw-like pieces of steel that protruded from the sand.

"What are those?" Helena asked.

"Those are piece of the hull."

"Why are they sticking up like that?"

"They're not sticking up, they're sticking in. At least we now know what sank this boat. Looks to have been a torpedo. Judging by the spread of those pieces of steel, the hole has to be huge. The ship would have gone down quickly."

"So, any survivors would have..." Helena started to say.

"I doubt there were any survivors. With the ship at this angle and the speed the ocean would have poured in, it would have been chaotic and deadly."

"But if they were over the Sands, couldn't that have helped some of them get out?"

"My guess is that they weren't directly above the sandbank when the ship was hit, and that when it went under it corkscrewed itself down onto an upslope of the barrier. Over time the wreck has obviously been consumed by the sand and ended up as you see it now."

"Didn't ships back then know about the Goodwin Sands?"

"Of course, they did," Jay replied. "By that point, it was clearly shown on all decent navigational charts."

"Then what was a British navy trawler doing this close if it was such a well-marked hazard?"

"Now that is a good question. We've got an hour of air left, let's see what else the old wreck has to show us."

The two poked around as many spaces as possible and

found nothing of any great consequence. It wasn't until they made their way to the foredeck of the ship that their excitement started to grow.

Lashed onto the deck less that a metre from the base of what was left of the ship's crane, and just above the level of the sand, was a rectangular box about two and a half metres long, one metre wide and one deep. It was covered by the remains of an oilskin cloth that had deteriorated into little more than a few streamers that waved in the tidal flow surrounding them.

The box itself appeared to have been made from some sort of local stone, which was now covered in barnacles and sea vegetation.

What intrigued both divers the most was that the box had been encircled with an over-abundance of chain – enough to make moving whatever it was extremely difficult.

Time and water had made the task far easier than the crew had doubtless intended. Where the chain ends met, the shackles that joined them together had rusted to a point where one hard twist of a screwdriver was enough to separate them.

"This must have been important to somebody for it to have been so well secured," Jay voiced. "As the wreck itself is not worth the cost or effort to salvage, we can at least hope that this thing contains something worthwhile."

"It looks heavy," Helena said as she tapped the stone with the butt end of her diving knife.

"The *Deep Knowledge*'s crane will have no trouble getting this on board."

Jay was right. After getting fresh oxygen tanks, he removed all the chain and fitted lifting straps around the box. He cut away the old leather strips that had been used to lash it to the deck then gave the signal for the crane operator on board the research ship to hoist away.

The journey up from the wreck to the research vessel took less than an hour.

The box was deposited on the foredeck of the *Deep Knowledge* and two crew members began hosing it down with fresh water. Once on board, Jay was so busy looking at the exterior of the box that he didn't hear Emma Tramis walk up behind him.

"Nice box!" she said, her voice rife with sarcasm.

"It's what's inside that matters," Jay shot back without even looking at his ex. "Shouldn't you be studying the *Lady Lovibond*?"

"I could say the same for you."

"I assumed that it would take days before it was washed down with fresh water to a point where I... sorry... we... could start going over her."

"And you would be right, hence my coming back here to see what you're up to. We are, after all, supposed to be sharing this research."

"We're sharing the *Lovibond*, not some old World War Two wreck."

"We'll see about that," Emma replied.

"I can't believe that you think you can just turn up and start demanding proprietorship for research of anything and everything that I find, just because you happen to be..."

Emma's face broke into a smile.

"I was joking, Jay. Remember when you used to have a sense of humour?"

"I remember you taking that with you when you left."

Emma rolled her eyes. "So, what's the deal with the sarcophagus?"

"What's a sarcophagus?" one of the crew members asked.

Emma looked the man up and down before answering.

"It's a coffin made from stone."

Before the crew member could respond, Brian appeared on deck.

"The folks at head office weren't much help, but the Admiralty was. After we sent the name you found on the bow, they were able to confirm that the HMS *Sea Hawk* was indeed a minesweeper – Bassett class apparently. She was reported lost in 1940."

"Did they happen to say what she was doing at the time?"

"They did not," Brian replied.

"Do they know or are they just not telling?"

"According to their records the ship had been moored in Dover for supplies when it was ordered to carry out a top-secret assignment."

"Of which, I assume, they have no record," Jay commented.

"The chap I was talking to seemed surprised at the lack of documentation. The only thing he could find was a note from the then acting director of the Admiralty that simply said 'HMS SH asg to DI K'."

"Did that mean anything to your contact?"

"He surmised that it could well have meant 'HMS Sea Hawk assigned to Deal Kent'. He also said that judging by the speed at which the trawler left port, mid-provisioning, the mission had to have been of some importance."

"How could transporting a coffin require that level of secrecy?" Jay questioned.

"Maybe they didn't want Dracula to get out," Emma replied, grinning.

CHAPTER SIX

The research vessel's captain, William Chase, was a burly man in his late fifties. His weathered features conveyed to all that he had spent his life at sea.

He had been watching the goings-on from one of the bridge wings and finally felt he needed to have his say. After joining the others on the bow, he took Jay by the arm and pulled him away.

"I have to raise an objection. I'm not happy with this being opened on board the *Deep Knowledge*. While it may not strictly be a government vessel, it still gets subcontracted quite frequently to the Royal Navy. Her owners would not be pleased if I tarnished that relationship just so you can avoid going through the appropriate protocols."

"I see your point," Jay replied. "If I don't open it here, how do you suggest we get this thing ashore without going through Dover?"

"Why all the cloak and dagger nonsense?" Helena said as she approached the two men. "Why not just follow procedure?"

"Because it would take reams of paperwork and potentially weeks to get clearance if we get it at all. I just want to get it ashore away from prying eyes so we can see what's inside. If there is anything of note, we will follow procedure and notify the right people."

"The best solution would be to see if Harry Zain is still in Dover with all his kit," the captain suggested. "He used to keep an old landing craft in the marina. That would be the best way to get it ashore without having to go through a port. You could just run it up on the beach then have a team waiting to carry the thing to a flatbed on the road. Obviously, that should be done in the wee hours so as not to attract too many curious eyes."

"Great idea. Want to give him a call?"

Once the captain was out of earshot, Emma got close to Jay so her whispering wouldn't be overheard.

"Getting it to shore is only half the challenge. Where are you going to put the thing? That sarcophagus is huge and very heavy. It'll have to be somewhere relatively big with sturdy floors."

"What about the town hall or..." Helena started.

Emma shook her head. "Every place in Deal is booked solid with *Lady Lovibond* events. That's another reason to go through formal channels. That way there's no subterfuge and the thing could go right into a customs shed."

"Where we most likely would never get a chance to study it before government officials disturb the contents to the point where any clues as to its history would almost certainly have been destroyed."

"I know that's a risk," she replied. "What I don't understand is why the sarcophagus is so important to you.

There might not even be anything inside at all. Have you considered that it might have been on its way to a burial of someone important?"

Jay was doing his best to keep focused but, with Emma standing so close to him, he could smell her favourite perfume and, like some Pavlovian response, sensed his own heart rate quicken.

"I somehow doubt that a naval vessel in the midst of a world war would be used to transport an empty coffin," Jay pointed out.

"What do you think could be in it?"

"I have no idea, but for a navy ship to be rushed to Deal under the cover of darkness has to mean something. That's why I want to open it. If the government gets involved, we'll never get near the sarcophagus or the truth," Jay insisted.

"You've already alerted them that you've found the wreck," she pointed out. "I'm surprised you haven't gotten some flack by now."

"I was wondering about that. I can only guess that whatever mischief the Admiralty was up to back then was never documented, and those involved have all turned to dust. I don't imagine that anyone official sees this wreck as anything more than that – just another wreck. I think if we formally log a report on the vessel's condition and survey results, we won't hear another word from them."

"I assume we will leave out the part about what was strapped to the trawler's bow?" Emma asked.

"I don't know what you're talking about."

Emma laughed. "You still haven't answered my question

about where you plan on hiding the thing once you get it on shore?"

"If you recall, I used to live a few miles north of here as a child, and one of my favourite pastimes was going to the cinema."

"That's fascinating, but what exactly does that have to do with the sarcophagus?"

"We'll use the old cinema to store the sarcophagus," Jay replied.

"Deal doesn't have a cinema. I checked. Besides when we were together and used to visit Deal, you yourself said that we had to go either to Dover or Margate to watch a movie," Emma reminded him.

"Deal absolutely does have a cinema, just not one that's currently operational."

"When did it close?" Emma asked.

"1963."

Emma gave Jay the expression he knew only too well. The one she used whenever she felt he was talking nonsense.

"If it was closed before you were born, please explain how you were able to watch movies in it?"

"I never said I watched movies," Jay replied with a smirk. "I said I used to go to the cinema when I lived near here. Back then, it was locked up tight and was slowly rotting away. Some childhood friends and I found a way in through a storage room window at the back and the place became our unofficial clubhouse."

"What's it used for now?"

"Not a thing. It's derelict."

"Then how do we get in?"

Jay smiled proudly.

"After our first break-in, one of the boys messed with the exit door so that we could get in and out that way."

"That was decades ago. Whoever own the place now must have changed the locks!"

"The exit doors don't have locks, they have a push-down bar that can only be used from the inside," Jay explained.

"Surely they must have replaced those?"

"You'd think so, but they haven't. When I arrived here for the *Lady Lovibond* project, I was curious and drove by. It's still the same old door. You have to understand, the place has had a few owners but none of them wanted to spend any money on it. They tried wrestling, bingo, you name it. Nothing paid off and the building just continued to deteriorate."

"And you think we can just stroll in there with a sarcophagus and no one will notice?"

"I'm counting on it."

*

Just before 1:00 in the morning, the sarcophagus was gently lowered into the well of a 1940s-era landing craft. Once on board, Harry Zain eased the throttle open and headed towards Deal. He was especially happy that, by a complete coincidence, a few years earlier he had swapped out the original diesel engine for an electric alternative. His reasoning had been based primarily on cost but also because the old engine sounded like a badly tuned Spitfire and could be heard from miles away. Though stealth had never been an issue before, being able to beach the craft in almost complete silence was going to be a big plus on that night.

As he approached the pebble beach just north of Deal Pier, dimmed headlights from a car suddenly turned on, illuminating a strip of shoreline. The moment that Harry grounded the landing craft, the lights went off, plunging the area back into darkness. Within seconds, Harry could hear the sound of heavy boots on the loose pebbles.

Sticking to the pre-arranged plan, he lowered the ramp and watched as the shadowy figures struggled to lift the stone coffin. Then, once their grips were set, they carried it up the beach and laid it onto a pickup truck bed. Thankfully, someone had had the forethought to chisel away enough of the sea growth from the stone so as not to shred fingers and hands. Four figures climbed up into the truck bed as the remaining two got into the cab. By the glow from the cab's interior light, Harry Zain, even from the shoreline, recognised Jay and Emma.

He closed the ramp, then put the vessel in reverse. Because of the electric motor, it hardly made a sound as it turned and headed back out to sea.

*

Jay drove out of the small parking lot and turned left onto Beach Street. After crossing over the Broad Street roundabout, he continued two blocks before turning right on South Street. Jay pulled the pickup over to the left side next to a battered-looking door recessed within an old brick wall.

Without a word, the six manoeuvred the sarcophagus to the end of the bed, then slowly dragged it out until they could all get a decent handhold. They carried it to the doorway, at which point Jay gently released his grip causing the others to grunt as they took up the extra weight.

He stepped up to the door, then slipped a heavy-duty screwdriver under one end between the reinforced wood and the worn concrete. He lifted with one hand as he rammed his shoulder against the door.

It opened, but not without a grinding sound that shattered the stillness of the early morning air. The others all froze in place listening intently in case the din awoke any of the townsfolk. All they heard in return was the sad lament from an errant seagull coming from somewhere amidst the crowded rooftops.

Jay resumed his place with the others as they quickly carried their prize inside away from prying eyes.

CHAPTER SEVEN

Once they were inside and the door was again locked, Jay turned on his cell phone flashlight so they could see where to put the sarcophagus.

"Well, this is different," Jay stated as he shone the light across the vast interior.

The once grand cinema with its vaulted ceilings and lavish interior had undergone a refit at some point after Jay and his friends had ceased using the space as a clubhouse. There was a lowered, false ceiling made up of what looked to be asbestos tiles in the midst of which were dated-looking neon light fittings. When it had been a cinema with a toweringly tall ceiling, the length of the room had been in perfect proportion. With its low grid-like replacement ceiling, it looked claustrophobically small and cheap.

To add to the disjointed appearance, faded pink chairs and tables filled the entire room where once the plush velvet seats had fanned up and away from the stage.

"I knew they refitted the place when it became a bingo hall, but this is offensive. It was such a beautiful building."

"While we are all enjoying your reflections of the past, this thing is just getting heavier by the minute," Emma said between grunts.

"Sorry. Let's get it to the stage and leave it there for the time being."

As the stage was only about four feet high, it was relatively easy for the six of them to deposit the stone coffin on its edge then push it the rest of the way.

"Mason," Jay said. "Go out to the pickup. Behind the driver's seat is a plastic bag. Would you mind fetching it."

The young crewman from the *Deep Knowledge* nodded and headed for the door as Jay turned the flashlight off.

"Try not to be seen," he called after him.

The man was back in less than a minute. Jay opened the door from the inside then shut it after him. He and the others, as if by telepathy, all turned on either their cell lights or the flashlights they had brought with them. Jay removed four battery-powered LED lanterns from the bag and began placing them strategically around the stone box.

"Right then. Crew members from the *Deep Knowledge*, thank you for your time and help," Jay said as he stepped up and handed them both some cash.

"That's one hundred each, as agreed. Please remember to not disclose what you were up to tonight. One of the *DK* dinghies should be on the shore by now, right at the end of this street."

Mason spoke for them both.

"A hundred quid each for an hour's work! Call us any time."

"I don't know if either of you are interested, but I may have an additional job for one of you," Jay advised.

"We're listening," Mason replied.

"I need someone to stay the night and make sure that nobody else tries to get in."

"How much are you paying?"

"How does two-fifty sound?"

"I'll do it," Mason said. "But I need to check with the captain first to make sure he's okay with that. I think they're staying at anchor out by the Sands till you decide if there's anything else needs doing on the wreck site."

Helena, who had hardly said a word since arriving on land, pulled Jay aside and whispered, "I'll do the night watch. I think it's better if someone from our team stay here. Don't you?"

"Are you suggesting that the crew might try and steal it?"

"No. I do, however, think that they may well try and have a look inside and do some damage. They are not professionals like us."

Jay had to keep a straight face as he looked down at the diminutive intern.

"Sorry, Mason. New plan. Helena is going to stay."

Mason gave her a leery stare. "Maybe she'd like some company," he suggested.

Helena's cold gaze was reply enough, and mumbling to themselves, the two crew members slipped out the exit door and made their way to the waiting dinghy.

Jay turned and faced Brian, Emma and Helena. "We have a huge decision to make. We can open it now and have a quick peek or get some rest and start fresh tomorrow. Helena, you will obviously be able to go off and get some sleep at your digs once we get here in the morning."

Brian was the first to speak. "While my curiosity is as piqued as everyone else's, I think we should get some rest. We have all day tomorrow to spend in here before we have to start the real work on the *Lady Lovibond*, so why don't we call it a night?"

Jay could see on Emma's face that she was about to disagree, but then, in a rare display of understanding, she saw the others nodding and decided to go with the flow.

"Right, then," Jay said. "Brian, you and I should get to our rooms in the Regal. Helena, you are staying here, but Emma... where are you staying?"

"As this project was last minute for me, I couldn't get a room anywhere. I had planned to stay on the ship. I'll have to radio for a dinghy to pick me up."

"Good. That's settled. Helena, do you need anything?" Jay asked, ignoring Emma's obvious hint for a bed for the night.

"I've got some water and Grant Fitzburton's latest paper on the desalination of artefacts. I'll be fine."

"Do you ever just have fun?" Emma asked.

"I can have fun when I retire."

Once the others had slipped out of the exit door. Helena sat at one of the pink tables and placed her water bottle next to a lantern, then retrieved her iPhone from her jacket pocket. She then opened the iBooks app so she could read more of the eight-hundred-page paper.

As diligent as she'd hoped to be with her time in the abandoned cinema, the quiet and repetitious nature of the document lulled her into a deep sleep.

*

Helena heard scratching.

At first the sound was distant, but as she became more aware of it, she could tell that it was getting louder. It didn't take long for her to trace the origin of the noise. It was coming from within the stone coffin. What unnerved her the most was that, along with the grating sound, she was convinced that she could hear breathing. It wasn't obvious, but under the din of the incessant scratching, there was the definite sound of a low-register, raspy panting, as if someone or something was having trouble getting enough oxygen. Then again, judging by the way the stones had been sealed together at every possible join, any air that might have been inside must have been exhausted decades earlier.

Helena reached out and rested her hands on top of the sarcophagus. She expected it to feel cold, as stone was apt to feel, but instead, it felt warm. Not a nice comforting warmth, rather a heat that reminded her of sticky humidity.

She withdrew her hands and checked where the lid was attached to the base, hoping to find an area where the adhesive had worn away. She wasn't planning to try and remove the top, but if she could pry even the tiniest part open, she might be able to get a little air into the thing and help save whatever was inside.

At the far end of the rectangular shape, Helena found a spot where the stone had, at some time, been chipped creating a minute crevasse that ran just below the lid.

She removed her miniature Swiss army knife and flipped open the corkscrew appliance. She began digging at the rotted sealant and before long managed to create a centimetre-wide hole.

Helena stared at the black opening and realised that the scratching had stopped. She listened but could hear nothing. Finally, the raspy panting started again, and she placed her ear against the tiny hole, hoping to hear it more clearly.

It took a few moments before Helena recognised that the sound wasn't emanating from within the sarcophagus. She felt a chill run down her back as it hit her that the breathing was, in fact, coming from somewhere behind her.

She jumped as three loud knocks filled the old cinema. As she turned towards the sound of the breathing, she saw, by the dim grey light of the battery-powered lanterns, a dark shadow rise up from the floor.

Whatever it was began moving towards her.

Three more knocks resounded within the space.

CHAPTER EIGHT

"Open the door please," a male voice shouted from somewhere outside the cinema.

Helena tried to shake away the nightmare she'd been having and saw that she was still seated at the pink table, though now, her head was resting upon it, and a thin trickle of sleeper's drool hung from her mouth.

As she sat up straight, another round of banging helped her pinpoint the source of the noise. It was coming from the old exit door.

Helena considered staying shtum, but the next words from the man changed her mind.

"We are government agents and must insist you open this door or else we will do so by force."

A different, harsher voice added," We're MI6 ma'am."

Helena tried Jay's mobile, but it went straight to voicemail. She checked the time on her phone and saw that it was only just past 3:00 in the morning and assumed that he had his set on night 'privacy' mode.

"Miss Malins, we know you are in there, so there is little point in pretending you're not."

Helena approached the door.

"What do you want?"

"You and your associates dived on a wreck yesterday and we believe that you are holding something you found at this location."

"Let's say that was true. Why would that be of interest to MI6?"

"If you open the door, we can discuss that further, but I have no intention of shouting our business in the middle of the street."

"Can you come back later when the others are here... around seven-ish?" she asked. "I don't feel comfortable opening this door to strangers."

"Yet you feel comfortable locking yourself in an abandoned building with a plundered object of questionable origin. I know which I would be more concerned about."

After pondering the man's words, Helena finally acquiesced and pushed down on the locking bar.

The door swung open, and she was faced with two young men who looked nothing like the image of agents she had acquired from watching shows like *Slow Horses* and *The Game*. Instead of seasoned and world-weary veterans, they looked like a couple of lads taking a break from university.

The pair entered the cinema then closed the door after them.

"I probably should have asked to see some sort of ID, shouldn't I?" Helena said nervously as she realised that she was now in a very precarious situation.

The thinner of the two stepped towards her and produced a folding leather wallet from which he removed a warrant card that looked not that dissimilar to the old-style UK driver's licence.

Helena briefly glanced at it though she had no idea if it was real or not.

"You do realise that you both look too young to be secret agents?" she asked almost as a reflex.

"We've heard that before," the thin one replied, smiling. "And you don't exactly fit the mould of a scientist."

"Why, because I'm a girl?" she shot back.

"No, because you have a double master's and a PhD yet aren't that hard on the eyes."

Helena laughed, or rather snorted, before she could stop herself.

"You're funny," she commented.

"It was unintentional."

She studied his boyish features to see if he was kidding and determined he was not. There was something about the coldness of his brown eyes that sent an unpleasant chill through her body.

Reluctantly, Helena gathered her few personal possessions, then in an act of pique, grabbed the four battery-powered lanterns as well.

"Oi. You can't take those; we'd be in the bloody dark," the other one snapped as he stepped between her and the exit door.

"They belong to the Marine Archaeology Trust. I would get a severe reprimand if I returned to London and reported that some equipment was missing."

The other agent was about to argue the point when the

tall one eased him aside and faced Helena.

"I'll tell you what," he said, his voice oozing with false charm, "how about you leave them with us just until the shops open, at which point, we'll buy our own and you will be welcome to come back and collect these?"

The moment she was back out on the street and the exit door was firmly closed behind her, she could distinctly hear the pair laughing.

*

"So, what do we do now?" Wilson, the thin one, asked. "We tracked them here and have the... whatever it is in our possession. Do we just sit here and stare at it all night?"

"We were told to find it, secure it and notify ops. We've done that. Now we just wait until we get further instructions," Calloway, the taller of the two, answered.

"Which will probably not be for a good few hours. I somehow doubt that anyone in London is going to lose sleep over some missing stone box that's been under water for eighty years," Wilson replied. "I'd suggest going out and seeing if I can find something to eat or drink, but this town looks like it's closed up tighter than a—"

"You can manage for a few more hours," Calloway interrupted before having to hear yet another off-colour analogy from his partner.

Even though Calloway was only a few years older than Wilson, he couldn't help noticing the decline in the quality of the newer recruits. When Calloway had been approached while finishing his master's at Oxford, there had still been an air of, if not sophistication, then at least, style within the agency. Not anymore. It was as if a decision had been reached to seek out new blood from the lowest ranks of the population.

"I say we have a look," Wilson said as he jumped up onto the stage and approached the sarcophagus.

"We had very specific instructions to not even get close to the thing," Calloway reminded him.

"I know, but it's hardly our fault that when we got here, we found that the twats from the Archaeology Trust had already opened it. At that point it was our responsibility to check inside and see what damage they'd done."

Calloway desperately wanted to nix his partner's idea, but Wilson was right. If they could blame the sarcophagus being opened on the girl and her associates, who would doubt their word? Especially as the Trust employees had already proved themselves to be a bit loose when it came to adhering to the letter of the law. Considering that they had brought the thing ashore with the specific intent of avoiding Customs and Excise, it was actually pretty obvious that they would want to check out their booty as soon as they could.

In fact, Calloway reflected, if they reported things with just the right slant, they could come off looking like heroes having stopped the smugglers before they could remove the contents from the coffin.

Calloway joined Wilson on the stage and studied the sarcophagus in a completely different light. Their objective had suddenly switched from being hands-off security agents to a couple of curious and bored boys desperate to find a way to kill some time.

"It looks to me," Wilson said as he held one of the lanterns close to the where the stone side met the two-inch-thick cap, "as if whoever built this created the four sides and bottom first then added the top. I know that sounds obvious, but it means the likelihood is that the weakest join will be around the top seal."

"That's all well and good, but how are we going to get it loose. Use our fingernails?"

"I've got a toolkit in the car. There'll be something in there that we can use."

"If we can't get it open within the next couple of hours we will have to give up. We have no idea what time that girl will come back with the others."

"My guess is that we'll have the top off in no time," Wilson said as he headed towards the emergency exit. "Don't start without me!" He slid out into the dark morning.

CHAPTER NINE

As the only parking spot, they could find was next to the Regal Hotel on the other side of the pier, it took Wilson almost fifteen minutes to return. At least, that was his excuse. Calloway might have accepted it were it not for the reek of bubble-gum flavoured tobacco that his partner vaped whenever possible. Yet another indication of just how low the standards of MI6 had sunk.

Calloway chose, with great difficulty, to not call the man out for having taken a cigarette break and instead feigned great interest as he watched Wilson unfold a vinyl-covered toolkit – the sort you could buy at Poundland for under a tenner.

Wilson selected the large flathead screwdriver and a half-sized rubber hammer with a bright blue handle.

"That's all we have?" Calloway asked, unimpressed by the cheap tools.

"It's all we need," Wilson replied as he placed the screwdriver blade against the greyish mortar beneath the stone capper.

"Ready?" he asked.

"Just try not to cause too much damage," Calloway

replied.

"That's what she said," Wilson replied with a wink and a leer.

The first strike with the toy hammer echoed within the abandoned cinema.

The pair studied the contact point and saw that the head of the screwdriver had indeed penetrated the old sealant. Wilson kept going and within two hours had chipped away enough of the mortar for the pair to attempt lifting the top. With muscles straining and veins bulging in their arms and necks, they used every ounce of strength they could muster, but to no avail.

"We are going to have to call it a day," Calloway stated. "We're cutting it too fine."

Wilson didn't reply. Something caught his eye down in the auditorium. In a pile next to the endless rows of pink padded chairs were spare metal frames. The chair bodies themselves were pretty much useless but the arm frames were a different story.

Each metal arm frame was fashioned into an L shape, with a plate on top where the cushion would be attached and the lower elongation where the arm unit would bolt to the underside of the seat assembly.

Calloway watched, confused, as Wilson grabbed a couple of arm frames and ran back up onto the stage. He pushed the lower elongation of one of them into the void where the mortar had been cleared then used the rest of it like a lever.

Understanding what his partner was doing, Calloway grabbed the other frame and did the same thing.

The top of the sarcophagus began to lift ever so slightly.

They kept at it until rivulets of sweat poured down their faces and necks and the top began to separate from the lower stones.

Driven on by their success, they slid their improvised prybars further along the rim and again threw themselves at the task of lifting off the stone top.

Suddenly and unexpectedly, the last of the aged sealant gave way and the top lifted then slid sideways onto the floor where it broke into three uneven pieces as the two men jumped aside.

"Gonna be hard to hide that," Calloway said as he gasped for air.

"We have nothing to hide. Those researchers caused all this damage – remember?"

"Let's hope it was worth all the trouble," Calloway said as he stepped to the side of the sarcophagus.

"It's got to be worth something," Wilson replied, moving closer.

They stood in complete silence as they looked down into the stone coffin. Briefly glancing at each other before staring down again, their shock and disappointment was mirrored on their sweat-covered faces.

The inside of the sarcophagus held nothing but a thin layer of fine, grey sand.

"Maybe there's something under it?" Wilson suggested.

Calloway gave him a doubting glance then combed his fingers through the sand from one end to the other.

"I don't understand," Wilson said, shaking his head. "Why the fuck did they need us to come down here in the middle of the night to guard a stone box filled with sand?"

"Maybe the value wasn't what was inside?" Calloway replied. "What if the stone box was the prize."

"And we just destroyed it! Brilliant. What a waste of a fucking night. We might as well get a few hours' kip before the shit hits the fan. At least we get to watch those researchers get blamed for all this. That should give us something to laugh about."

Wilson stepped off the stage and sprawled across two chairs in an effort to get himself into a sleeping position. Calloway kept looking at the sand trying to understand what was so important about the stone box. As he stared at it, he thought for a second that he saw something move. He lifted one of the lanterns closer and lowered it between the stone sides.

The sand was as still as the night.

*

Something woke Calloway up. He wasn't sure if it was a noise or just the extreme discomfort of trying to sleep in a sitting position on a pink chair whose padding had rotted away many years earlier. He checked his phone and saw that only forty-five minutes had passed.

He closed his eyes and tried to let sleep drag him back down into its dark embrace when he distinctly heard a noise. It sounded like his mother's damn cat when it was using its litter box. After opening his eyes and listening with more directional curiosity, he knew where the sound was coming from.

Calloway got to his feet, grabbed one of the lanterns and

turned it back on. He glanced at Wilson who had decided to sprawl across one of the pink tables and had a sizeable string of drool running from the corner of his mouth to the faded tabletop.

What made his partner's position even more comical was that Wilson's legs were jerking in place. Calloway assumed that the man was chasing something or someone, but when Wilson let out a long moan, he realised that maybe he was dreaming about being chased.

Once on the stage, Calloway approached the sarcophagus and peered into it.

Things had changed.

The sand, if that was indeed what it was, had formed into dozens of small clusters, each of which reminded him of uncooked manicotti pasta.

Curious, Calloway dragged his fingers through the piles and was pleased to see that they devolved back into the fine sand he had observed when they originally opened the thing.

Though curious at how and why sand would accumulate in specific areas of the coffin and even appear to take on odd shapes, exhaustion took over and he returned to his uncomfortable chair hoping to grab at least a few more hours' sleep.

*

Wilson was the first to wake up. It was gone 7:00 in the morning, and he felt surprisingly rested despite the looping dream he'd had where a wolf-like creature was chasing him through a dark and claustrophobic forest.

As he tried to shift his weight and slide off the table, one of its legs gave way tipping itself over and spilling Wilson onto the floor. The din woke Calloway who took a moment to understand the comical tableau that was transpiring only a few feet from him.

"Sleep well?" he asked Wilson.

"Up until now, yes," his partner replied as he managed to untangle himself from leftover bingo furniture.

Laughing to himself, Calloway stood, stretched, grabbed a lantern and walked up onto the stage. He half expected to see that the sand had formed into little pasta piles again but was greeted with something far stranger.

The sand was gone.

All of it.

The only things left in the bottom of the sarcophagus were some smears of a mucus-like gel.

"Everything alright over there?" Wilson asked as he reached for another of the lanterns.

Calloway looked over at him and was about to respond when Wilson's light came on. In the few seconds that the lantern was still, Calloway saw Wilson grinning as a dark grey shadow rose up behind him.

For a brief moment, Calloway believed that maybe it was simply a shadow, right up until he saw the razor-sharp teeth wrapping around Wilson's neck.

CHAPTER TEN

The pain made it clear that it was alive. Even as its body was still reconstituting itself, its brain began to function. As bones grew and skin formed, it felt everything. Though the agony filled most of its consciousness, one sensation somehow managed to rise to the surface.

Hunger.

It had no concept of the passage of time or that it had been reduced to little more than a sandy residue as it lay entombed on the bow of a sunken ship.

It had no memory of youth, just as it had no memory of where it came from. All it knew was that it had to kill, and it had to eat. The two humans in the dark space had eased the pangs for a brief moment, but that satiation never lasted and never abated.

Every part of its brain seemed wired for one single function.

Hunting.

*

When Helena reached the Regal Hotel after the MI6 goons

had basically thrown her out of the old cinema, she had intended to advise Jay and Brian about what had happened. Maybe it was the cold night air or the indignity of her treatment at the hands of the agents, but she had suddenly felt exhausted and decided to have one of her fifteen-minute powernaps before waking her two superiors. She doubted that a few minutes would make that much of a difference considering the early hour.

What she had never considered was that her usual unfailing internal time clock would, on that occasion, fail her.

As a swatch of sunlight found its way into her room and began to caress her sleeping face, Helena felt the warmth and was about to roll over for a few more minutes' kip when her brain kicked in.

"Shit, shit, shit!" she growled as she ran into her en-suite bathroom and splashed water on her face. She squeezed a dollop of toothpaste directly into her mouth, chewed it, sluiced it and spat the remains out. She didn't feel she had the time to use something as irrelevant as her toothbrush.

She couldn't even remember the last time she'd slept beyond 6:00 a.m., yet her phone clearly showed that it was past 7:00. As she ran out into the hallway, she knew that her decision to grab that fifteen minutes would almost certainly cost her job and, most likely, her entire career.

As Jay's room doubled as their operation centre, all three members of the team had a copy of the key card. Helena knocked first, waited only a few seconds then tapped the card against the reader.

By this time, she was hyperventilating and badly needed

to pee. She had expected the room to still be in darkness, but found the drapes drawn and no one there.

Helena ran down two flights of stairs and headed for the reception desk, hoping they would know where Jay might have gone.

As she dashed across the main lounge, she caught sight of Jay and Brian sitting by a window apparently having what looked to be a leisurely breakfast. For some reason, that frustrated her still further.

Helena stood before them and began a jumbled and speedy rendition of what had transpired during the night.

Jay held up his palm to stop her.

"We know. I got a call from Sir Michael at around four o'clock. He was notified that the sarcophagus was now under the protection of two gentlemen from MI6 and that you had been removed from the cinema."

All she could do was stare dumbly back at him.

"I should have told you," she finally mumbled.

"You must have been exhausted. When I finished with the call, I confirmed with the front desk that you had made it back in one piece and decided to let you sleep," Jay explained.

"You don't seem that upset," Helena said.

"No reason to. We're down here to study what's left of the *Lady Lovibond*. Finding that sarcophagus, while enticing, was never part of the plan anyway. If the agency feels they need to scuttle off and bury our find in some remote government hiding place, I say good luck to them."

"Aren't you at all curious about what was inside it?"

"Of course, I am, but not to the degree that it's going to ruin my day. Why don't you sit down and have some breakfast."

"I have to stop by the cinema and pick up our lanterns. I let them keep them overnight, so they didn't have to sit there in the dark."

"Perfect. Let's fill our bellies, then we can swing by the cinema on the way to Dover."

"You've got to try the sausages," Brian said as he skewered one off his plate and held it up for her to see. "They're bloody delicious."

"You know full well that I'm vegan."

"I feel that it's become my life's calling to bring you back into the light."

Helena flagged down a plump waitress with a nose ring and ordered plain porridge with almond milk.

"That's a fine meal for a goat," Brian joked.

"That's a fine meal for a stroke," she said pointing at his plate."

"At least I'll die happy," he shot back while chomping down on the aforementioned sausage.

"More than can be said for that poor pig."

"Will you two give it a rest. Breakfast is my zen time. Please don't spoil it," Jay said, interrupting their verbal jousting.

Brian and Helena glanced at each other, both trying to supress a smile. Their banter was SOP whenever they were out of the office and on a project, and though it occasionally weighed on Jay's nerves, there was something almost quaint about having two such brainy colleagues who seemed to, despite the thirty-year age difference, find pleasure in oral sparring.

*

Jay pulled his car, a pristine 1968 Jensen Interceptor, over to the right side of the street, directly across from the cinema exit door. He hoped that the town's traffic wardens had better things to do first thing in the morning than ticket him for stopping on a double yellow line for what would probably be no more than a couple of minutes.

As they stepped out of the car, they were hit with the sounds and smells of the seaside town. The morning seagull chorus was almost kennel-like, with very little of their language sounding even remotely as if it had originated from a bird. One particularly large specimen was standing on top of a streetlight, glaring at them while making noises that were eerily like a cross between a crying baby and a cat in heat.

The air, while smelling fresh, still managed to carry the scent of brewing coffee and old fish with a subtle back aroma of sewage.

"Ah," Jay said as he took an exaggeratedly big breath of air. "There's nothing like the smell of the British seaside."

The three crossed the narrow street and though tempted to use his tried-and-true break-in method, Jay decided not to add fuel to the exchange before it even got started.

He knocked three times then looked to the others with a

forced smile.

"Let's just get our lights and be on our way. Stay professional and don't let them goad you into anything they can report on later. Clear?"

Jay waited as long as his patience would allow then knocked again, only harder.

There was still no response.

"They've obviously gone out to get some food and I would imagine, find a toilet."

"I didn't know that MI6 agents were that well house trained," Brian whispered to Helena.

"Let's just grab the lamps and go. If they try and raise a stink, I'll remind them that they were the ones who weren't at their post."

Jay removed a large screwdriver from his windbreaker pocket.

"You always carry that?" Brian asked, grinning.

"Always," Jay shot back.

Jay jimmied the bottom of the door then used his shoulder to push. Not wanting to attract too much attention, the moment it opened the three stepped inside and quickly shut the door behind them.

The cinema was pitch black.

"You'd think they'd leave at least one of the lights on," Helena observed.

"By the smell of the place, I was right about their lack of house training. It's rank in here!" Brian added.

Jay switched on his phone light and sought out one of the lanterns that Helena had left.

"You two stay by the door," he said with as much calm as he could muster. The trouble was, he wasn't feeling anything close to calm. Brian had been right about the smell, just not the full spectrum of the odour. There was definitely excrement in the mix, but there was something else – something coppery and sweet.

Once the lantern was on, it took Jay a moment to understand what exactly he was seeing. The blood was instantly recognisable. The level and spread of the carnage was not.

He could hear Helena gasp at the same time as Brian began retching near the exit door.

He couldn't blame either reaction. Even by the limited light from one battery-powered lantern, he could clearly see the blood that had been splattered in almost every direction. Chunks of what he assumed had to be human flesh were dotted around the space and by the look of them, were the result of some sort of frenzied feeding.

Jay knew from Helena's recounting that there had been two men in the cinema. There was no part that he could see that was large enough or intact enough to help in their identification.

"What did this?" Helena asked as she took a step away from Brian who was still having trouble with his retching reflex.

"I couldn't begin to guess."

Jay found a second lantern and switched it on as well. He left in on a central table then used the other to guide him towards the stage. Once the arc of the illumination reached the sarcophagus, he could see that it had been opened and the lid severely damaged. He stepped towards it and peered inside.

It was completely empty.

"Just a thought," Helena said from her position of perceived safety by the door. "How do we know that whatever did this isn't still in here with us?"

Jay felt as if he'd been slapped. Helena's question was all too logical, yet his interest had been driven by academic curiosity rather than safety for himself and the others.

Jay switched his lantern to torch mode and an ultra-bright beam immediately shot from the front-facing lens. He angled it up at the ceiling tiles hoping to see some sort of disturbance that could be proof that whatever did this had found a way out. The tiles were still in place.

Helena approached the stage and joined Jay at what remained of the sarcophagus.

"Do you think whatever did this was inside this thing?" she asked.

"Normally I would say no, and that you've been watching too many horror movies. However, faced with what's happened here, I think it's a good possibility that that may well be the case."

"What could it have been?"

"Something that seems to like feeding on humans."

"Liked feeding on them, or that was the only thing available at the time?" Helena suggested.

Jay shrugged and glanced across the cinema floor. At the very end of the lantern's reach, he could make out something on the furthest table. Two ball-shaped objects sat side by side on what had been the pink Formica top, the surface of which seemed darker than the others at that end of the room.

As Jay intensified his focus, he realised that the two items he'd assumed were balls were not uniformly round but were, in fact, egg-shaped.

"I think I'm going to throw up," Brian said from his position at the door.

Before Jay could reply, his brain completed its interpolation of the data. With a feeling of extreme disassociation, he determined that the two object at the far end of the room were severed heads sitting in a congealed pool of blood.

"Get back to the door," he whispered to Helena.

Before she could move, Jay had a flash of realisation. The heads obviously belonged to the two missing MI6 agents. That was a given. What wasn't, was the reason why the bodies of the two men had been violently eviscerated and strewn across the cinema floor yet their heads had been placed and balanced upright on the table's surface.

That act was in direct conflict with the animal-like and seemingly non-sentient slaughter of the men. Placing their heads like that had to have been intentional and the only reason Jay could think of for anyone or anything to do that was as a form of pride.

The thing kept the heads as trophies.

"I'm definitely going to be sick," Brian said, gagging.

Jay wasn't certain if it was a trick of the light or his own mind, but he thought he could see the two heads slowly move away from each other.

"I gotta go outside," Brian groaned as he reached for the exit door.

Jay was so fixated on the heads that it took him a moment to realise why they seemed to be moving. They were being pushed apart by a long black snout that had appeared out of the shadows.

"Don't open that door," Jay shouted, but it was too late.

Brian had already put his weight against the metal bar and took a step towards the outdoors.

All Jay could see was a streak of something greyish-black as it flew across the room and intersected with his colleague. His shocked brain wasn't able to determine the true shape of the anamorphous entity. There was something canine about it while at the same time, it had an almost humanoid poise when it landed on the other side of the exit.

At first it looked as though the creature had simply pushed Brian aside, then, almost as if in slow motion, his head separated from his body. A geyser of blood rose up from his severed neck before Brian's body crumpled to the ground.

Helena began screaming. Jay froze in shock as he felt a sense of dark foreboding, knowing that they had just inadvertently released something truly horrific onto the quiet and scenic streets of Deal.

CHAPTER ELEVEN

After feeding on the humans that it had found within the darkened space, it felt somewhat sated, yet the urge returned almost instantaneously. When the other humans arrived, bringing with them illumination and the odours that humans carry upon them, it knew to stay in the shadows until the moment was right.

After the night's nourishment, it had rediscovered that it could change its shape from the form it seemed to naturally take, to one of a human male. It had sat in the blood-drenched cinema for hours, altering itself back and forth between species. As it had the ability to see in the dark, it became fascinated watching its front paws turn into slender, hairless hands right before its eyes.

Strangely, such was its urge to consume any and all human flesh it encountered, each time it looked down at its own human-like appendages, its first instinct was to devour them. Thankfully, when in human form, it did not take on their scent, rather a hint of its own canine-like pheromonal redolence remained, which probably saved it from consuming itself.

When light came to the big room, it saw that there were

three humans. They spread apart, which it did not find conducive to a hunt. It wasn't until the older male – who even from a distance reeked of fear and malaise – opened a portal to the outside that it knew what to do.

Once the human was down, it ran into the daylight and for a brief moment was disoriented and thought of returning to the dark space and the two remaining humans.

Then, distant memories began populating its awakened mind. Memories of the town in another time. Memories of feeding within that same town.

It suddenly knew where it was and where it needed to go, but first, it morphed itself into human form.

*

As a marine archaeologist, Jay's job had never involved dealing with work-related death, especially something as hideously macabre as the scene inside the old cinema. Though he initially felt that he should contact Sir Michael at the Trust, he realised that the safety of the townspeople had to come first.

Once he and Helena had cautiously stepped over the decapitated corpse of their fallen colleague and walked out into the morning sunshine, Jay closed and secured the door then dialled 999. It took a while before he was finally transferred to someone at the nearest police station, which was located eight miles away in Dover.

The officer who answered sounded young and inexperienced. By the time Jay had given him an abridged overview of what they had found at the cinema, the young policeman was actually stuttering.

When Jay asked him what he planned to do, the line went quiet until the constable admitted that it was his first week on the job and he had been assigned morning call duty as crime was usually at its lowest ebb at that time.

Jay suggested that he contact his superior and treat the incident as still active with lives at risk. The officer agreed but advised that his supervisor was on holiday in France and that he would have to call the operations division commander. As it was still early, he felt he should wait until at least 10:00 before disturbing him.

Jay stressed the importance of the matter, but the young constable seemed bent on ensuring the commander had a good lie-in rather than hear about violent death in Deal. The officer did, however, tell Jay that he and Helena should stay where they were, and that they would be contacted as soon as possible, then hung up the phone without taking any contact information from him.

"I don't feel that I made my case very well," Jay commented.

"You did all you could. Maybe Sir Michael will be able to get in touch with the right people," Helena replied.

"That could take forever. We have to notify the authorities immediately before whatever that was decides to strike again."

"First of all, it's probably as scared as we are and now free from both the sarcophagus and the cinema, will most likely find somewhere safe as far from the likes of us as possible. Secondly, there is one body we could contact that would be in a very good position to react appropriately to what's happened here."

"Who's that?" Jay asked.

"The two men in there – they were MI6. Considering they were sent down here in record time, presumably after Brian did some checking on the origin of the wreck with the Admiralty, it makes sense that someone up in London is expecting reports from them."

"Are you suggesting we call MI6?"

"Why not? They are in the best position to raise the flag and get help down here. Plus, you said you saw one of their IDs, so we have a name."

Helena gave him an embarrassed look.

"What's wrong?" Jay asked.

"I sort of looked at it but to be honest, I didn't actually read what it said. I was too nervous. We may just have to call MI6 and hope that someone knows who was assigned down here and why."

"That may be worth a shot, it's just..."

"Just what, Jay?"

"We don't have any idea how to call the right department at MI6."

"There must be a number online," Helena suggested.

"Whatever number we find online will doubtless be a switchboard which will do us no good whatsoever." Jay paused, thinking. Then an idea occurred to him. "I may know where we can get the number," he said.

Helena cringed before she spoke.

"I hope you're not suggesting that we go back in there?"

"We need to get some ID and at least one of their phones," Jay replied.

"How exactly do we do that? Did you see what I saw in there? It's not like we can just remove a phone or ID from one of their pockets. Their body parts are pretty much scattered throughout the cinema, and that's just the bits that weren't consumed."

"Look, we know that whatever attacked them definitely left the scene. All that's in there now are some dead bodies."

"Including Brian's," she added.

"Yes. Including his. My point being that we know they can't harm us. I'm not suggesting it will be pleasant, but at least by going in again, we might hopefully find their identification and at least one of their phones."

"What's the importance of finding one of their phones?" Helena asked. "Especially as, even if we do find one, it will doubtless be locked."

"I'm hoping that they will have a speed dial set up to whoever was their minder."

"Won't help us much if the phone's locked," she reminded him.

"We'll just have to unlock it then, won't we," Jay said as he broke eye contact.

"How are we supposed to do that, exactly?"

"I couldn't help noticing just before that thing attacked Brian that there was a..." – Jay tried to find the right words – "a hand. I'm relatively certain that I saw a severed hand lying close to the sarcophagus. It didn't look too badly mauled and it's possible that the fingerprints could still be intact."

Helena's jaw dropped open as she stared back at Jay in shock.

"Whichever one it belonged to won't mind," he advised. "In fact, by using what's left of him, we just might save other lives."

"You're serious, aren't you?" Helena asked, shaking her head.

"Of course, I am. I'm surprised, as a researcher, you're not somewhat intrigued yourself," Jay replied, oblivious to just how disgusted his colleague had become.

"I research and examine old ships and their artefacts. That... that..." – she pointed towards the cinema exit door – "looks as if an abattoir exploded."

"Imagine the scene as something from a movie," Jay suggested.

"I don't go to the movies, and if I did, it would most definitely not be one with scenes like that in it."

"I suppose I could go in alone."

"I'm hardly going to let you do that, am I?" Helena took a deep breath before heading back towards the door.

"Thank you," Jay said, catching up with her.

"There is one small thing we have forgotten to consider," Helena said as she watched Jay do his trick with the bottom of the exit door.

"What's that?"

"How do we know that there was only one of those creatures inside that box?"

CHAPTER TWELVE

Helena's words rang heavy in Jay's mind as they stepped into the cinema and turned on their phone lights. Without saying a word, Jay knelt next to Brian's body and gingerly moved the head so that it was at least back to being close to where it was supposed to be.

"I'm sorry, old friend," he said in a whisper.

Helena tried to see what Jay was doing but felt her eyes immediately mist over and had to turn away.

"The police aren't going to be happy about you tampering with evidence," Helena commented.

"Fuck 'em," Jay replied as he stood up and made for the first lantern.

Finding any identification within the shadow-filled space was next to impossible. The creature appeared to have shredded all the men's clothing as it fed on their lifeless corpses. Finally, Helena found a blood-soaked mound under one of the tables, and after prodding it with her foot, it rolled over revealing that it was the midsection of a body. The upper torso was gone as were the legs, but for some reason the beast hadn't fed upon the meat between the waist and the groin.

Stranger still, after additional foot prodding, Helena could see that khaki material still somehow covered that one remaining part.

"Jay, I need help," she said in barely a whisper.

"Are you alright?" Jay replied instantly.

"I've got something, but I can't... I can't touch it."

Jay joined Helena and stared down at what she'd found.

"I don't know which one that belonged to," she voiced more to herself than to anyone else.

Jay retrieved one of the same chair arm assemblies that the agents had used to open the sarcophagus and used one end to wipe away some of the gore. He managed to find a back pocket and, with zero finesse, used the metal bar to tear it open revealing a thin leather wallet that appeared to have miraculously not been splattered with blood.

Cringing all the while, Jay bent over and daintily removed it. As he started to open it, a claxon alarm sounded somewhere within the room causing both of them to jump. The sound repeated for about ten seconds then stopped.

Jay looked over to see if Helena had any idea what had just happened but she was making her way towards the stage end of the room.

"I got a phone," she said as she raised a blood-soaked Galaxy S24 into the air. She tried to open it but was faced with a locked screen which she showed to Jay.

"I'll see if I can find that hand I saw," Jay replied as he headed for the stage.

Helena considered helping but decided that she had already done more than her share of treasure hunting within the charnel-like interior of the cinema.

Jay approached the sarcophagus and looked down at where the remains of the hand had been earlier in the day.

It was gone.

A small smear of blood stretched out towards a floor-to-ceiling grey curtain that looked to be slowly rotting from the ground up.

The blood trail disappeared under a fallen clump of material. Jay was about to move it aside when he thought he heard a rustling coming from somewhere behind it. He stopped and listened more intently, but the noise didn't re-occur.

Shaking his head at his own discomfort, he bent over and lifted the curtain segment out of the way.

Helena saw Jay's body stiffen then back away from the rear of the stage.

"You alright?" she called out.

Jay gestured with the palm of one hand for her to stop talking while he slowly moved backwards to the front of the stage.

"Fuck!" Jay suddenly yelled as he turned and leapt to the lower level. Helena had no idea what was happening until she saw a veritable wave of black, wriggling rodents crest the stage and drop to the cinema floor.

"Rats!" Jay shouted as he headed for the exit.

Like anyone else, Helena had her own set of fears and foibles, but rats, or any other rodent for that matter, weren't among them. She calmly made for the stage allowing the flowing tide of vermin to scamper over her feet as they headed off towards the back of the auditorium.

Jay stood by the open exit door and watched in amazement

as Helena climbed onto the stage and approached the spot where he had first encountered the horde. He'd had a fear of just about anything that crept or crawled ever since falling through a rotten floorboard while 'exploring' an abandoned house when he was only ten. The basement room where he'd landed unceremoniously on his back had literally been alive with a truly astonishing quantity of spiders, beetles and rodents.

Watching Helena stride through the fleeing rats, made him feel both embarrassed at his own frailty and in awe at Helena's fortitude and determination.

"Jay," she called from the stage. "You really should see this."

Jay tried not to look too obvious as he scanned the area between himself and where Helena was standing. With his route devoid of vermin, he walked over to the stage and was about to step up when one lone rodent straggler scooted by him and leapt down onto the floor.

Jay let out a shriek before he could stop himself. It wasn't a big one, but it was of sufficient volume to cause Helena to inadvertently laugh.

"Wasn't expecting that one," Jay said, trying to sound unaffected by the last encounter.

"Obviously," she replied as she tried to stop grinning.

"So, what have you found?" Jay stepped beside her.

In an almost theatrical gesture, Helena pulled the damaged curtain aside.

Jay stared in disbelief at the sight before him.

"It would appear that our little furry friends have been busy while we stood outside."

"Indeed," Jay said, nodding.

Piled against the back wall was a foot-high mound of small body parts that the rats had obviously decided to collect and keep in one safe place.

While many of the parts were impossible to identify, some were still intact enough to be recognisable.

"I count three hands," Jay stated. "There may be part of a foot in there, but I'm not sure. I think I also see what could be part of an elbow."

"I don't consider myself to be much of a maths whizz, but by my reconning we have enough hands now to give us a seventy-five percent chance of unlocking the phone."

"I wonder why they chose to keep the hands?" Jay pondered.

"Probably because they were easy to drag up here." Helena pretended to bite down on her index finger and mimed dragging it away.

"I've got some wet wipes in the car. You are going to need to clean the fingers before trying to swipe on the phone," Jay said, trying not to show the revulsion he was feeling.

"What's with the '*You* are going to need...'?" Helena replied, smiling. "Aren't you going to help?"

"Of course. I just meant that—"

"I'm just pulling your leg. I'm fine with wiping down the fingers so long as you don't mind holding the phone."

"That I can do. I'll be back in thirty seconds," Jay said as he headed for the door.

"Where do you think you're going?" Helena asked.

"To get the wet wipes."

"And leave me in here alone. No chance. Hold that door

for me."

"I thought you were fine with everything?" Jay said with a straight face.

"I'm not *fine* with any of this. I just appear to be made of stronger stuff than you."

Jay was about to respond with something snarky as Helena passed him on the way out.

"By the way," she whispered. "There's a rat on your foot."

Helena smiled as she stepped into the sunlight when Jay cried out and ran into the street while trying to shake a non-existent rodent off his foot.

Once he'd managed to regain some degree of composure, Jay walked to the back of his Jensen and opened the boot. Tucked next to his travel bag was a black tote, which he unzipped and held open for Helena to see.

"I'm impressed and concerned at the same time," she commented.

The tote was filled with a treasure trove of post-Covid supplies. Along with a selection of different strength wet wipes, there was a pump dispenser of hand sanitiser, an assortment of rubber gloves and three different types of face masks ranging from the cheap disposable ones to the once sought-after holy grail, the famed N95.

"What should I bring?" Jay asked.

Helena glanced across the street then back at him.

"All of it!"

CHAPTER THIRTEEN

In an attempt to not garner too much attention, they crossed the road at a leisurely pace trying to appear like run-of-the-mill tourists. After tipping the contents of the tote onto a table, Helena was delighted to find that Jay had also included a couple of full body, single use, PPE suits.

They chose to don those, the gloves and face masks. While Helena thought they may be overdoing the due diligence by a smidge, Jay wished he'd thought to pack a full hazmat suit.

Suitably attired, they made their way to the stage and, as Jay watched, the phone in his hand at the ready, Helena gently removed the three hands from the bloody pile and set them down on a relatively clean area of flooring.

While she was chuffed that Jay thought of her as being immune to the carnage around them, he couldn't have been more wrong. He'd mistaken her lack of fear at the rat horde for general bravery. Nothing could have been further from the truth.

She hated the sight of blood. Seeing strewn body parts that had been partially chewed was way worse. Though trying to act as stoic as possible, inside, she was a roiling mass of nerves, fear and nausea.

Helena picked up one of the hands, a right one, and with the same care she would have given to the living, gently wiped as much of the gore off the index finger as was possible. She then held the finger against the biometric icon on the home screen.

Nothing happened.

"Not to worry," Jay encouraged her. "There's two left."

Helena placed the hand back on the floor and selected the only other right hand. She again cleaned the index finger, but again, to no avail.

"Looks like the phone belonged to a lefty," Jay offered.

"Or the owner never activated the fingerprint app."

"Those phones have biometric face recognition too, don't they?" Jay asked.

Even as he spoke, he realised the stupidity of his comment. He and Helena both glanced towards where the two heads were still in place on one of the tables. Even though neither had spent much time evaluating them, they could both recall that whatever facial tissue remained had been torn and severely chewed.

Helena collected the final hand and after cleaning it, held it against the phone.

Nothing.

"Hmmm," Jay mumbled.

"What?" Helena looked over at him, frustrated that their phone plan had failed so dismally.

She was shocked to see that Jay was holding up his left hand and appeared to be giving her the finger.

"That's a bit rude!" she stated.

"Use the middle finger. If someone was holding a phone that size in their left hand and the other hand was in use, it would be very hard to touch the sensor with the index finger. The middle one would be much easier."

Helena gave him a doubting look but cleaned the gore off the end of the middle finger. She held it against the sensor orienting it as if the phone was cradled in the hand.

The screen instantly came to life showing the shorter agent standing in front of an Aston Martin DB5 holding a silenced handgun in the iconic James Bond pose. She desperately wanted to make some disparaging comment about the man, but decided that considering his recent fate, she should, for once, keep such a thought to herself.

"Let's go through the contact list and see if we can find anything that might look like an MI6 number," Jay said as he tapped the address book icon.

"I thought that you were some sort of technical genius," Helena replied. She gently took the phone in her hand, then pressed the hot button on the left side. "Hi, Bixby, call MI6."

Nothing happened.

She tried again, her voice louder and more precise, again with no result.

Jay held his hand out for Helena to return the phone to him.

"I don't understand," Helena voiced in frustration. "I use it all the time on my phone."

"While I may not be a technical genius, I do know that you have to set your phone up with Bixby so that it recognises your voice," Jay said with a slight smile.

Once back in his hand, Jay opened the contacts app, and after checking for MI6 and secret service with no success, entered *W* and found an entry for *WORK* with three subheadings: *PW*, *Gen* and *OPS*.

He pressed *OPS* then looked at Helena with a hopeful, raised eyebrow.

A series of beeps indicated that there was no signal inside the decrepit old building.

Jay sighed.

"Want to step outside with me?" he asked.

"I'm certainly not staying in here by myself."

Once outside and seeing that two bars had begrudgingly appeared at the top of the screen, Jay tried again.

After only two rings, a gruff voice came on the line.

"Where the fuck have you two been. I've been trying to call you for hours."

Once Jay explained the situation, the gruffness left Richard Wilding's voice. When he learned that two of his direct reports were dead, his demeanour changed instantly.

"And you say you've contacted the local police?" he asked.

"Yes, however I'm not sure that the constable I spoke with understands the severity of what I was saying. I think he misinterpreted it as there having been a dog attack or something."

"How do you know it wasn't a dog of some sort?"

"Because, even in the dark it seemed huge and must have jumped at least five metres to escape, th—"

"While unusual, I'm still not sure..." Wilding interrupted.

"—then," Jay talked over him. "It managed to sever the head of my friend and colleague who stood well over six feet tall."

"Do you think whatever it was had something to do with the item you brought ashore?"

"I can only assume it did. When my colleague left in the early hours of the morning, the sarcophagus was intact, and your two men were alive. When we went in less than an hour ago, the sarcophagus had been opened and human remains were strewn across the interior of the space."

There was silence from the other end of the call.

"You still there?" Jay asked.

"Sorry," Wilding answered. "Everything you've said so far has been transposed into text and sent on up the ladder. I'm just reading the initial responses."

"That brings up an relevant point," Jay said. "Why exactly is MI6 so interested in an old stone box that we retrieved from a sunken wreck? I thought you lot only dealt with foreign threats."

"Wish I could tell you. The extent of my knowledge is that two of my colleagues were to go down to Deal and secure the item."

"Is that usual for you to be kept in the dark about what your team is actually doing?"

"You're joking, right. This is MI6. I'm kept in the dark so often I'm afraid to go out in the sun in case it blinds me."

"What about us? What should we do now?"

"I'm just reading..." Wilding stated. "A go-team is being dispatched as we speak. They should be with you shortly."

"That's fast, isn't it?" Jay asked.

"Apparently your constable took you more seriously than you thought. Word reached the top floor here before you even called us."

"I'm not sure I feel comfortable just standing here next to a building filled with dead bodies while we wait for—"

A deafening racket caused Jay and Helena to look upward just as a black Wildcat helicopter roared overhead only a few feet above the rooftops. It came to an abrupt stop just past them then hovered in place for a moment before turning 180 degrees and flying off.

"Would your lot come by helicopter?" Jay asked.

"Possibly. I guess from the noise that one just flew overhead."

"Yes, it did," Jay confirmed.

"Then they're with you already. If I may offer a quick word of advice: cooperate with them."

"That almost sounds like a threat."

"Just play nice. That's all I'm saying."

CHAPTER FOURTEEN

It kept to the shadows as it ran down the southernmost end of Middle Street then found the narrow pathway that led west to South Court. Though the names meant nothing to it, the creature knew the geography as if only days had passed rather than eighty years. The fact that Deal had gone out of its way to preserve the old homes and buildings was a great help.

Once in the narrow passage, it found the same gap in a wall that allowed access to a set of stone steps leading down to a poorly maintained door. Though locked, it had no trouble forcing its weight and great strength against the rotted wood until it gave way.

Beyond were more worn stone steps that reeked of age and human secretions. These led down to the labyrinth that lay beneath the quiet town. These were the tunnels that were built even as the town was being constructed above, one home at a time.

They had been used by smugglers and pirates, and the hidden entries and hand-hewn passageways connected almost half the houses between the High Street and the coast. Though Deal prided itself on its maritime and Royal

Marine Corps history, it was smuggling and piracy that had originally been the financial lifeblood of the town.

Ignorant of these facts, the creature only cared that the underground network was still intact so that it could use it to find new prey and feast on human flesh.

*

It didn't take long before the MI6 support arrived. Less than five minutes after the low fly-by, two Land Rovers pulled up next to the cinema exit door, in effect, blocking the street.

Four men stepped out of the first one. They were identically dressed in black trousers, black T-shirts and black windbreakers. They were young and looked prematurely hardened by life. One of them stepped to the second vehicle and opened the back door.

An older man, who looked uncannily like the actor Charles Dance, emerged wearing an impeccably tailored pinstriped suit under a tan-coloured camel-hair coat. He removed a well-worn trilby and, squinting at the bright sunlight, scanned the area once before striding towards Jay and Helena, who had opted to wait on the other side of the street.

"I assume that you are Ms Malins and Mr Sallinger?"

"We are," Jay replied, mildly surprised by the man's strong Scottish accent.

"My name's Cameron and I gather you've had a rough time of it down here. Hopefully we can find out exactly who or what did this and put a stop to it."

"I assumed you already knew what did this," Helena stated. "Otherwise, why are MI6 involved?"

Cameron smiled. "Sir Michael told me you were wont to say your piece. The reason MI6 is involved is that if, as we suspect, whatever killed those men in there" – he gestured with his head towards the cinema – "came ashore within the stone box that your team located and claimed, you have, in effect, brought a deadly threat to these shores making this a potential terrorist event."

"Whatever came out of that sarcophagus was not a terrorist. It wasn't even human," Jay said.

"That remains to be seen," Cameron replied as he turned away from the pair, about to head to the exit door.

"May I enquire as to what exactly your responsibility is down here?" Jay asked.

"You may," the man said as he crossed the street and joined the four agents standing at the closed cinema door.

"Do you want us to go inside with you? There's a trick to opening that door," Jay called after him.

Cameron ignored him and watched as one of his men placed a small black object under the lock plate. Once he was a safe distance from the door, he entered something into his oversized smart phone. There was a puff of white smoke and hardly any sound, yet a football sized hole appeared where the lock had been, and the door swung open.

"They seem to have their own tricks," Helena said, shaking her head.

Before Jay could respond, a familiar figure appeared, heading straight for them.

"Just what we need," Jay said as he offered his ex-wife a forced smile and lacklustre wave.

"What's going on?" Emma asked as she stopped next to them just in time to see the MI6 team enter the cinema. "I get the distinct feeling that I missed something."

"You did," Jay replied. "First of all, I need to tell you that Brian is dead."

Emma visibly paled as she took a reflexive step backwards. "How?"

"There was an incident last night in the cinema. After you left, Helena was evicted by two agents from MI6. When we returned this morning to pick up our lanterns, we found them both dead. They'd been attacked by something."

"What do you mean attacked by something?"

"We think that whatever killed them came out of the sarcophagus."

"This is a joke, right?"

"I wish it was. When we were in the cinema, Brian started to open the exit door and the creature killed him then fled outside."

"Who are those men I saw going in a moment ago?"

"I believe they belong to something called a go-team within MI6."

"Why MI6? Shouldn't this be a police matter?" Emma asked. "None of this makes any sense."

Jay's phone rang. He answered it and listened intently to what the caller was saying. After less than a minute, he disconnected the call and sighed.

"That was Sir Michael. He appears not to be very pleased

with me this morning."

"I was never pleased with you on any morning," Emma quipped.

"In no uncertain terms, I have been advised to leave the agents in peace and get back to work. We are to drive to Dover immediately and start our evaluation of the *Lovibond* wreck."

"Despite your close friend and team member having been killed a few hours ago?" Emma asked. "Did he even know?"

"He knew and he is holding me directly responsible for his death. He pointed out that if we had just done what we were supposed to do here, Brian would still be alive. As for us being allowed some time to grieve, Sir Michael advised that we would have plenty of time once we finish with the *Lovibond* and have returned to London to begin serving out our suspension."

Helena gasped. She had never in her life had so much as a scolding let alone a suspension.

"Sorry," Jay said patting her arm. "I didn't mean to get you into any trouble."

"Yet, you did," Emma pointed out. "May I suggest that we head to Dover and get started."

"I don't think either of us feel like doing much work, plus the fact that I don't think it would be right to just leave Brian in there alone," Jay voiced.

"Brian's not in there," Helena replied. "That's just a shell that housed him while he was alive. I know one thing for certain and that's that he would be livid if he thought we were going to just stand around moping. I say we do as Sir Michael instructed and get to work on the wreckage. It's bloody obvious that the Gestapo over there aren't going to let us in, so we may as well keep busy in the meantime."

"Someone should at least notify his family," Emma suggested.

"He didn't have one. He was an only child, his parents are gone and when his wife died five years ago, he decided life was less painful alone," Jay explained.

"That's a sad statement," Emma said shaking her head.

"That was Brian." Jay opened the passenger door of the Jensen and tilted the seat forward revealing the cramped rear. "Emma, why don't you sit in the back."

*

Jay drove along The Strand then veered right onto the Dover Road as he passed through Walmer. He pointed out a few spots where he'd gotten into mischief as a child then, just as they were leaving the town proper, he had to slam on his brakes as traffic seemed to be backed up the rest of the way up the hill.

He assumed it was another of the temporary traffic lights that seemed to pop up without any notice within the sleepy town. They crawled along at about two miles an hour until they finally crested the rise and could see the rolling hills and fields in the distance.

Oddly, there appeared to be a pair of military helicopters parked on either side of the road less than a mile ahead.

"What's going on up there?" Jay called to a frustrated-looking man in a car who was also stuck in traffic but heading the opposite direction.

"They've bloody closed the fucking road," he snarled.

"Why?"

"They wouldn't say. But judging by the number of soldiers that are gathering up there, there must be some sort of a training exercise."

As the man moved off, Jay looked ahead at the helicopters and could just make out tents being erected in one of the adjacent fields.

Jay was not a believer in coincidences and for the road to be closed and a military presence appearing right after MI6 sent a team into the town, it was pretty obvious that it was all because of whatever they had brought ashore in that sarcophagus.

Jay grabbed his cell phone and opened the Waze app. He chose Sandwich, which was in the other direction, then waited as his route was being calculated.

Seconds later he felt his blood run cold.

Every single road, including the single lane farm tracks were glowing red and showing stationary traffic before the screen went black and the words NO SIGNAL appeared at the top.

CHAPTER FIFTEEN

Peter Cates was exhausted. The restoration project on the three-hundred-year-old town house was running way over budget both in time and money. As lead contractor, Peter had been exceptionally careful with his original estimate and still believed it could have been achieved were it not for the draconian involvement of the local council.

Peter had restored countless properties in and around Deal and had always known what he could and couldn't do when working on a listed property. Unfortunately, the building planning supervisor had been forced to take emergency leave due to illness, which meant that all decisions now fell to his assistant, one David Kotwas, the nephew of the mayor of Dover.

Kotwas was lazy, pompous beyond his thirty-two years and a bully. The moment he took the reins he began a campaign of reviewing all his predecessor's current projects and he made a point of visiting each site and either modifying or revoking every permit that had already been issued. Were it because of actual concerns over the progress or adherence to the plans of the project, it would have been one thing, but that wasn't the case for Kotwas. His sole motivation was to make life difficult for as many homeowners and contractors as possible.

In his latest mandate, he had modified (again) the permit for the house Peter was currently restoring. The basement had a flimsy half door at one end that had once opened onto an ancient stone stairway leading to a partially collapsed tunnel dug centuries earlier. As this issue cropped up in a lot of the older homes in Deal, the council had, over the years, come to approve removing the doors and walling up the openings. Kotwas, however, decided that the old smugglers' hatches were as historic as any other part of the house and deemed that access should not just be maintained, but fully restored.

Peter sat drinking a Diet Coke on the top of the stairs leading down to the basement while Kotwas, as part of an unexpected inspection, evaluated the work that had already been done hoping to find yet another reason to modify the planning approval.

The interim planning supervisor studied the sturdy door that Peter had installed only days earlier and despite wanting to discover even the slightest irregularity, couldn't find fault. He then opened it.

Peter took a deep breath and prepared himself for what he knew was coming.

"This won't do," Kotwas said as he glared back at him. "My notification clearly stated that the access to the tunnels had to be preserved. Yet you've gone and built a bloody wall."

Peter stepped down into the basement proper and stood

next to the new doorway.

"We walled this up weeks ago before your latest notice," Peter replied as he admired his own handiwork. "You've got to admit it's a nice piece of wall."

"I don't care when you built it, my notice was completely clear. This access has to be unobstructed."

"Even though the request to wall it up was approved by the council months ago?"

"I've taken over from the person who gave that approval, and my decisions are final."

"Even if they're retroactive?" Peter said, trying not to lose his temper.

"I want this wall down right now," Kotwas insisted, ignoring Peter's last question.

"Then you'll have to knock it down yourself because I'm not going to do it. You're nothing but a low-level, power-hungry bureaucrat bully and I for one am not going to take it anymore."

Kotwas smiled coldly as he looked at the various construction tools that were scattered around the basement. His eyes came to rest on a sledgehammer. He picked it up and Peter could see that he was surprised by its weight, forcing him to drag it across the concrete floor.

Peter shook his head and climbed out of the basement so he could get some air and not have to watch the pudgy civil servant demolish a perfectly good wall.

Kotwas didn't notice that the other man had left until he was about to assault the exposed brick. Disappointed that he wouldn't have an audience for his little lesson on council notice adherence, he tried to swing the weighted metal end towards the wall. The impact was slow and almost powerless, doing little more than scarring one brick.

Determined to make his point, Kotwas tried a different method. Instead of going for the more traditional full-arc swing, he moved his hands halfway up the handle and managed to actually get a little force behind the blow.

With one brick cracked and mortar loosened in a foot-wide radius, Kotwas kept at it until he had knocked a hole in the wall that was big enough to squeeze through, not that he had any intention of attempting such a feat at his age and weight.

Instead, he continued with his barrage, focussing on the bricks at the circumference of the hole. Finally, though nowhere near fully destroyed, the wall was sufficiently ruined for him to feel that his work was done.

Though he had certainly caused some tangible damage, the real reason he'd stopped was that he hardly had enough strength left to continue standing, let alone bang away at some stupid pile of bricks. Kotwas leaned against the adjacent plastered wall and allowed himself to slowly slide down until he was sitting on his haunches.

He closed his eyes and took some deep breaths trying to steady his heart and also get rid of the self-inflicted ringing in his ears that he'd earned by not using ear protectors while hammering inside an enclosed space.

Unfortunately for Kotwas, the tinnitus was not simply annoying, it also masked any other sounds that he might otherwise have heard.

When he eventually opened his eyes, he was stunned to find a naked man standing in front of him. His initial, fleeting thought was that it must be the owner of the house and he'd come down to check out the noise.

The man was looking down at him with a mix of curiosity and lust. Kotwas was about to tell the bloke that he didn't dance to that tune when his brain began to register some subtle anomalies in the owner's face and body. The man's skin didn't look like skin... not exactly, anyway. It looked more like one of the waxwork sculptures at Madame Tussauds in London.

Then there was the fact that his entire musculature didn't look right. The muscles were too tightly bundled and seemed to be constantly twitching beneath the waxy skin. As if those oddities weren't strange enough, the man suddenly began sprouting thick, black, wiry hair across his entire body.

Then things got bad.

*

Though it had initially felt at ease once it recognised the town and, more especially, the underground network of tunnels, things were not exactly as they had been. Many of the familiar passageways had crumbled and some were now even blocked. What made matters worse was that a good number of the buildings in which it had expected to feed were now mostly sealed up.

With its hunger unsated and the option of where to feed safely becoming a major factor, it was considering waiting until nightfall at which point it would have no choice but to venture outside of the tunnels.

Just as it was about to give up on one particular passageway, it heard the sound of humans. It followed the noise until it came to a set of crumbling steps leading to what, judging by the smell, was a new wall with its red stones held together with fresh mortar. As it stood at the bottom of the steps, it could hear anger in the humans' voices.

It explored the wall to see if it was secure or whether it had, by chance, been built with any space around it that could provide access.

The structure was solid and against hard rock. Disappointed, it began to walk further down the tunnel when it heard something impact the wall. Though the noise itself was intriguing, what it found most interesting was the grunting of the human on the other side. It could tell that the it was male and, by the sound of it, in poor health.

As it crouched in the darkness and watched, a second blow hit the wall, letting thin rivulets of light pierce the darkness within the tunnel.

After a third impact, an opening appeared providing light as well as the smell of its prey.

*

Peter finished his cigarette and felt that he'd got his anger sufficiently in check to go back down to the basement and see the extent of the damage the man had wrought. As he walked into the ground floor entry, he heard what could have been a scream, but because it only lasted a millisecond, he couldn't be sure that it wasn't an odd cry from an errant seagull.

Peter started down to the basement where he was hit with the smell of copper mixed with something dankly feral. As he rounded the tight, steep turn of the stairway, the basement came into full view.

The newly plastered and undercoated walls were covered with what Peter at first assumed was paint. For a split second, he felt anger that Kotwas had decided to vandalise the property. Then he saw a portion of what, until very recently, had been the acting supervisor of building planning.

It appeared as if the man had been ripped in two. Peter had spotted what was left of the man's lower half. The top part was being held in the jaws of what looked to be a massive canine of a size and shape that he knew didn't and couldn't exist.

The creature stared up at Peter, Kotwas' innards seemingly still pulsating within its maw. The creature glared into Peter's eyes without any show of surprise or fear at having been disturbed. If anything, it looked to be calculating whether to abandon its current meal so it could focus on the fresh meat that had just appeared or simply take what it had already claimed.

As Peter watched, frozen in place, the beast partially transformed into something vaguely human then spun around and, with what was left of Kotwas in its jaws, dived through the uneven opening that had just been created in the brick wall.

Peter stood there shivering, his mind flooded by way too much adrenaline to make sense of anything he had just seen. Finally, after what seemed like an eternity, Peter stumbled back upstairs and made it out into the open air.

Having just witnessed horrors beyond anything his mind could have ever imagined, the peaceful, seaside rhythm of life seemed almost surreal, as if it were the fabrication not what he'd just witnessed.

Peter fumbled for his phone and managed, with palsied hands, to dial 999.

Nothing happened.

He tried again with the same results.

At that moment, the owner of the next-door fish and chip shop walked by and saw that Peter was having trouble making a call.

"I wouldn't bother trying," the man said. "Every telecom tower within ten miles is down. Haven't been able to make a call all morning."

The man then noticed Peter's fraught condition.

"Don't look so upset. They always come back on eventually."

"Do you have a landline in your shop?" Peter asked.

"Yes, I do."

Peter felt a brief moment of relief.

"Funny thing is," the man continued, "that's on the fritz as well!"

CHAPTER SIXTEEN

Still stuck in an unmoving line of traffic trying to return to town, Helena switched from one radio station to another hoping to find some snippet of news regarding what exactly was going on around them.

"This is odd," Emma said as she stared at the message on her phone. "I haven't been able to get service for the past fifteen minutes."

"That's probably because we've only moved a quarter of a mile in that time." Helena looked out at the traffic jam that had developed on both lanes of the Dover Road.

"Let's try a trick that sometimes works down here," Jay suggested, and he turned right, down Walmer Castle Road, a narrow street that led towards the coast.

The two women sat in silence as Jay drove from one dangerously small lane to another until they finally emerged onto Kingsdown Road that ran parallel with the shore. He made a right and stomped on the old car's accelerator.

"If you plan on killing us all, you may as well tell us where you're taking us," Emma said.

Jay ignored her comment and, just as the road split into two even narrower tracks, he turned left onto a steep, unpaved lane. On the right was an unobstructed view of the White Cliffs of Dover and on the left was a row of charming old fishermen's cottages, most of which had been modernised and glammed up.

The lane ended in a dirt parking area.

"Why are we here?" Helena asked.

"There's a pub here," Jay advised. "It's literally on the beach."

Emma turned in her seat and felt a wave of emotion wash over her.

"Oh my God," she said.

"You remember." Jay looked back at her.

"Of course, I do. This is where you proposed."

"Seriously?" Helena chirped in. "How cool. It looks very romantic."

"He could do that occasionally," Emma said with a sigh. "As touching as this is, shouldn't we be trying to get help?"

"Check your phones," Jay replied.

All three did just that. Initially the phones showed no signal whatsoever, then, one by one, bars appeared at the top of their screens.

Helena was the first to speak. "I'm picking up French telecom."

"So am I," Emma said.

"Not a bad trick, huh?" Jay bowed his head. "It's something to do with the cliffs. We lose the UK carriers and pick up French roaming."

Helena started fiddling with her phone, then after a moment, held up her screen so the others could see.

"What are we looking at?" Emma asked.

"This is a site that tracks mobile phone outages and shows you where they are on a map. You see that orange circle that looks to be around fifteen miles across. That's why we can't use our phones… except down here."

"How could an area that big go out?" Jay asked.

"It can't, at least not unintentionally," Helena pointed out. "It's shared by too many providers using dozens of leased towers."

"So, the military closing the roads and now all communications being blocked is likely not a coincidence," Emma stated. "Jesus, Jay. What exactly did you bring back from that ship?"

"I don't know but at least now we can communicate outside this area," Jay replied.

While his words still hung in the air, all three phones lost their signal from France.

"How is that even possible?" Emma asked as an icy chill ran the length of her spine.

"This is nothing to do with the UK towers. The French signal is obviously now being jammed as well," Jay said.

"What the hell is going on?" Helena asked. "What could warrant going to these extremes to make sure we can't communicate with the outside world?"

"I have no idea, but I know someone who does. I think it's time we had a little chat with that Cameron fella, don't you?"

"What makes you think that he will be any more willing to talk now than he was a few hours ago?" Helena asked.

"It's just possible that I have something that he might find valuable."

"I'm not sure he needs an expert on vintage cars and single malt Scotch right at this moment," Emma commented from the back.

"If I was that creature, I know where I would hide out," Jay commented. "I'll wager you that it has found its way into the smugglers' tunnels under the town."

"How does that make you any more valuable to MI6?" Helena said with a roll of her eyes.

"When I was doing my master's in marine archaeology, I chose the Goodwin Sands as part of my thesis. I also documented the tunnel network beneath Deal, as it was in constant use back in the piracy days. As the Sands claimed countless smugglers' ships, I felt the tunnels should be part of the same narrative."

"I'm not sure that Brigadier Rod-Up-Bum is going to want any help, no matter what," Helena opined.

"I guarantee he will after that thing starts feeding on the town population."

"That's if it doesn't find a way into the open countryside. It would be far safer there than in the centre of town," Helena replied.

"That's the thing. I don't believe it cares about safety. From what it did in the cinema, my guess is that its full focus is on killing and feeding."

"It could do that in the countryside as well. Think of all the livestock."

"I think it wants to feed on humans. Not only that, but

did you see the way it placed the two agents' heads on that table? It was like it was displaying its kills."

"While we appear to be outside a pub, maybe we should check to see if they have a landline. Theirs may not yet be cut," Emma said, trying desperately to change the subject.

Once inside, Jay took the opportunity to chat up the publican to see if she knew what was going on with the road closures and the telephone blackout.

"First I heard of it," Belinda Fielding replied as she picked up the land line handset and heard nothing but a low frequency buzz. Belinda was a slight woman in her late sixties and, despite her blue-rinsed, overly permed hair, she looked as tough as nails. "Let's see if there's anything on the radio?"

"We've been trying that for an hour. We get nothing," Helena advised.

"I bet that's because you tried the big stations. Did you know that Deal has its own station, aptly named, Deal Radio? If you want to know what's happening in town, that's who you'll want to be listening to!"

She opened her iPad, which was attached to the pub's AV system, and tapped an app icon.

It wouldn't open. She tried again with the same results. Belinda then moved a stack of napkins from in front of the pub's router and saw that all of the LED light that should have been green were yellow and flickering.

"That's odd, we seem to have lost all data as well as phone. Never mind, we can always go back to the basics."

Belinda reached into a low cupboard and after a

moment's rummaging, produced an old-fashioned analogue radio. She turned it on and dialled in a frequency in the AM range. There was a lot of static, but after fiddling with the extendable antenna, a station finally came through, clear as a bell.

A man's voice sounded both serious and concerned.

'... especially as nobody knows why we have lost communications. We sent one of our technicians up to the roadblock on the Dover Road, but the officer in charge claimed to know nothing about a communications blackout. Whether he was being honest we simply don't know. To repeat, all roads in and out of Deal are closed. No trains are running, and all phone and internet appears to have been cut. While some in Walmer and further south have come by and told us that they were able to connect to French telecom by switching their roaming on, we have just learned that that too has just ceased to be possible.'

As the radio presenter read a list of closed roads, Belinda turned down the volume.

"It seems you were correct," she said to Emma.

"Has anything like this happened before?" Jay asked.

"Not since the war."

"Which one?" Emma asked.

"WW2. My parents used to tell me about how, for three entire days, this whole area was locked down. Supposedly, a couple of unexploded bombs fell near here and the ministry felt they were of a size to warrant evacuation, but apparently the folks in Deal flatly refused to leave their town unattended."

Emma turned to face Jay. "Could this be for the same reason?"

Jay steered her out of earshot of Belinda.

"First of all, I don't think the two occurrences are linked. During the war, people were told to evacuate, which makes sense. With regards to our situation, I somehow doubt that it has become common practice to force everyone to stay in an area where unexploded munitions have been found. Secondly, all of this started soon after the MI6 go-team turned up. I think it's pretty clear that whatever we brought ashore is the root of the problem."

"Surely the government wouldn't go to these lengths over an oversized dog, no matter how dangerous. Besides, wouldn't they want as many people to leave the area as fast as possible rather that trap us all here?"

"Yes, I think they would. That means that they are more worried about the creature slipping out of the area than protecting the towns and villages within the cordoned-off zone."

"Are you saying that our lives aren't as valuable as that oversized canine you described?"

"No," Jay said, lowering his voice. "I believe that they are thinking that leaving us here as a food source for the creature is preferrable to it getting loose and having the entire country as a buffet."

CHAPTER SEVENTEEN

Charles Haley, the mayor of Deal, was recovering from the excessive amount of alcohol he'd managed to consume the previous night. The mine opening had ended with an impromptu champagne party at the Deal Hoy pub. The ride owners and Deal dignitaries had all been invited as a thank you for having helped pave the way for the attraction to become a reality.

The small crowd that had been expected for the opening had doubled, then quadrupled, as the public became more and more frustrated at how little they could see of the *Lady Lovibond* recovery from the shore. People by the drove had made their way through the narrow lanes until they found Cannon Street. From that point, signage led them a further three hundred yards to the site of the grand opening of the mine tunnel.

Few had any great interest in the mine itself but having heard that there was to be free soft drinks and sweets for the children as well as live music and beer for the adults, they followed the crowd like the lemmings they were.

The actual opening had taken less than an hour. Three speeches and a ribbon cutting were immediately followed by the inaugural VIP descent down the newly constructed lift to Shaft 57.

Haley had severe claustrophobia and had consumed three pints of cheap lager just to get him to a point whereby he could pretend to be enjoying himself. Before descending, a staffer had handed them each a brand-new mining helmet complete with built-in light. As the lift started its descent and the air became warmer and staler, Haley felt beads of sweat forming on his hairless scalp. The trip down seemed to take forever. Even though he'd been warned that during the descent the lights would intentionally flicker as part of the 'ambience' of the ride, the first time it happened he'd let out an involuntary, fearful gasp, though the other ten guest inside the lift chose to pretend not to notice.

Once they reached the bottom, Haley was shocked at how realistic the tunnel appeared. He had known from the plans that the owners had intended to keep it as true as they could to how it was for the miners back in the day, but he'd expected bright lights, at least, and something closer to a Disney attraction. Instead, the tunnel had a hard earth-packed floor with a string of low-wattage bulbs draped along one wall. The support beams looked ancient, and Haley couldn't help wondering how safe they could be if they were as original as they appeared.

The one mildly calming feature was that the shaft was much bigger than he expected. It had to be five metres wide and three metres tall. Down the centre ran a pair of steel rails, on which sat a small locomotive and six mine cars that had been converted to hold six passengers each.

Though surprisingly warm, the air in the shaft smelled damp and earthy. Haley looked beyond the locomotive, hoping to be able to see the length of the tunnel. What he saw instead was about a hundred metres of weak illumination from the strung bulbs, then nothing but blackness as the tunnel curved off to the right.

As if reading his mind, the owner, one Sasha Glenn, began speaking.

"When we were planning out the attraction, we decided that we needed to keep everything as realistic as possible. The lights you see here at the arrival point were our only concession to illumination. Once you are in the cars, you will have to switch on your helmet light, like this." He demonstrated by pushing a switch directly above the light housing. "Then you will be able to get a view of the shaft just as the miners did."

"How did you get the locomotive and cars down here?" a manly looking woman asked.

"We were amazed at just how much equipment had been abandoned within the shaft once we were able to actually see in. Apparently, bringing the old machinery to the surface would have cost a small fortune and, as there was little market for outdated and well-used mining equipment at that time, the decision was made to let it stay down where it was. We were initially concerned that we might not be able to proceed because of all the detritus left behind."

"You dug a hole all the way down here just so you could see that it couldn't be used?" a member of the chamber of commerce asked incredulously. "That seems like a waste of money."

"We didn't have to dig at all, initially. We were able to access an old ventilation shaft and snake a camera down into the tunnel. Once we'd filmed as much as we could we went over to the Betteshanger Museum and met with a group of miners that now act as volunteers. They'd all worked in Shaft 57 at some point in the past and knew it to be a junk yard. They showed us a video that had been taken just before the mine owners sealed this shaft. They hadn't exaggerated.

"Then where is it all now?"

"The locomotive and cars that you see before you were found abandoned almost where they sit now. We first converted the locomotive to electric then used it and the cars to move everything back to what had been the start of the shaft or tunnel, almost a mile away. Then once it was clear, we were able to fully inspect the area that we planned to use and carry out whatever repairs or maintenance was needed to ensure that all was safe and secure. After that work was done, we added the lights, modernised the ventilation and completed the lift and stairway."

"Stairway?" Haley asked.

"It's adjacent to the lift but separated by enough concrete to survive a nuclear blast. That was one of the biggest caveats of building this attraction. The government and council were adamant that there had to be two points of ingress and egress. They are right of course. Can you imagine being down here and have the lift fail?"

Haley felt the colour drain from his face. Until that moment, he hadn't thought of such a possibility. Even knowing that there were backup stairs did little to calm his nerves. Overweight and adverse to anything close to exercise, he had trouble climbing the single flight of stairs in the town hall to get to his office. The thought of climbing stairs all the way back to the surface made his stomach do backflips.

After a quick safety briefing, the host assigned seating within the cars, then climbed into the rear of the converted locomotive. Seconds later his voice came through concealed speakers in each car.

"Welcome aboard the express coal train," he said before using a touch screen to start the locomotive's journey into the sheer blackness of the shaft beyond.

Haley sat miserably within the clanking and oddly bouncy coal car. Once out of range of the illumination near the lift, he had to turn his entire head to throw any light on the passing walls and support structures. He could feel his claustrophobia kicking into high gear, but knew that, as mayor of Deal, any visible sign of weakness would only end in ridicule from the town's population.

Then, after about five minutes, the owner's voice resumed as he described the conditions the miners had worked in during the earliest days of the mine. The train followed the old tracks around a slow curve before stopping next to an exposed area of open coal face.

A lifelike pair of stationary manikins were dressed in full miners' gear and were posed with pickaxes in hand, striking at the black surface as a faux gas lamp provided minimal light at their feet. A soundtrack of miners at work came through the speaker.

There was something so twee and low budget about the display that Haley couldn't help laughing. It wasn't until they continued further along the shaft that his mirth dried up and fear took its place.

He had almost managed to get his breathing and panic in check when the owner questioned, in an exaggeratedly dour tone, whether any of the guests could imagine what it was like to spend over seventy-two hours a week in such an inhospitable location. The owner then pointed out that before the mid-twentieth century, miners would often have to do twelve-hour days, six days a week.

Haley did his best to specifically not think about such things and managed to keep his mind focused on happier times, when the wooden shaft support they were passing under suddenly groaned, seconds before one of the vertical load-bearing struts split in two.

The air filled with the sound of collapsing wood and dirt. Finally, an overhead light came on revealing that the collapse had been staged and that the *real* support structure was right next to the false one and was still very much intact.

Haley had been very concerned about his bowels and gag reflex for the entire return journey, while at the same time had vowed to himself to never visit Deal's new attraction ever again in his life.

*

Once in the pub, Haley had drowned the memory of the

mine shaft in copious amounts of champagne, and by 9:00 the following morning was still dead to the world. It wasn't until his deputy, who had been trying to reach him by phone right up until all mobile service suddenly ended, hammered on the mayor's door.

Barry Halford had only joined the mayor's office out of boredom. As neither the deputy nor the mayor himself were paid an actual salary, it had been the lure of helping the town that had first attracted him. Eighteen months later, Barry knew only too well that the current mayor seemed more interested in helping himself than actually improving the town. The only reason he still hung on was that he knew, judging by Haley's ill health, alcoholism and gluttonous diet, the man was bound to drop dead at some point in the very near future.

Once the mayor opened the door, Barry found himself babbling as Haley, clearly still inebriated, struggled to understand what he was saying. After finally managing to get Haley to focus, he talked in a calm and measured tone, advising the mayor about the latest goings-on in their town. He explained that there were a government helicopters on Walmer Green, the military had set up roadblocks stopping anyone from entering or exiting the area and, most recently, that there was no phone or internet service within the cordon.

"Has anyone contacted the police in Dover?" Haley asked.

Barry stared at him with total dismay. "As I just mentioned, we have no means of communicating with anyone." He watched as Haley's booze-soaked brain tried to compute what he was being told. Finally, he noticed a brief spark in the other man's eyes.

"What about the seafront?" Haley asked. "Why can't the RNLI launch their boats and get word to Dover?"

"We already thought of that, but there are three Royal Navy vessels off the coast, and they are under orders not to let anyone in or out."

Haley looked back at his deputy in confusion. "They let hundreds of asylum seekers land on our shores every week, but when they finally decide to use the military, it's to stop us from leaving! What the bloody hell is going on?"

"We have no idea. There's some kerfuffle over at the old cinema, but apart from that, everything seems normal. The only rumour I've heard is that there may be unexploded ordinance involved, but that doesn't exactly ring true. One would hope that if there were bombs discovered here, the first thing they would do would be to get us away from the danger, not keep us trapped here."

"So, who's keeping the residents and tourists under control. They must be going mad."

"The majority are still sleeping, but with check out from the hotels and B & Bs fast approaching, things will most likely escalate."

"Then, who's in charge when there's no help from the government or the police?" Haley asked.

"You, I presume," Barry replied with a shrug.

Before he could respond, a figure appeared on the front stoop and calmly stared in at the mayor and his deputy.

"Glad you're both here," Peter Cates said. "I thought

someone should let you know that there seems to be a slight problem in Deal at the moment."

"We know all about the roads and the phones," Haley replied dismissively. "Shouldn't you be off painting something?"

"I was doing just that, but when the planning inspector arrived, I thought it best to stick with him."

"Then why aren't you with him now?"

"That's why I'm here. I can't be certain, but I think he was eaten."

"Why have you come to tell me that a building inspector was eating? I presume that you yourself must have done the same thing this morning?"

Peter shook his head. "Not eating... eaten. Something came into the basement I'm working in and was making a right meal of the bloke before I startled it, and it ran off with what was left of the inspector in its mouth."

"I haven't got time for one of your incredulous sagas, Mr Cates. The town has a real emergency going on. Why not, just this once, let us get on with—"

Peter held out his phone so the two men could see the photo he'd taken of what was left of Kotwas' body.

The reaction was instantaneous.

Barry slumped against the wall as the colour drained from his face while Haley began projectile vomiting still-undigested champagne, hamburger and pork scratchings onto his hallway mirror.

"Sorry." Peter tried to supress a grin. "Was it something I said?"

CHAPTER EIGHTEEN

It sat in utter darkness below the town. Though it had recently fed on the fatty human, it hadn't enjoyed the meal. The male had tasted sour, and the layers of fatty tissue had made finding the rich, red meat far more difficult. What was even more frustrating was that the feeding immediately after its rebirth the previous day hadn't been satisfying enough. Even though it had saved its favourite parts of the human anatomy, the legs and lower back, as a treat once it had fully destroyed the carcasses, it was interrupted by the arrival of the two males and one female.

Just like the deep-rooted urge to feed, the overpowering need to ravage the human remains was ingrained within its consciousness. It knew that such action did nothing to enhance its meal, yet it did so with an unconscious drive. While capable of simple sentient thought, even enough to move unobserved among humans by assuming their form, its mind was not capable of memory recall, self-awareness, or even questioning why it had the need to kill and kill again.

After the last unsatisfying feeding, it had moved through the system of tunnels until it again picked up the aroma of raw meat. It most definitely wasn't human, but still, it smelled healthy and fresh. Four metres under Middle Street, it had to crawl flat on its belly to climb over a partially collapsed section of earthen ceiling. Once on the other side of the obstruction, the smell of meat was even stronger.

It moved silently in the blackness, allowing its nose to guide the way. The tunnel suddenly branched – the main part continuing straight ahead, the other heading east, away from the coast. Its olfactory sense led it to choose the eastern branch.

After only a few seconds within the narrower and damper section, the intensity of the meat odour quadrupled. It stepped carefully through muddy sludge and found an even smaller tributary tunnel that sloped upward to drier ground. This one was hardly taller than its back when in canine form.

A solid wooden door attracted its full attention. Even though closed, the aroma of raw flesh came flooding through the sealed portal. It closely examined the wooden barrier, hoping to find it as rotten and fragile as many it had encountered below ground. Instead, it smelled newer, and after a few pushes with its head, the creature recognised that it was not going to be able to breach the portal. It studied the ground and sought any sign of recent human activity outside the barrier.

There was none.

Frustrated, and with its hunger growing by the second, it wondered whether hunting on the surface would be worth the risk, but something instinctual told it that it was better to hunt below ground than to risk detection above.

It was about to give up on its search of that part of the

tunnel branch when something caught its eye thanks to its enhanced scotopia, which allowed it to see as well in the dark as at night.

Only a few feet away from the door that blocked access to the fragrant raw meat, rows and rows of bottles filled wooden shelves that had been mounted into a hand-hewn earthen wall that led to yet another door. This one was nowhere near as fortified, and much to the creature's delight, did not appear to be fully closed either.

It rested its head against the worn wood and listened. There were human voices that seemed to be coming from somewhere beyond the doorway but were not close enough to warrant a forced entry until it knew more. It decided to stay just out of sight of the doorway and observe.

*

Jay, Helena and Emma reached the corner of Beach and South Street and were surprised to see that armed soldiers were blocking access both at their end and on Victoria Road to the west. Frustrated, Jay took the next left then turned into a narrow roadway and pulled up in front of the Kings Head Pub.

Once free of the car, he led them through a series of alleys until they arrived back on South Street, having avoided the guards. Acting as if they had every right to be there, they marched up to a soldier who was stationed in front of the closed exit door of the cinema.

"We need to see Cameron," Jay stated.

"Please move on," the soldier said in a monotone.

"I think if he finds out that I know where the thing has gone, yet you sent me away, he might be a tad peeved. Then again, a few years serving your country in the Falklands might be your idea of heaven."

"Wait here." The soldier gave Jay a healthy glare before stepping into the cinema.

The three stood silently for less than a minute, then the door opened, and Cameron emerged, blinking, his eyes unaccustomed to daylight.

"As I explained earlier, your country thanks you for your efforts, but at this point you are no longer needed."

"I disagree," Jay said with a smile. "What if I was to tell you that I not only know where the creature is likely to be hiding, but could also help you navigate your way to it?"

"We have people stationed throughout the town. As soon as it makes a move, we will know, and at that point be able to put an end to this unfortunate mishap."

"Mishap? My closest friend is lying dead behind this door and two of your own people have basically been consumed. I would hardly call that a mishap, and as far as you hoping that there will be a sighting, that's not going to happen."

"If you are suggesting that the beast is hiding out in the tunnels under the town, a network you wrote about in your master's thesis, we have already considered and dismissed such an idea. We believe it is waiting for nightfall so it can leave the town unseen and make its way into the more remote countryside."

"And if you are wrong?" Jay asked trying to keep the

frustration he was feeling out of his voice.

"In the unlikely event that we need an expert on the collapsed tunnel system beneath Deal, I will personally ask for your help. In the meantime, may I suggest that you return to your hotel and relax. Deal's a beautiful little town. Enjoy it."

Jay knew that they would most likely never hear from him again. He decided that trying to force the issue, especially against such a dismissive and stubborn individual, was pointless. Jay realised that the best option was to wait. After all, if he was right, there would be other deaths in Deal, and they would doubtless be linked to the tunnel system beneath the town. If not, and the creature did try and escape the town and its cordon, the military would be able to deal with the problem without his help.

Cameron smiled as the three walked off. As Jay led Emma and Helena away from the old cinema, Cameron turned to the soldier that had been guarding the door.

"Don't let them get anywhere near this place again."

"How am I supposed to do that?"

"If they try, shoot them."

*

As Jay drove into the Regal Hotel parking lot, Emma said, "Since I don't seem to have a way to get back to my ship and I don't have a room here, where do you suggest I go?"

"I'm sure they'll have something available," Jay replied.

Once they were inside, the throng of angry guests put

pay to that idea. What Jay hadn't realised was that with departing guests unable to leave the town and some newcomers having reached Deal before the barricades went up, rooms were suddenly a scarce commodity.

Two young women behind the reception desk were trying to pacify a growing crowd with little success. The most vocal participants seemed to be those who had already checked out but had been blocked from leaving the area. They felt it was the hotel's responsibility to give them their original rooms back despite others having already checked in.

"This must be going on all over town," Helena commented. "Not just at the hotels either. Can you imagine the skirmishes that must be happening at the Airbnbs?"

"That brings up an interesting point," Jay said. "Food is going to become an issue. We should hit Sainsbury's before everyone gets the same idea."

"I somehow doubt that every restaurant is going to run out of food," Helena replied.

"Good thinking. I'll be right back."

Before anyone could ask for some clarity on his 'good thinking' comment, Jay spun around and charged out of the hotel.

"What's he up to?" Helena asked Emma.

"I didn't know when we were married, and I certainly have no idea now. Far more of a worry is the issue of where I am supposed to sleep tonight."

Helena could see the anxious expression on the other woman's face and after a brief internal battle decided to push aside her almost phobic hatred of sharing a bedroom with any other human being.

"My room has a second bed. You're welcome to camp out with me until this nonsense gets sorted out," Helena offered.

"Really? That's awfully nice of you."

"I was a little surprised that Jay didn't make the same offer, so I thought I'd better step up."

"Knowing my ex as I do, I doubt he ever even gave it a moment's thought. He's always too busy within his own head to think as linearly as we mere mortals tend to do," Emma suggested. "I am curious, however, as to where he's gone."

The two made small talk for a few more minutes and were about to head upstairs when Jay returned, breathless and sweaty.

"We're covered for dinner tonight," Jay said as he pushed through the growing crowd. "I booked a table at Victor's."

"How can you think of food after what happened to Brian — to say nothing of the fact that the entire town is starting to come unravelled?" Emma asked.

"We have to eat, and I thought we may as well eat somewhere secluded. Ron is still the manager there and he was able to squeeze us in."

"I feel strange about eating at a posh restaurant with Brian lying in a body bag somewhere," Helena whispered.

"Brian would be the first person to insist that instead of dwelling on what happened to him, our priority is to look after ourselves. Food is near the top of the list. By evening, the natives will have grown hungry and restless."

"And knowing you Brits, they will be compensating by drinking away their displeasure," Emma added.

"And let's not forget that there won't be any police presence in town until after the roadblocks have been lifted," Helena commented.

"Good point," Jay said, nodding. "Victor's might just be the perfect place to hide out, away from the sozzled masses. If I may suggest, we should battle our way to the front desk and see if there is anything they can do about a room for Emma, then we can hit Sainsbury's for supplies before it gets mobbed."

"I'm going to share Helena's room, so you can put away your shining armour," Emma said sarcastically.

"Hopefully she can find a way to blank out your snoring," Jay replied, smiling.

"That's not fair. I had adenoid trouble back then. I'll have you know that I had them removed soon after we were divorced."

"That's funny," Jay replied with a straight face. "My haemorrhoids went away around the same time."

"While this banter is a delightful addition to the day, perhaps we should get on with it and get the shopping out of the way," Helena suggested.

Jay knew she was right, but he was enjoying the exchange between himself and his ex. What Helena couldn't have known was that, even during the darker days of the marriage, the repartee between them was always a pleasant respite from all the insidious poison that was creeping into their relationship.

With Jay leading, the three exited the hotel and wound their way through the centre of the town. Emma knew the place reasonably well from her days with Jay, but it was all very new and interesting to Helena. Almost every other building had some sort of dark history, and Jay seemed to know every detail.

Once they reached the High Street, Jay could see that the peaceful little town was going to have some problems, sooner rather than later. Usually on a weekday morning, the street would be dotted with locals and holiday makers quietly window shopping or just plain milling about without any particular destination in mind.

That was not the case on this day. Word had spread through the community that everyone was trapped within the cordon. Being English, they reacted as they usually did when faced with adversity.

They drank.

Heavily.

With no police presence and pubs, bars and restaurants treating the lock-in as more of a business boom than an emergency, it looked as if a large portion of the population was already well on its way to intoxication, even at 11:00 in the morning. While most were content to sit on the exterior seats and benches that the establishments had provided once interior space was filled, the rowdier members of the crowd saw fit to stagger along the busy street with a minimum of one cocktail clutched in hand.

Profanity and vomit were plentiful as were early skirmishes as the youth of the nation felt the need to air their alpha tendencies in plain view for one and all.

"This is going to get nasty," Jay whispered to the others. "By mid-afternoon this bunch is going to be uncontrollable."

"I'm not sure they haven't reached that stage already," Emma commented.

The three crossed the road quickly and darted down a path that ran between the Rose Hotel and St George's Church. Within only a few steps, the troubling vibrations that were emanating from the centre of town died out as they entered a small park with leafy trees overhanging almost the entire spread of well-tended lawn.

Once they reached Sainsbury's, Jay was surprised to see how quiet the car park was. Even on a slow day it would have been at least two-thirds full, yet that morning, there was only a smattering of vehicles. What made the sight even stranger was that one of the home delivery vans pulled out in front of them and headed north, presumably sticking to its home-shopping schedule despite the lock-in.

Once inside, the sense of otherworldliness grew exponentially. There were hardly any shoppers, and the shelves were well stocked and neatly arranged. It was almost as if everyone was treating the lock-in as some sort of holiday rather than the entire town and surrounding areas having been put under an unscheduled quarantine.

Jay couldn't help wondering how the revelling population would feel if they were aware of the real reason for the military's presence. He doubted they would be in quite such a partying mood if they knew that a violent creature that seemed to prey on human flesh was loose among them.

Then again, if they continued drinking themselves stupid, he doubted they would be in a fit condition to care.

As their hotel rooms came without a fridge or hot plate, and they had no ability to cook or even heat up any food, they opted for energy bars, some fruit, water, and at Emma's insistence, a bottle of VSOP brandy (for emergency use only).

"I noticed that they sell clothes here," Helena commented, pointing to the far end of the supermarket.

"I don't usually buy clothes at the same place I buy toilet paper," Emma replied, despite the realisation that with all her belongings stuck on the research ship, she would need both clothes and supplies.

"I don't think you want to shop on the High Street at the moment, so hopefully they'll have something you like here," Jay suggested.

There was a surprisingly large selection of women's clothing. All brightly coloured and oddly shapeless. Perfect for post beach wear.

"Some of this looks halfway decent," he mentioned. "Try something on."

Emma turned and stared at him with a concerned look.

"You really never knew me, did you?" she asked, shocked that Jay would think she would ever be willing to be seen in such unflattering garments.

"I'm trying to avoid getting anywhere near the mob. These are" – he gestured to the nearest rack – "perfect to blend in with the tourists. I'm not expecting you to adopt this casual a lifestyle. It's just something to wear until we can reunite you with your own clothes."

"I'll just keep wearing what I have on."

She hesitated at a section selling bras and panties sets for a ridiculously low price. She found her size and grabbed two multipacks and shoved them to the bottom of the shopping cart.

"Now if you don't mind, find me the cosmetic section."

CHAPTER NINETEEN

Once back in the hotel, the three opted to hunker down in Jay's room, as the lounge areas were even more crowded than earlier.

The three ate sandwiches they had bought in Sainsbury's, satisfied to use the time to try and get some sort of a grip on what they had endured so far that day.

Once everyone had finished and policed their own crumbs and detritus, Emma, without a word, opened the brandy and poured each of them a double shot into two hotel-provided water glasses and one teacup. Before Jay could question her motives, Emma raised her cup and said, "To Brian."

Helena and Jay could have added more but felt that the simplicity of his ex's toast was all that was really needed.

An hour later, the three left the hotel so that Jay could provide them with an overview of the old smugglers' tunnel system. He felt that they should have some idea of just how vast it was, and how easy it would be for the creature to stay hidden within its underground labyrinth of dark, abandoned passageways.

Jay led them along the seafront, then through a circuitous

route to the south end of Middle Street, careful to avoid getting too close to the old cinema and the MI6 contingent.

Middle Street was one of Deal's greatest treasures. Because of a strict and obsessively monitored conservancy that required the entire street be kept as close as possible to its original condition, some parts dated as far back as the fifteenth century and looked almost exactly as they had when new. The only real variance to the architectural charter was where WW2 bombs had destroyed original structures and newer, less quaint versions had been erected.

Jay pointed out a number of buildings that he knew from experience housed entryways to the subterranean tunnels. He described in detail the access through an old coal chute at the side of a detached two-storey house. He explained how the tunnel ran under Queen Street then, once under the main section of Middle Street, branched and fed countless homes throughout the old part of Deal.

As they walked along the ancient road, Jay pointed out a number of homes that held much darker histories than their brightly coloured paint jobs implied. He pointed out that it had been an area of press-ganging, where drunken citizenry were clubbed unconscious and carried onto waiting merchant ships to become unwilling and unpaid members of the crew. It was also the main thoroughfare used by smugglers to move the booty they had either brought ashore themselves or stolen from those who had already undertaken such work.

Jay further explained that countless homes that had, over the years, walled in or simply covered the old tunnel access points, had more recently reversed the trend and had made the quaint hatchways and doors a feature.

"Do people still go down into the tunnels?" Helena asked as the tour finished at Alfred Square.

"I suppose some of the tunnels are partially functional, but they would be damp, crumbling and almost certain to be filled with rats and the like," Jay replied.

"Deal has rats?" Helena asked, with a straight face and a twinkle in her eye.

Jay knew full well that she was goading him after the rat encounter at the old cinema but chose to ignore the jibe. "Just about anywhere has rats. So long as we continue to create refuse, they will multiply and enjoy the pickings."

"Is that why the bins always seem to have been picked over during the night?"

"Actually, the seagulls are the main culprits, with foxes running a close second."

"Foxes?"

"Absolutely," Jay replied. "If you walk along these back streets just before dawn, you'll see them everywhere."

"I thought they were supposed to be woodland creatures?"

"They were, but as we keep paving over their habitat to build more and more bland brick housing, they have fewer and fewer choices of where to hunt, and eventually have to turn to scavenging. A little like us."

"We're not scavengers," she insisted.

"Of course, we are. Humans used to hunt or at least forage for their food. Now we depend on others to do that work for us so that we may walk through aisles and aisles of premade meals and pick and choose what to consume next."

Helena looked to Emma as if hoping for some sort of moral support against Jay's strong opinion on the decline of civilisation's food sourcing.

"Hasn't he blessed you with one of his 'mankind is ruining the planet' diatribes before now?" Emma asked.

"I was saving them up until I felt she was ready," Jay said, smiling.

As the three walked back to the hotel, they noticed that there appeared to be a growing military presence dotted around the town. Soldiers in teams of three were stationed at almost every intersection. Jay couldn't help wondering if the troops had any real idea as to what was going on. He assumed that, just as the town was being kept in the dark, the soldiers were doubtless no more well informed than the civilians.

Then again, Jay was finding it hard to understand why the show of military might, coupled with the stringent lockdown were even necessary. Sure, the creature was oversized and vicious, but so were some of the XL dog breeds that seemed to have become popular with gang members and the like. Jay's recall after the creature had killed Brian was that it seemed to have some sort of human traits. In the cold light of day and with the edges of his memory fraying with each passing hour, he questioned his earlier observation. After all, since he had just witnessed his close friend and colleague be decapitated by the beast before it sprang out of the cinema, some degree of shock was bound to have caused confusion and distortion of his memory.

"Does anyone else think that all of this is just a little over the top for a dog attack?" he voiced.

"A dog, if that's what it was, has killed three people since last night," Helena pointed out.

"Still, soldiers at every corner and everyone blocked from leaving. There's more afoot than searching for a wild dog. I think it's time to find someone local with authority. Deal must at least have a mayor or something close to it."

"If there is, he or she would be wise to keep their head down until all of this lunacy subsides a bit," Emma stated. "Fear, frustration and alcohol are not a particularly calming mix. Add confinement and an armed military presence and you have a recipe for disaster."

"You don't sound as if you have too much faith in the locals being able to sort this out," Helena said.

"The problem I foresee is them not being mentally or emotionally able to resolve an issue like this. Remember the torch-carrying villagers in *Frankenstein*? This has all the makings of a re-enactment, only at least the villagers knew what they were marching upon. My biggest fear is a gang of drunken louts getting it into their sozzled heads that the military is to blame and trying to go after them."

"You don't have a lot of faith in humankind, do you?" Jay asked.

"As soon as we become a sentient and responsible race, I'll be the first one to sing our praises. Until that time, I prefer to sleep with one eye open and when awake keep one eye closed."

"What does that even mean?" Jay said shaking his head.

"It makes more sense in French. Let's go back to the hotel so I can have a long hot bath before dinner."

"My room only has a shower," Helena pointed out.

"Barbarians. All of you," Emma said as she strode off back towards the Regal.

While finding her comments frustratingly obtuse, at least to his way of thinking, Jay couldn't help reflecting on that characteristic being what originally attracted him to Emma.

Emma had been born to academic parents. Both were tenured lecturers at the Sorbonne in Paris, and both treated their only child as they would any other student. In their minds there was no life outside learning. The search for knowledge was, to them, the only reason to exist.

Needless to say, Emma's school years were an exhausting rollercoaster of studying and pedagogic tyranny from her parents. Their expectations vastly surpassed their own achievements causing them to offload their hopes upon her, something that Emma found to be untenable, and totally unfair. Her days consisted of rising at 5:00, reviewing the previous night's homework, attending school, then returning directly home to continue studying.

Emma was not permitted to play sports, or to undertake any extra-curricular activities that did not directly revolve around learning. Even before puberty, she had felt trapped without understanding why.

Once in her teens and with hormones beginning to edge out of the shadows, thoughts of boys began to invade her already crammed mind. Emma started to realise that the search for knowledge was by no means the be-all and end-all of existence. Her parent's attempts at trying to brainwash her away from any thoughts that weren't directly tied to her classes, only made Emma more aware of just how controlling a force they had been up to that point. As she began to observe her classmates go out on dates and to parties, she started to rebel against what she felt were the draconian edicts that her parents had foisted upon her.

When it came time to focus on university, her parents advised that she didn't need to worry about that as she already had a place reserved at the Sorbonne where they both still lectured. Emma rebelled and flatly refused to even consider such an option. The very thought of having to study right under their noses was simply too much to bear.

Not only did she baulk at their insistence she attend the Sorbonne but was so upset at their meddling that she felt the need to go her own way and managed to get a full scholarship to the Aix-Marseille University. In a final burst of rebelliousness, she chose to major in marine archaeology, a field so new that the university was only offering it for the first time that September. It wasn't even going to get full academic accreditation for another five years. But choosing it had the desired effect.

Her parents completely lost the plot. To them, pure archaeology was a calling – as devout a science as could ever have existed. They had never heard of marine archaeology and after reading the syllabus, deemed it to be little more than ocean-floor piracy. They initially attempted to sway their daughter's mind, having assumed that she must have some temporary malaise that had somehow managed to puncture her usually rational bubble.

The more they attempted to cajole her, the more Emma fought back and resolved to leave home and move south to Marseille. Ironically, she had initially declared her new major out of sheer frustration at her parents; however, after a number of pre-admission meetings at the university, she became enthralled with the scope of the subject matter. In her eyes, it was a science with far more depth, no pun intended, than straight archaeology.

After all, digging around the surface of the planet just so you could confirm something that was already most likely a known fact was hardly ground-breaking. Studying ruins on the ocean floor was a chance to re-write the history books. As if to emphasise that point, the university used the example of the *Titanic* wreckage. Prior to its discovery, it was thought likely to be in one piece. It was even fantasised that one day the wreck might be refloated.

It wasn't until researchers from the Woods Hole Oceanographic Institution managed to not only locate the wreck but also photograph it that the truth became known. Though the images were grainy and the light poor, those initial robotic dives informed the world that the great vessel would never rise again.

A few days before she was due to start at the university, and with few words passing between her and her parents, Emma stepped out of the family town house in the 16th arrondissement in Paris and journeyed down to the south coast, alone and terrified.

By the time Emma had obtained both her graduate and master's equivalencies (the Marseille university was still one year away from having the courses formally certified by the Ministère de l'Enseignement Supérieur et de la Recherche – the government body that strictly oversaw the higher education process in France) much of the distance between her and her parents had been bridged.

"Of course, you're going to teach," her father stated one evening when Emma had come up to visit. "There's no real future in trying to make a life out of practical archaeology. It's one of those subjects that must be taught, not toiled!"

"That is the most illogical statement I've ever heard. The whole point of spending the last four years in Marseille, as well as having put in countless hours as an unpaid intern on more undersea projects than I can remember, was so that I could get the necessary credentials to allow me to make it my career."

"What utter nonsense," her mother exclaimed, shaking her head.

Before long, the emotional gunpowder was reignited, and a standoff began again in earnest. No matter how she tried to convince her parents that spending her life as a marine archaeologist would be highly rewarding, they dismissed such 'childish drivel' as the result of a poor educational foundation and an immature mind.

Almost a year later, Emma was still fuming over her parents' refusal to take her seriously. It was with thoughts of making them eat their scholastic words, and possibly even finding some way to make them apologise for their short-sighted parenting, that Emma boarded an Air France jet in Marseille on her way to Athens to attend a three-day symposium on the latest technologies for deep sea archaeological recovery.

As the boarding was about to end, the very last passenger stepped into the fuselage. Dishevelled, unshaven and with a lock of greasy black hair covering his eyes, the man's appearance told Emma two things: he was what her parents would call 'the wrong sort' and there was an irresistible force pulling her towards him.

Jay Sallinger gave her a subtle nod as he passed her row then continued to the back of the plane, not knowing that he had just shared a glance with the woman who would ultimately change his life forever.

CHAPTER TWENTY

Helena and Emma stood on their room's narrow balcony and stared out at the Deal Pier as it became slowly enshrouded in thick sea fog.

"That's one thing that terrifies me," Helena commented. "I know it's just water droplets, but there's something very creepy about it."

"Perhaps that's because it's been the backdrop of just about every story involving unnatural death since film and TV were invented," Emma suggested matter-of-factly.

"Maybe that's it, but I seem to remember being scared of fog long before seeing any of those movies. The way it slowly swirls as it blankets anything that stands in its way. It's almost as if it's consuming everything it touches."

Emma replied, "I find it strangely comforting. I like the way it blurs reality as it approaches, then slowly turns everything grey, removing all colour. It's like some sort of magic trick."

"I've always heard that the French can romanticise just about anything."

Emma shrugged. "We do what we can."

Helena laughed as she checked her watch. "We'd better

get going. Jay will be downstairs waiting for us."

"Sometimes it's good to have the man wait."

"I haven't really had much time or interest in that kind of stuff. So far, I get all the satisfaction I need from science journals."

Helena sighed and shook her head. "That's not satisfaction, that's simply filling a void."

"If it's satisfying for me, then logically, I must be satisfied," Helena insisted.

"*Ma chèrie*, once this is over, you and I must have a lengthy talk. You have already proven yourself to be far superior to most males. It's time to relax and enjoy all the benefits that can bring."

Helena was tempted to ask what Emma meant by that, but before she could say anything more, Emma stepped back into the room, grabbed the cheap windbreaker she'd bought in the supermarket and headed to the door.

*

Marvin hated Deal. He was one of the most successful managers at Rockflow, the UK's biggest bookseller, and felt that having to temporarily manage the shop in Deal High Street while the regular manager was on leave was a slap in the face. His Canterbury shop was considered one of the jewels in Rockflow's crown with sales numbers that were always among the top of the group's, yet here he was stuck in Deal for the foreseeable future.

Marvin had arrived a day early. He was glad he had

chosen to take the reins so far ahead of schedule as, from what he was hearing, the town was now impossible to either enter or leave. Rumours of why they were under lockdown ranged wildly from unexploded munitions to some sort of terrorist attack.

Marvin waited among the throng of binge drinking locals until the regular staff had closed for the night then let himself in with a set of keys provided by head office. He wanted to go over the books without interruption and sat with the shop lights off so that he couldn't be seen from the street as he looked over the sales and diary entries. In the calendar of events, he was shocked to see that the regular manager seemed to have a different author booked every other Saturday for a signing event.

Marvin went through the names and shook his head at his colleague's sad attempt at garnering business by supporting local up-and-coming writers. In the Canterbury shop, signing events were a rarity and only ever featured best-selling authors. Crowds regularly lined up outside the shop and it wasn't uncommon to sell close to five hundred copies or more per event.

Judging by the list of writers that were scheduled to do a signing within the next six months, Marvin doubted they would sell more than twenty or thirty copies per event. He didn't care if it was beneficial to the town and the struggling writers – in his mind that wasn't what they were there for. Rockflow was not some sort of charity. It was a for-profit company, and he had every intention of ensuring that during his time in Deal, precious floor space would not be squandered on a bunch of unknown hacks whose books he wouldn't have on the shelves let alone at the signing table.

Marvin tried to get onto the company email site but couldn't get online. Instead, her typed a generic letter into notes, planning to copy it over to an email when the system was up and running. He planned to send the letter to all the authors in the calendar.

It said simply:

Dear Mr/Ms…

Unfortunately, there has been a problem with stock delivery, and we will therefore have to cancel your signing event. We will be in touch when we have more information.

Marvin planned to set up a distribution protocol whereby each writer would get his or her email only a few days before their signing event. That way there wouldn't be time for them to make too much of a fuss.

He was halfway through creating the list when he heard a creaking sound coming from the basement.

*

It didn't want to leave the tunnel near the overwhelming meat smell, but the craving to find another human target was simply too great. It eased out of the narrow tributary and headed south under the town's main shopping precinct. Even being that deep beneath the surface, it could hear the chaos above ground. Though muffled and distorted, it knew that in some way, it was responsible for the growing unrest in the streets.

Despite recognising that the drunken mele directly above it meant that there was an almost unlimited supply of young human flesh, it also knew instinctually that tempting as it was to separate a few bodies from the horde, doing so could be dangerous. It had found out during its earlier time within the town that a drunken mob could suddenly direct their fears into a vengeful and determined mass. Maybe if there were more creatures like itself, so that they too could hunt together in a pack, things would be different, but as a lone hunter, it knew that it had to use some degree of caution no matter how much the cravings escalated.

It travelled through a part of the underground system it did not recognise. In places the tunnels appeared better constructed while at the same time, disuse and decay had taken a greater toll. One entire section of wall had collapsed inward making it awkward to crawl over the damp, fetid earth to reach an undamaged section beyond.

It located many old access portals that should have provided entry to the dwellings above, but all had been sealed up tight. It was about to give up on that particular tunnel section when a familiar scent reached its olfactory senses. The odour of a human was unique. It was complex and acted upon its system before it was even aware of what was happening. Its eyes adjusted even more fully to the darkness of the tunnel while, at the same moment, its hearing became more acute. If there was still any trace of ambiguity about the sensory on-rush, the extra flood of saliva that began to fill its massive jaws told the whole story.

The only scent that triggered that instantaneous reaction was human.

It sought out and soon found a small vertical hatchway that had at some point been sealed shut with a thin bead of cheap putty. Over time in the humid tunnel, the sealant had flaked away in places, allowing trace odours to pass through and reach its highly modified nasal senses.

It clawed gently at the partially rotted wood as well as the putty and within minutes was able to force the hatchway open exposing the access hole. It intuitively knew not to climb too far up within the structure without an inkling of whether it would be visible to the humans on the street.

Instead of climbing to seek out its prey, it chose to try and tempt the human down to its level. It morphed the upper part of its body and head into a partial human form. It knew that in that mode its attack capabilities would be diminished but it needed to access one of its human talents in order to arouse the human.

It closed its eyes and straightened its neck, then after a moment's deep concentration, let out the sound of a human baby crying. Though it had some use of its vocal cords and could even utter single words if required, it felt that the sound of an infant in distress was more likely to bring the male down to the sub-basement.

*

Marvin listened intently, but the creaking sound appeared to have stopped. He went back to the list of who would receive his ego-destroying email. After entering a few more names, he heard a new sound. At first, he thought it was a cat meowing somewhere in the basement, but as he listened more intently, he realised that he was, in fact, hearing a baby crying.

For a moment he felt anger, assuming that one of the second-rate assistants had not only brought a child to work but had forgotten it in their haste to shut up shop and leave. He considered doing nothing and letting whoever had left the child deal with the aftermath in the morning, then realised that neither staff member who had been on duty that day was likely to have brought a child with them.

Marvin's curiosity finally got the better of him and he descended the narrow and poorly lit staircase to the storage area in the lower basement. It was his first time down there and like with the rest of the shop, he wasn't impressed. He understood that many parts of the town dated back to the sixteen hundreds, but he didn't understand why that should negate anyone from fully modernising their homes or businesses.

The space was dark and claustrophobic. The ceiling was less than five feet above the ancient wooden floor and the employees clearly treated the area like some sort of literary dumping ground. As thoughts of just how to sack the existing staff entered his mind, the crying suddenly took on a more urgent tone.

Marvin followed the sound through the piles of cardboard boxes and loose books until he came to what looked like a loft hatch, except it was situated on the side of a brick wall only inches above floor height.

The first thing he noticed was that the hatchway seemed to be partially rotted away. The second was that the crying sound appeared to be coming from the other side of it. As Marvin knelt to have a better look, he was hit with a strong scent of something feral. As his brain started to compute what exactly could be the origin of such a strong odour, the hatchway disintegrated and a long, black snout poked out of the hole.

For a brief moment, Marvin saw humour in the total absurdity of the situation.

Then the rest of the head emerged. Before Marvin could react, the creature lunged, closing its massive jaws on his midsection. For a microsecond, Marvin considered fighting back.

That idea never fully populated his brain before he was pulled, with impossible ease, right through the narrow hatchway and into the tunnel beyond.

Marvin's last thought was to question how he could still be alive as the monstrous dog began devouring his stomach.

CHAPTER TWENTY-ONE

"Patrick, could you go down to the storage area and bring up a couple of bottles of the Chateau Mireux," Ron called out from the bar. "The mayor is dining here tonight and I'm sure he'll ask for it."

Patrick appeared from the kitchen and shook his head as he smiled at Ron.

"I don't know why he likes that muck. It's too sweet and too oaky."

"You know that, and I know that, but ever since being appointed mayor he seems to feel that he's deserving of free drinks wherever he goes in Deal," Ron explained. "When we found cases of the plonk in Calais being sold for less than a couple of quid a bottle, I came up with the plan. A friend of ours complained loudly in front of His Honour that they were shocked how much the restaurant charged for Chateau Mireux – even if it was one of the best wines they'd ever had – and the mayor fell for it, and now, it's all he ever asks for. The fact that he wouldn't know a Sauvignon from a Sauternes has saved us a small fortune."

"What happens if one of the other restaurants spills the beans?" Patrick asked as he tightened the rubber band holding his long blond hair in place.

"They wouldn't dare. They've all found some low-cost option that they've conned him into liking. They know that if one of us falls, we all fall."

"Wouldn't it just be easier if everyone refused the man free drinks?" Patrick suggested.

"And bring down the wrath of the town hall?" Ron replied. "Ever wondered why this alley of ours is better maintained than some of the main streets in town? That's called having a good relationship with the powers that be. Plus, think about it; we give him free wine about once every two weeks – wine that cost us just over two Euros a bottle. Think of the alternative. What if instead of wanting something we've managed to convince him is a secret and treasured estate wine, he expected his meal to be comped. The mayor might not have a clue about what he drinks, but he is a world class gourmand and glutton and could, in that scenario, do us some serious financial damage."

Patrick rolled his eyes and grabbed an old-fashioned iron key from a hook next to the bar till. Just as he was about to head down two levels to the reclaimed tunnel area that they used for storage, he stopped and looked over at his uncle.

"Are we going to be okay tonight? I mean, with all the chaos that's happening on the High Street, is it even safe for us to open?"

Ron patted him on the back and internally shivered at the sight of his nephew's ludicrously long snake tattoo that, despite every attempt to conceal it, seemed to be creeping up his neck beyond his black linen shirt.

"The only thing we have to worry about is if the High Street premises run out of alcohol. Just in case though, I am planning to shut up shop no later than 10:00. That way the mob should still be focused on destroying their livers rather than releasing all that pent-up, alcohol-infused angst. I have little doubt that come the wee hours it won't be safe for man nor beast to be out there."

*

In the derelict cinema, Cameron and his team were finishing up their investigation of the site. Video had been taken of every square centimetre using both LED and ultraviolet light. Tissue samples had been taken from each piece of human remains as well as smears from all blood spots within the cavernous auditorium.

A team of 'recovery specialists' had then packed away all remaining pieces of the two agents in vacuum-sealed self-refrigerating containers. Brian's body and head were carefully sealed within a black double-lined body bag and would travel with the rest of the evidence, even though his remains were of far less interest than those of Wilson and Calloway. The reason being that his death had been immediate and almost surgical whereas the other two had been literally eviscerated and consumed, resulting in a substantial amount of trace evidence from the attacker.

Once everything was packed and ready to be transported, the interior of the cinema was sprayed top to bottom with military grade bleach.

Cameron had been briefed before his arrival in Deal via a phone call with Angela Clarkson, head of MI6. He wasn't told exactly what was suspected to have killed their agents as, at that point, she had not even read the full contents of black file 1076. All she knew was that the attack in Deal may well have had both military and terrorist implications.

He was told via a secure sat phone link that they were likely to be dealing with what was believed to be a large 'modified' canine that was capable of great savagery coupled with a strong sense of self-preservation.

Cameron was not told, as Clarkson herself was not yet aware, that the entity was also capable of self-resurrection. That the creature could reconstitute itself from its own ashes once it had come into contact with oxygen, had been witnessed by Wilson and Calloway; however, they never passed that information along before meeting their own unfortunate end.

Because of the extreme secrecy coupled with security-related bureaucracy that dated back to the 1940s, Cameron was left mostly in the dark and thought that they were dealing with some sort of genetically modified dog that had been designed to be bigger and meaner. He assumed its purpose was somehow battlefield-related, but in an age of precision drones and weapons that could be controlled from thousands of miles away, he wasn't quite sure what a dog, no matter how big, could bring to a theatre of war.

Then there was the matter of the unusually large military presence that had descended on the area. Cameron understood that the creature was indeed lethal. After all, he had seen the results first-hand. But to quarantine a town over a loose animal made no sense, not that sense always accompanied his orders.

Cameron stood outside the cinema watching the samples that had been boxed up or bagged be loaded into a fleet of Range Rovers. Together with the recovery team, they were about to be taken back to Walmer Green where three Dauphin 2 helicopters were standing by to whisk them to the Porton Down campus near Salisbury, in Wiltshire.

The fact that the destination was the UK's most secretive and controversial research facility was another anomalous cog in the operation and should have set off any number of alarms for Cameron. However, after over thirty years of acting as a senior on-site investigator for countless covert government operations, he had stopped wondering about the why and instead found it far safer to simply follow his orders even if they didn't make any sense.

His secure sat phone began buzzing, interrupting his thoughts.

After listening to a revised set of instructions, Cameron learned that he was not to accompany the recovery team and was instead to remain in Deal and meet up with some senior officers who would be arriving just after 8:00 that evening. He was to bring them up to speed on what had transpired at the cinema as well as provide them with whatever logistical and informational help they may require in order to resolve the current issue. In addition, there would be a consultant from Porton Down arriving at the same time who would, as they termed it, need some special handling.

As he watched the SUVs drive off, Cameron walked back into Deal avoiding the main area of town where a sort of inebriated chaos had taken hold. He couldn't help wondering if any of the drunken revellers would end up face to face with the supposed canine and whether, at some point, he would have to supervise the scraping up of their remains for future study.

His current client, MI6, had managed to find him a seafront home that was usually available for short-term rental, but had, in this instance, been commandeered for his use until such time as his skills were no longer needed in the area. The property was a three-storey Regency town house that, according to its promotional blurb online, 'could easily sleep ten'.

Cameron managed to wrestle the key from the lockbox that had, for some unexplained reason, been attached to the property at ground level behind a substantial bush. Once inside, his keen eye could see beyond the cleverly coordinated shades of blue and the endless array of seaside paraphernalia to the rotting wood of the vintage sash windows, the warped floorboards and the walls that were clearly fighting a brave battle against damp. Such was the hidden tragedy behind ownership of a grade I listed property.

Cameron knew all too well that the draconian rules that forbade modernising and fully weatherproofing such properties to ensure a historic purity within a conservation area only led to a slow but inevitable deterioration of the very buildings they intended to preserve.

He was exhausted. Despite being in great health and

fitness for his age, staying up for almost thirty-six hours and overseeing the investigation into the brutal slaughter of two MI6 agents, took a toll. One of his most rigid regimens was to ensure that he ate healthy and balanced meals even when on the road. The current assignment had made it impossible to stick to his strict diet. He had had to eat the same food as his go-team, which amounted to petrol station sandwiches, crisps and packaged pasties, all washed down with truly awful coffee.

He felt drained and troubled by his stomach's growing protestations over what it had been forced to process. Cameron, in a wise move only hours after arriving in Deal, had had the foresight to book himself a table at a highly rated restaurant for later that same evening. While normally a very frugal individual – the main catalyst to having two failed marriages – he'd sensed that food would become an issue and that, for once, his penny-pinching needed to be brushed aside in favour of a guaranteed decent meal, somewhere tucked away from the growing mob.

He fervently hoped that he could eat with some degree of anonymity. The last thing he wanted was to be peppered with questions he couldn't answer while trying to enjoy a quiet meal by himself.

Having walked down the side alley where the restaurant was located, Cameron felt reassured that it was not a place one would accidentally come across and that Victor's might just prove to be an oasis of peace.

CHAPTER TWENTY-TWO

"Has anyone seen Patrick?" Ron called out from behind the bar.

After the staff all replied in the negative, Ron was about to head down into the sub-basement to retrieve the mayor's favourite wine when the front door opened, and the first diners of the night arrived. By the time he had seated them in the upper level and then managed to calm his chef over what he perceived was the poor quality of the raspberries that were destined to be the garnish for the chocolate ganache cake, he had forgotten all about the wine as yet more guest began arriving.

Just as Ron started to feel that he had forgotten something, Jay, accompanied by his ex-wife and a young woman he didn't know, stepped inside the restaurant.

After exchanging pleasantries, Ron seated the three, then returned minutes later with a complimentary glass of Prosecco for each of them.

"Thank you, Ron. I'm glad to see that this place seems unaffected by the lunacy out on the High Street."

"That reminds me," Ron said, suddenly looking flustered.

The three watched as Ron drew the inside curtains across

the three windows that faced out onto the alley, making the room seem far more intimate, while at the same time ensuring that any prying eyes couldn't see what was going on inside the restaurant.

Jay gave Ron an approving thumbs up just as the front door opened and Cameron stepped in.

"This should be interesting," Jay said to Emma and Helena, who both turned to see what exactly had prompted such a comment.

As Cameron was shown to his table next to the curtained window, he sensed that he was being observed and casually scanned the dining room. His eyes met those of the three diners on table eight, and he felt his blood run cold. Here he was trying to have a quiet dinner away from the chaos in Deal, and who should be seated only inches away? The very man that had chosen to bring the artefact to shore. The man who, with the help of his team, had almost certainly opened the sarcophagus, resulting in the current state of confusion that was plaguing his investigation. All this nonsense about something from within the sarcophagus having attacked the men, was, in his opinion, just another example of a government that had lost the plot. Yes, the stone box had been tampered with, but whatever had violently ripped those men apart had doubtless already been within the abandoned cinema long before the artefact was ever placed there. His minimal brief that a large canine might have been responsible for the murders just made the whole endeavour even more ludicrous.

"Do you have a table in a different area?" Cameron asked.

"I'm sorry, we don't. The upstairs is booked for one large group, so this" – Ron gestured to the small dining area – "is all we have."

Cameron weighed up having to be in close proximity to Jay or having to take his chances trying to find food among the inebriated townsfolk who had pretty much laid claim to the High Street. A waft of air coming from the kitchen carried with it the aroma of roasting meat and Provençal spices.

Cameron took the seat facing away from Jay's table and sat down with a sigh just as the front door opened and a loud booming voice echoed through the small space.

"Where's Ron? I need a bloody big glass of that plonk he insists on serving me," the mayor said as he squeezed through the narrow doorway.

Ron immediately remembered what it was that he had forgotten. He stopped one of his waitresses and whispered for her to go down to the sub-basement and see what the hell happened to Patrick.

"Tell the little bugger to stop skiving off. Tell him that the mayor's just shown up and we need some of that Chateau Mireux up here."

"So, how are things going?" Jay asked, smiling, as he, uninvited, took the empty seat across from Cameron.

As Jay's arrival coincided exactly with the delivery of a double Tanqueray and tonic, Cameron was unable to let loose with as nasty a response as he would have liked, so as not to offend, or even scare, the young waitress. Instead, he thanked her, poured half the Fever Tree bottle into the glass then took a long swig.

Jay kept a straight face despite the amusement he was feeling at the other man's obvious discomfort.

"You look as if you needed that," Jay said, gesturing to the half empty glass.

"I don't suppose you would consider leaving me the fuck alone, would you?" Cameron said in little more than a whisper.

"I just hoped that you would have some interest in hearing our perspective about what went on at the cinema."

"Did you or any member of your team witness the murders of the two agents?" Cameron asked.

"If you are referring to the two MI6 agents, then, no. We did not."

"Then I don't understand why you feel that you can offer me any insight into to what exactly went on early this morning."

"Are you ready to order?" the waitress asked, her note pad at the ready.

"Is the venison good?"

"I've probably had venison here over a dozen times and I can, on this subject, be highly instructive," Jay advised. "It's always delicious."

Cameron studied Jay carefully then smiled up at the waitress. "I'll have the haddock tart to start, then..." He again looked over at Jay. "And I'll try the venison."

"Good choice," Jay said, smiling. "As for the other matter, we were in the cinema shortly after those men were killed and witnessed my friend and colleague be decapitated by what, most likely, killed your men."

"I believe you told the ops leader on the phone that it appeared to have been an oversized canine of some sort," Cameron commented.

"It was far more than a canine. I was so shocked the instant it happened that my mind was unable to correlate what I'd just seen."

"So, it wasn't just a dog."

"The creature that attacked my friend did appear to be canine — though of a size that was beyond any breed I've ever heard about — but microseconds after ripping Brian's head off it started to transform into something else entirely."

"Such as?" Cameron asked.

"I only saw it for a moment before it disappeared out of my viewpoint, but it almost looked as if it turned itself into something humanoid."

"Humanoid?" Cameron replied shaking his head. "Do you not think that we'd have heard of dogs that can change into people. I'm pretty sure the internet would have somehow produced a veritable flurry of images on that little beastie."

"You don't believe me?"

"Why would I?"

"You were sent down here with a team only minutes after I called the local police. By the time I called MI6, you were already in the air. That's not the normal response to a murder, no matter how violent. Then a few hours ago, I was standing on my balcony at the hotel and distinctly saw the same three helicopters you lot arrived in take-off and head inland, I assume with all the evidence on board. If I was to hazard a guess, I'd say that they were heading for some highly secure government facility where whatever they find would remain secret."

"That's quite a web of intrigue you're weaving in that mind of yours, and I'm crushed to have to be the one to inform you that you've got the wrong end of the proverbial stick. The go-team that was sent down here was SOP for any multiple-fatality agency crime scene."

"Then why the military presence and the full lockdown of the area?" Jay asked.

"Standard precaution. Obviously, whomever killed the two agents and your friend is indeed a monster, but most likely of the humankind. All of this is simply precautionary."

"So, what was in the sarcophagus?"

"I have no idea, but, if I were forced to guess, I'd say a valuable relic of some sort. Something that was worth killing for."

Jay stared at the other man and shook his head.

Cameron finished his gin and tonic before meeting Jay's gaze.

"Why was it so important to speak with me?" he asked.

"I had hoped that you might talk to whoever the big wigs are up in Whitehall and tell them my side of the story. That way, they could actually send down someone who knows what we brought ashore, and we might finally be in a position to go after the thing."

"We?" Cameron replied. "Whatever gives you the notion that you would be part of such an exercise? Yes, you brought the damn box ashore and circumvented customs and security, but that's the total extent of your involvement.

You are basically just a low-end pirate, and our association ended this morning."

"You're not understanding—"

"What I understand is that you breached so many laws and regulations that you will be very lucky – and I include your team in this – you'll be lucky if you don't get awarded some serious custodial time in one of His Majesty's more unpleasant incarceration facilities."

Jay slowly got to his feet and looked down at Cameron's smiling face.

"Enjoy the venison."

*

Carrie, the waitress who'd gone down to the sub-basement storage area to look for Patrick, stopped on the narrow staircase only a few steps from the bottom. She heard what she thought was a hissing sound coming from somewhere near the old, partially rotted doorway that led to an unused tunnel.

She reached for the archaic wall switch and flipped on the light. The low-wattage bulb flickered a few times before providing a dim but steady glow. Patrick was sitting on the stone floor taking heavy drags on a substantial-looking spliff.

"You prat," she said shaking her head. "The place stinks of weed and Ron is about to go off on one if you don't bring up that wine he wanted."

Patrick squinted then held the loosely rolled spliff out to her. She sighed then glanced up the stairs. Seeing no imminent threat, she grabbed it and toked hard until her lungs were full to capacity. She held her breath as long as possible, coughed once, then handed it back to Patrick.

"Nice," she said before trotting back up the stairs.

Patrick took one more hit from the joint and began to head back to work, but stopped, feeling there was something he'd forgotten – some legit reason for him to have come down to the lower basement in the first place. He tried to get his stoned brain to kick into gear, when a draught wafted over him from the direction of the old tunnel door.

*

Once Carrie re-entered the restaurant proper, Ron rushed to her side.

"Did you find him?"

"He wasn't in the basement or sub-basement."

"Did you check the tunnel storage area?"

"Absolutely not. It's a death trap down there."

Before Ron could respond, Mayor Haley called out to him and waved him over.

"Firstly, where's my vino, secondly, tell me more about this twice roasted pork belly. I don't think I've had that before, have I?"

"You have not. We only added it to the menu last week, and I assure you, you will love it. We created a spice mix that's somewhere between Cajun and Thai. It comes with a mango and chilli pepper salsa and celeriac fritters."

"That sounds delicious. I'll definitely have that and will

decide on my starter once I get my wine."

"I'll see to that immediately," Ron said as he glared across the room at Carrie who was just coming out of the kitchen.

Ron was about to head down to the overflow wine storage area when he had a thought. He stepped into the small but highly efficient kitchen and asked the chef if he had used the bottle of red wine he'd given him earlier in the week so he could make a boeuf bourguignon as a birthday surprise for his pregnant wife.

"Of course, I didn't use that muck. I went to the Saturday market and bought a bottle of something decent."

The chef reached under one of the prep stations and retrieved an unopened bottle of Chateau Mireux. Ron grabbed a corkscrew from the back of the bar and a red wine glass from the hanging rack, then plastered a smile on his face and made for the mayor's table.

While Ron was pouring the wine for His Honour, Jay, Helena and Emma placed their orders, which included a bottle of house Prosecco with which to toast Brian.

Once the waitress headed off with their order, Helena glanced over at Cameron then back at Jay.

"That exchange didn't look particularly friendly," she commented.

"It wasn't."

"Yet you still had to go over there, knowing full well how he felt about you... and us," Emma said.

"To be fair, I wasn't certain whether he felt any real animosity to us or not. At least I found out."

"Just so you know," Emma said as she turned to Helena.

"There isn't an awkward situation that Jay here won't waltz into and somehow make exponentially worse."

"I wanted to feel him out and see if he knew more than he was letting on," Jay replied defensively.

"And did he?" Emma asked.

"Unless he's one of the best actors in the world, his handlers have kept him on an extremely short leash. He doesn't seem to know what he's up against."

"To be fair," Helena jumped in. "Neither do we."

"Maybe not specifically, but we certainly know that whatever attacked Brian and the two agents came out of that sarcophagus. There had to be a very good reason why that thing was lashed to the sunken trawler. If we add the fact that the military has encircled the town, then I'd say that everything points to some sort of massive government cover-up that may have started as far back as the Second World War."

"While that seems to fit the current scenario, I am having trouble understanding why there's all this fuss for what sounds like a rabid dog," Emma stated.

"Only somebody who hasn't seen the creature would categorise it as something as simple a dog."

"I know I haven't personally caught a glimpse of—"

Emma's comment was cut short by a woman's piercing scream.

Jay made it to the bar at almost the exact moment as Cameron. Jay had only had time to arm himself with a steak knife from their table. Cameron, however, had drawn a Glock 17 and was aiming it at where he felt the scream had emanated.

The sight that met them would have been comical had either man been in the mood for levity.

Sitting at the bar was a pretty young woman staring at a man of about the same age who was kneeling next to her as he held out a diamond engagement ring.

The woman screamed her delight once again until she noticed the two armed men crouching on either side of the archway between the main dining room and the bar area. Both with their weapons pointed in her direction.

She screamed again, but this time it wasn't from delight.

Jay and Cameron both relaxed and began apologising profusely while Ron tried to dispel the soured mood with free Prosecco for everyone.

As he started to pour the first glass, the basement door behind him opened and Patrick stepped out into the light.

At least, Ron thought for a nanosecond that it was Patrick until his brain registered that the man in the doorway was naked and that there was something very wrong with him. Firstly, he was entirely hairless, next, he didn't seem to have any genitals at all, and lastly, his skin looked more like the skin on an inexpensive child's doll rather than anything human.

"Ron," Jay said in a forced whisper, "step over here. Now."

Ron was about to ask why, when the faux Patrick face suddenly protruded and formed into a long, fang-filled snout. All resemblance to a human vanished as the thing changed into something between an enormous wolf and a hyena. Its jaws snapped open as it lunged towards Ron's throat.

The mayor chose that moment to step into the bar to tell Ron what starter he'd selected. The room again filled with a girlish scream, this time from His Honour as he spun around and literally dived back into the dining area.

In an astonishingly lucky defensive reflex, Ron fell backwards in fear, yet at the same time, managed to throw the Prosecco bottle at the gaping maw of the creature. Somehow the bottle stayed upright and for a brief moment became wedged between the top and bottom of the canine's jaw.

It was enough of a distraction to allow Ron to slither out from around the bar and for Cameron to open fire. Even in the ensuing chaos of hysterical screams from the patrons and staff while the creature gnawed on the glass bottle until it shattered, Jay saw that every single shot from Cameron's Glock appeared to hit the target.

Though hurt, the thing didn't seem to have been slowed down. It retreated into the kitchen to get away from the volley of bullets only to be met with Peter, the head chef, standing in its way. He was holding two large culinary blow torches and, as the beast made a move for him, used them at the high setting, turning them into a pair of very effective flame throwers.

The creature's fur caught fire and it morphed into its quasi-human form as it raced back down into the cellar.

Nobody chose to go after it.

Jay, his hands shaking, placed the steak knife on the bar then turned to Cameron.

"Believe me now?"

CHAPTER TWENTY-THREE

It felt pain. After feasting on the body of the human who had been sitting in the dark surrounded by a pungent cloud of smoke, it had felt a glorious intoxication. Its already finely honed senses seemed to become sharper even as it began chewing on the human flesh. One of the first things it noticed was the flavour. The human tasted a little like the smoke that had surrounded him, and with each mawful, the taste intensified and its urge to consume flesh grew exponentially stronger with each bite.

Even once it was, or should have been, sated from the meal, the sounds and smells of other humans a short distance above it fuelled an irresistible urge to venture higher in the structure to seek out more fresh meat.

Despite its thinking being dampened by the cannabis it had unknowingly ingested, it still knew to be careful. Though hazy and fleeting, the memories of being hunted and almost destroyed well over half a century earlier still dwelled in its psyche.

Once the human had been sufficiently digested to a point where the DNA could trigger its mimicking cells, it took on the deceased male's form.

As it rose higher in the old building, the smell of raw human meat was joined by the scent of burned animal flesh, something it knew the humans fed upon.

Normally it should have been able to slaughter and feast on numerous humans at a time, but as it stepped into the light, a female let out a shocked squeal despite not even looking in its direction.

The horrific din, coupled with its groggy mind, caused it to freeze in place allowing an older male to begin firing metal projectiles into its body. Even as it tried to rip the throat from a different male, he somehow fell out of range while managing to place a foreign object in its jaws. It fled to the nearest room – the one from which the smell of burned meat was emanating – only to find another male who used fire against it.

With its brain befuddled and its fur burning, it chose to retreat, knowing that as bad as the wounds were, they would heal and it could then find the humans with the projectiles and the flames, and, more especially, the one who had been holding a metal tool and staring at it with pure, open hatred.

It knew that human. It had seen him in the dark cavernous place after it had fed on the two young males immediately upon its latest rebirth. That human had seen him in the shadows and then again as it fled into the daylight, taking the life of another as it passed through the open portal.

For that same human to have been present at two different locations – locations from where it had been forced to flee – it instinctually knew that the male was hunting it.

Even through the pain that always seemed worse as its

body healed, it knew that the human could not be allowed to continue in such an endeavour.

The only way it knew how to stop being hunted was to become the hunter.

*

Cameron, Jay, Emma and Helena sat in a quiet corner of the restaurant with Ron and a bottle of complimentary Hennessy brandy. With the exception of the mayor, who still sat at his original table, all the other diners and staff had vanished immediately after the assault. Two members of an elite SAS assault team stood vigil by the front door as a third guarded the stairs leading to the lower levels.

Despite the soldiers' initial insistence that they give chase to the creature, Cameron had nixed such an idea as being far too dangerous considering the fact that the beast knew its way around the tunnel network, whereas they did not. Jay had been amazed when the men stormed into the restaurant only seconds after the creature had fled. Cameron was even more surprised by their arrival considering that he had been offered twenty-four-hour security but had vehemently declined it. He now realised that it hadn't been an offer at all, rather, a decision made with or without his approval.

"Ron," the mayor called out, "would you mind sending someone to get another bottle of this delightful *vin rouge*."

"It's in the lower basement in the tunnel. The doors are unlocked. Help yourself."

Mayor Haley's eyes widened like a deer's in headlights

while his already pallid complexion paled still further.

One of the soldiers sniggered before he could stop himself as Cameron shook his head. "Your honour, why don't you come and sit with us and have a nice snifter or two."

Seeing Cameron's offer as a face-saving alternative, the mayor rose and walked unsteadily to their table. While Ron retrieved a snifter for him, Emma reached across and patted him on the knee.

"It must be especially horrid for you, this being your town," Emma said in a soothing tone.

"It has been a very strange couple of days," he admitted. "What with the *Lady Lovibond* event, the quarantine and now this, I'm at loss as to what exactly I should be doing. I mean, have you seen the High Street? It hasn't been that bad since my predecessor tried to start a monthly late night shopping event."

"What could have gone wrong with that?" Emma asked.

"For the inaugural evening, almost every shop offered free food and drinks to any and all shoppers. Word spread as far as Dover to the south and Ramsgate to the north. Suffice it to say that the scene was not that different to what's occurring at this very minute."

"That must have been quite a sight," Helena commented.

"It was, especially after the alcohol ran out and the revellers decided to ransack the High Street. At least on that day there were no fatalities."

"How did you hear about the killing at the cinema?" Cameron asked.

"The cinema?" Haley said, confused. "That place has

been closed up for decades, I'm talking about the poor building inspector."

"What happened to the building inspector?" Jay asked as he felt a chill worm its way up his back.

"If that contractor, Peter Cates, is to be believed, and considering he has photos to prove what he was saying, he may well be telling the truth, the man was attacked in a basement that was undergoing restoration. The thing is, it appears as if whatever attacked him was in the process of eating him when Peter interrupted it."

"Did this Peter gentlemen happen to see where the thing went at that point?"

"He did. It seems it ran into one of the old smuggler tunnels. The house Peter is working on used to have an access door in the basement that led right into one of them."

"When you say, 'used to have'?" Jay asked.

"The contractor had just finished bricking up the opening," Haley explained. "Apparently, when the council inspector arrived, he became so upset at the contractor for having closed off the access to the tunnel that he started to knock down the wall himself. It seems, at least according to Peter, that once the man had created an opening in the brickwork, the creature was able to access the lower basement and attack the man."

"Have there been any more reported deaths as a result of an animal attack within the last twenty-four hours?" Cameron enquired.

"Well, obviously there was the waiter here and the one you mentioned in the old cinema, but other than those, I don't believe there was anyone else."

"That we know of," Emma added.

Jay looked to the mayor with concern. "How many access points still exist for the tunnels within the old town?"

"Are we talking about the ones that have been fully filled in as well?"

"No. Just the ones that are either still in use for whatever reason, or ones that have been partially closed off, but with force could be breached."

"That's really more of a question for Dover Council, but if I had to guess, taking into consideration that we're talking about an area from the Castle to Alfred Square and from the coast to the High Street, I'd say there are easily a couple of hundred that still have some sort of access that could be used at a pinch."

Jay turned to Cameron. "Not wanting to use the old adage 'I told you so', but I do feel that it's time that we focus our efforts on the tunnel infrastructure."

"Would you mind moving to the other room while Jay, his accomplices and I have a little *tête-à-tête*?" Cameron said to the mayor.

"You could sit at the bar," Ron suggested.

"That includes you as well," Cameron replied with a cold smile.

"You do realise that this is my restaurant, don't you?" Ron declared.

"Yes, I do."

Cameron then stared at Ron until the other man became fidgety and confused. Finally, the mayor got unsteadily to his feet and gestured for Ron to join him at the other table.

Nobody said a word until the others were out of earshot.

"You keep referring to the things that we need to do. May I remind you that there is no *we* in this scenario—" Cameron said, following on from Jay's earlier words.

"Oh, shut up, you silly man," Emma interrupted.

"I may not know exactly what the hell is going on down here," Jay stated. "But I am the only person in this town that knows the tunnel system well enough to help your lot kill or capture whatever has decided to eat the good people of Deal."

"The thing that you lot brought ashore," Cameron shot back nodding towards Jay.

"Will you please let that go. I have no doubt that I will be held accountable at some point, and when I say I, I mean me. It was my idea to bring the sarcophagus ashore and mine alone. In the meantime, when you call whoever it is that you report to, will you please get approval to involve me so that we may work together on this. Remember, my closest friend was one of the men killed today."

"Are you asking to be involved on the basis of wanting vengeance?" Cameron asked, his eyebrows raised.

"Call it what you like. The fact is that I am probably the best resource you have for locating this creature. You've now seen it first-hand. This is no steroidal canine. I think it might be a good idea to have your people read you in on exactly what it is that's attacking this town."

Cameron took a long time to swill the brandy within the snifter and take a sip of the amber liquid.

"While you were trying to comfort your team and persuade the other diners to go elsewhere, I made that call. We will be getting reinforcements shortly, and you are already approved to help with your knowledge of the tunnels."

Jay looked at Cameron with a confused expression. "Why didn't you tell us that earlier?" he asked.

"And lose the chance to wind you up a little?" Cameron smiled.

A commotion from the entry area caused everyone at the table to face that way. A man that could easily have been Cameron's clone, were it not for his dark hair and being dressed in battle fatigues, stepped into the room.

"That was quick," Cameron commented as the man approached.

"I felt that haste was vital if we're to get this situation taken care of. I've had a chopper on standby since this started and we even managed to stop on the way down and collect what I hope will prove to be the best weapon yet within our arsenal."

"Colonel, these are the people we discussed earlier," Cameron said as he gestured to Jay, Emma and Helena.

"Ah. You must be Mr Sallinger." The colonel held out his hand. "My name is Colonel Hartfield."

Jay didn't get to his feet, rather chose to shake the offered hand while still seated.

Jay introduced Emma and Helena at which point Hartfield turned to the front entry and nodded once at the guarding soldiers.

"I think it's time that you were all introduced to our secret weapon."

The front door opened, and for a surprisingly long time, nothing happened. Then the oldest man Jay had ever seen slowly shuffled inside.

CHAPTER TWENTY-FOUR

One of the soldiers held the man's arm and helped him to where Jay and the others were seated.

"Doctor," the colonel gestured to Cameron. I'd like you to meet our contractor for this operation. This is Cameron..." He waited for Cameron to offer his last name.

"Just Cameron."

The elderly gentleman held out a frail hand.

"One name is plenty for me," he said, his voice weak and raspy. "I am Doctor Randoph Wiseman."

Cameron shook the offered hand then introduced the doctor to the others. After two chairs were dragged over from another table, Wiseman and Hartfield sat among the group.

"Doctor of what exactly?" Jay asked.

Wiseman laughed. "Direct young man aren't you. Suffice it to say that my area of expertise is quite broad and my three doctorates only mesh with about half of my areas of responsibility, at least they did when I was still working."

"You're retired?" Cameron asked, surprised that a person of such advanced years could be so vital to the operation, especially when he wasn't still actively involved.

"Have been for over forty years. I'll let you in on a little secret. When I retired in '92, my intent was to have nothing more to do with my working life ever again."

"Yet, here you are," Cameron commented as he shot the colonel a questioning glance.

"Are you hungry, would you like a drink?" Emma offered.

"I had a questionable sandwich on the chopper ride down, but I wouldn't say no to a drink. Any chance of a whisky Mac?"

As the colonel started to get up, Emma signalled for him to stay.

"You lot keep talking. I'll see if Ron has any ginger wine."

Wiseman stared fixedly at Emma's rear as she walked out of the room. There was no attempt from him to hide his interest.

"What a stunner," Wiseman said as he slowly turned back to the others. "Why are you lot all staring at me? If you think that all this new age woke nonsense is going to have any bearing on my life, you have another think coming. Besides, all I can do nowadays is look, so, what's the harm in that?"

"Perhaps you'd care to explain to the group exactly what it was that you did when you were working," Hartfield suggested.

"That's permitted?" the doctor asked, surprised.

"To a point and within this very small group, yes."

"Very well," he said clearing his throat. "Back in the day, I was the director of what we called 'the special projects division' at Porton Down. I assume that you have all at least heard of the place?"

"It was some sort of military think tank for boffins," Jay

offered.

"Still is, or so I am told," Wiseman replied. "But it was way more than a simple think tank. It's undoubtably the most comprehensive facility in the UK for the development of military weaponry. Not just hardware, mind you. Our team of mad scientists were, and I suppose still are, delving into software, microorganisms, animal and even human mutation... Basically anything and everything that could kill or at least disarm our enemies."

"You mentioned mutations?" Jay said. "May one assume that your specialisation in that arena has something to do with what's happening down here?"

"From my understanding of the situation, I would have to say yes."

"I don't want to seem unappreciative of your abilities, but how can you help us deal with a creature that you have never seen and only know from the reports that have been shared with you?" Jay asked.

Before Wiseman could respond, Emma returned with a half-filled whisky glass.

"I hope I didn't over pour," she said as she placed it in front of him.

"Nonsense, I'm rather glad you did," he said as he raised the glass to his chapped lips and downed half the contents in one. After a small belch, he sighed then turned back to Jay.

"My dear boy, I know a little more about the creature than that. It was my team that created it."

"I'm not sure you should divulge quite that level of—"

"Poppycock!" Wiseman snorted. "If you expect these people, to say nothing of the soldiers that are amassed just outside the town, to proceed with any expectation of success without knowing what it is exactly that they will be battling, then you are a poor commander."

"As I explained on the way down, we feel that a general overview is all that's needed here. I thought you agreed."

"You thought wrong. These people need to know what we created and what it's capable of."

The colonel glared across the table at Wiseman hoping that his gaze would somehow deter the old man from divulging one of the country's best and longest kept secrets.

"If you think that glowering will in some way intimidate me, then you are sorely mistaken. I have been stared down by the likes of Churchill and Mountbatten, so put away that air of superiority and let me tell these people what they will be up against."

With thinly veiled frustration and anger, Colonel Hartfield, got to his feet.

"I hope you understand that I cannot be privy to you leaking such information. I will therefore take my leave and go watch the antics in the High Street. When you've finished being in violation of the Official Secrets Act, have Cameron give me a call on his sat phone."

With that, Hartfield stormed out of the restaurant.

"Officious little prig," Wiseman said as he took another gulp of his drink. "As I started to explain, my team actually created the Lusus."

"Lusus?" Emma asked.

"Lusus Naturae, to give it its full title. That's the formal term for an abomination of nature. While the ministry wanted to give it one of their silly code names, we continued calling it Lusus. Initially, the project was indeed meant to mutate a regular dog into a much larger and much more vicious version. We soon found out that such an animal could never be pre-programmed to carry out any specific action; rather, the earliest test subject simply went berserk and killed everything in the lab including the other dogs. We realised that to have size and ferocity coupled with a programmable brain, we needed to create more of a hybrid."

Cameron looked on in horror.

"A hybrid of what?" he asked.

"Why of a dog and a human of course," Wiseman replied.

"Before you go on," Cameron said, "why exactly was there the need to create such a creature in the first place, and in the second, how on earth was research like that even sanctioned?"

"You have to understand the pressure that we were under in 1940.

"Hold on," Jay interrupted. "1940. You must have been a child back then."

"Thank you for the compliment, but I was eighteen at the time and was considered to be something of a boy genius. A veritable savant. Anyway, we were at war with Germany, and at that time, there was a real fear that England would lose. We were tasked by the War Office to create living, autonomous weapons that could be released into Nazi Germany and would be able to kill a vast number of German soldiers before they even knew what hit them. It couldn't just be something as simple as a bomb. It had to be able to not just kill but to hunt out as many targets as possible."

"What would be the point?" Jay asked. "I mean, once the

enemy realised that it was only a dog, all be it a very large one, they could simply shoot it."

"Exactly our thinking at the time. We had to create an entity that could attack targets at night, while they were at rest and ill-prepared to fight back. Once a Lusus had attacked, let's say, a barracks and slaughtered all those inside, it would vanish into the night, travelling to where its senses would lead to still more unprepared soldiers.

"At some point, it was bound to be shot and killed. We knew that up front. So, what we managed to do was create a creature that, even after death, could use the oxygen in the air to basically reconstitute itself. It meant designing an entirely new genome that could self-repair almost any damage that may have been inflicted upon itself. The more damage, the longer it would take, but we found a way to create a creature that could be reduced to nothing but ash and still reconstitute itself, again, only if oxygen was present."

"How did you accomplish that?" Emma asked. "It's not possible."

"You would be amazed, if not terrified, to learn just what was possible back then given unlimited funding and complete free rein to do what was necessary without fear of moral or legal challenge."

"There is more to the Lusus than just being able to self-resurrect, isn't there, Doctor?" Cameron asked.

"Ah." Wiseman finished the last of his whisky Mac. "You must be referring to its chameleon gene. It took long months, but once we had found a way to splice the genes of our oversized canine with those of a human, things got interesting. After countless trials, we found that by adding the genes of creatures that exist right here on earth, many of them aquatic, we were able to make the initial Lusus physically morph from the canine form to the human one at will."

"I'm confused," Emma stated. "To create such a mutant would take countless generations of modification before getting anywhere near the creature that you envisioned."

"That would indeed be the case if we had chosen to go down that slow and winding road. The problem was, we didn't have time for the luxury of waiting for generational genetic change."

"Then how—" Jay started to ask.

Wiseman grinned back at them. "While some of the internal organs could be... cheated chemically to create the necessary bodily reactions, most of the core construction was managed in surgery."

"That's vivisection," Helena said shaking her head in disgust.

"You're quite right, it was exactly that."

"Those poor animals," Helena said as she stared down at the table.

"Actually, the testing on live dogs was almost secondary. The human body was designated as the preferred core state of the creature; therefore, human volunteers had to be used for the majority of the trials."

CHAPTER TWENTY-FIVE

"Can we go back to that resurrection ability you mentioned?" Emma asked, revolted, yet fascinated. "How is it possible to create anything living that can be killed and the death then be reversed? It's impossible."

The doctor laughed. "It's not impossible at all. I'm sure you've seen video of fish that have been dead for days being found on shorelines and after a little douse with water coming back to life. You've also undoubtedly seen or at least know that lizards are able to lose their entire tail yet regrow it back to its original shape and size. All we had to do was find the correct blend of genes and develop a way for the process to take place at a vastly increased pace."

"Even if you did what you say, there is no way to grow back a head... what about the brain? That's not going to grow back!"

"Every single part of the human body is made up of trillions of cells. Once we focused our efforts on individual cell types, we found that targeted mutational protocols were indeed possible."

Jay shook his head. "If what you are saying is true, doesn't that mean that you had basically unlocked the door to a medical breakthrough that could have cured everything from cancer to ALS?"

"We may have opened the door, but everything we accomplished was, and still is, some of the most top-secret data that has ever existed. We were at war. You have to understand that our findings and subsequent successful creation of the Lusus was never published nor shared with any other scientific body both inside or outside of this country."

"But the war has been over for more than eighty years," Jay insisted. "Keeping the greatest discovery in the history of medical science a secret at this point is criminal."

"That war may be over," Wiseman replied. "But we still have enemies spread across the globe. Imagine if a terrorist group or a country like North Korea managed to get hold of the data. While it most certainly could cure a multitude of diseases and ailments, think for a minute what those nations who don't live by any moral compass could create using that very same data."

"Armies of mutants," Helena said in little more than a whisper as she wiped away a tear that had formed in the corner of her eye.

"Exactly, miss. Exactly."

"If we could get back to the task at hand," Cameron said. "How do we kill the bloody thing?"

"There is only one way. We had to test numerous substances in the lab till we found one that could terminate any subjects in the event that they went rogue or became too damaged to continue with the mutation trial."

"Did the Nazis know about you?" Jay asked. "You sound like just the sort of chap they would have welcomed into their fold."

"I believe they knew of me, but thankfully did not have any details of who or where I was," Wiseman answered, ignorant of the sarcasm in Jay's tone.

"What is this substance?" Cameron asked.

"It's now called Fluoroantimonic acid. For those of you who aren't aware, it was and still is one of the most corrosive substances on the planet. Though it was supposedly invented in the late sixties, we had been dabbling with it over twenty years earlier. The wonderful thing about this super acid is that when combined with water there is an explosive reaction as it turns into hydrogen fluoride gas, which is also corrosive, and once airborne, it can be inhaled and destroys the subject from the inside out."

"You do make that sound like such a beneficial invention for all mankind," Emma commented.

Wiseman smiled, again missing the sarcasm entirely. "Thank you. We found that by using it on our test subjects, it destroyed the mutated cells before any regeneration can take place. The ashy remnants of the Lusus would simply seep into the ground and be of no further consequence."

"I'm not sure that the locals would agree. Something like that has got to be highly dangerous when it settles into the ground water," Jay pointed out.

"Let's stay focused on getting this thing destroyed," Cameron interjected. "How much of this acid did you have on hand?"

"There was no need to keep any on site after all the testing and then the cancelling of the project."

"Why exactly was the project cancelled?" Jay asked.

"Because of the very reason we are here. Once we had created a fully functional Lusus, we then had only one final on-site test to carry out."

"On site, as in the lab? Cameron asked.

"No. On-site testing was planned to take place in German occupied France. It was to be released in a garrison just outside Calais. We wanted to see how many troops it could kill before it was terminated and, hopefully, reanimated."

"I take it that never happened?" Jay asked.

Unfortunately, while we were transporting the Lusus to Dover, in preparation of sneaking it across the Channel, the lorry carrying the test specimen crashed on the A2. Even though it was sealed in an oxygen-free environment, and it was in an only partially reconstituted state, the metal container was breached by the force of the crash, oxygen leaked in and—"

"It re-formed and found its way to Deal," Jay said, finishing the doctor's statement. "That's why the trawler had to pick up the sarcophagus from Deal Pier."

"Correct. Once we heard that something dog-like had been captured after slaughtering and consuming a number of townsfolk, we knew that the Lusus had regenerated itself and made for the nearest supply of living human flesh. By the time we arrived, the Lusus had been killed for the second time with the help of locally stationed marines after which, they sealed it inside an airless stone coffin that had originally been commissioned by the Guilford estate for a ceremonial burial at Waldershare House.

"As the Lusus was at that point denied all oxygen, the creature stayed decomposed and dormant. Faced with an entombed weapon, we came up with a revised plan to cross the Channel under cover of darkness and leave the box on shore by the town of Wimereux, which was at the time Nazi occupied. We believed that curiosity would prevail, and the German sentries would feel obligated to open it.

"Unfortunately, our plans were scuppered when the trawler was spotted by a U-boat only eight miles offshore and sunk with a single torpedo. The trawler captain apparently made a valiant effort to ground his craft on the Goodwin Sands but didn't quite make it."

"Was there any attempt to recover it?" Jay asked.

"There was going to be, but after a godawful three-day gale in the Channel, the wreck couldn't be located," Wiseman replied. "We know, thanks to your efforts, that it must have been forced onto the Sands at some point during the storm and was consumed as the waves swept the top layer of the barrier away, only to be replaced with even more sand as the whole place went through something akin to a washing machine's more violent spin cycle."

"Going back to the discussion about that acid you claimed could kill the creature – if the lab no longer has a supply of it, where do we get it?" Cameron asked.

"It's really quite simple to synthesise. It's just a mixture of hydrogen fluoride and antimony pentafluoride plus a blend of cations and anions."

"That doesn't sound at all simple," Helena mumbled.

"Not to worry. It's available to purchase on the open market if you have the right licences."

"If we need to buy a large quantity of that acid, where would we go?" Cameron asked.

"You have to understand that what is available today has undergone years of tweaking and is not quite the same as the formula we were using," Wiseman advised.

"Will today's version of the acid still kill the thing?"

"Yes, but it won't have the same punch."

"If we could ensure that a layer of water was already in the tunnels before adding the acid, would that do the job?" Cameron asked.

"Just exactly how big an area are we talking about?" Wiseman questioned.

Jay, as if reading Cameron's mind, answered first. "It's a tunnel system that's approximately one mile long with branches that spread out a hundred metres wide."

Wiseman stared at Jay as if the other man had suddenly lost his mind. He looked to Cameron for support but saw that he was actually nodding his approval of Jay's estimation.

"Why that's almost the size of a town!" Wiseman exclaimed.

"It's certainly the size of this town," Jay stated. "At least the old part."

CHAPTER TWENTY-SIX

Once Wiseman had been filled in on the specifics of what had happened that day in the restaurant and within the town, he came to accept the notion of using the tunnels in order to destroy the creature.

"I understand your plan, but you would need tens of thousands of gallons of acid to ensure even minimal coverage in that sort of area."

"We know that; hence my question about where we might find that sort of quantity," Cameron explained.

"You won't. There has never been the need for that volume of acid. If you can settle for a few hundred gallons you should call the petrochemical consortium in London. That industry uses a lot of it and may be able to help."

Cameron's face began to redden in frustration. "You know the area in question. How are a few hundred gallons going to help us?"

"If I may make a suggestion," Jay said. "If we were to somehow force the creature into one specific tunnel branch, we could already have a layer of water in it then add the acid at the right moment."

"How the hell are we supposed to find just the right

tunnel to use?"

Jay theatrically pointed at himself.

"I keep telling you that I could be the answer to your problem. I still have my schematics of the tunnel system. I scanned them years ago and uploaded them to my cloud storage. I could have them for you in seconds."

"That just might work," Wiseman said as he waved his empty glass at one of the soldiers.

Cameron sighed and studied Jay before finally throwing his hands in the air in a gesture of defeat.

"Fine. You will be the tunnel expert, while I try and get Whitehall to blag the acid from the petrol folks. In the meantime, you together with a small team of soldiers will do a visual survey of possible areas where we could trap the thing."

The colour drained from Jay's face. "I think there's been some sort of misunderstanding. My idea was to coordinate all the tunnel work from up here, not... down there," he said gesturing with his head.

"You wanted in. You're in."

"What about this Lusus creature. It'll be down there as well," Jay pointed out.

"That's why you'll have a military entourage. They'll be equipped with some serious firepower. Tell me if I'm mistaken, Doctor," he said to Wiseman who was still trying to get a soldier's attention. "If there's a choice of dining option for the Lusus, will it go for the armed soldiers or unarmed civilians?"

"It will always go for the easier target. It was programmed

to protect itself so that its mission could last almost indefinitely," Wiseman replied.

"That brings up a good question," Jay said. "How were you going to recall the Lusus once it had consumed sufficient enemy personnel in France during the war?"

"Let me take that from you," Helena said getting to her feet and relieving Wiseman of his empty glass. "Whisky Mac?"

"Yes, please," he said before turning back to Jay. "Our expectation was that the Germans would eventually kill the thing with sufficient weaponry to scatter its body parts far enough away from one another so that it couldn't re-form."

"Wait a minute." Cameron sat up straight. "If we can just blow the thing up, why the need for the acid at all?"

"The size of explosion that would spread it far enough would have to be something in the range of a direct impact from a howitzer shell, or in today's parlance, a cruise missile. While that's an option, attempting that size of blast under Deal would likely destroy most, if not all, of the old town, and even then, because of the enclosed environment of the tunnels, it would very likely not be sufficiently dispersed and would still reconstitute itself."

"Does it need all of its original self to reconstitute?" Emma asked.

"Very good question," Wiseman said. "The answer is no... to a point. Its molecular structure is programmed to re-form only into the specific assigned parts and organs. For example, if the brain were to have been completely disintegrated, the creature could perhaps partially re-form, but it wouldn't be able to function at all. If, however, it was simply musculature and skin that had gone, it could still restructure itself, though depending on the severity of the damage, it would not necessarily be able to take on exactly the same shape and form."

"That doesn't sound very promising," Cameron commented.

"It was designed to be a self-reliant, semi-sentient weapon. Destroying it was never meant to be easy."

"Was there never a consideration about how to destroy it if conventional methods failed?" Jay asked.

"The acid was the only viable way to ensure full destruction of the creature."

"What if there wasn't a way or the means to bring the Lusus into contact with the acid. What then? I can't believe that you would have created something so horrifically lethal and not have some sort of a failsafe switch with which to deactivate the thing."

"That, I'm afraid, is an area that we are not able to discuss," Hartfield said causing everyone to jump having not seen nor sensed his return to the dining room. "I think we've infringed enough on Doctor Wiseman's time tonight."

"Before we do that," Wiseman said. "May I see where the man was attacked here?"

"I don't think that would be wise," Hartfield replied. "It's been sealed off and—"

"It is not out of curiosity. Seeing the site will give me some idea of the Lusas's thinking process in relation to its ferocity and focus. I should be able to tell whether it is working with full functionality or whether such a long period of oxygen-deprived desiccation has damaged its capabilities. This we will need to know if we are to successfully kill the creature."

"You keep saying we," Hartfield commented. "You are being flown home right after this meeting."

"Unless you plan on doing so by force, I intend to stay and observe as well as consult, in case my experience and knowledge might come in handy," Wiseman replied with a forced smile.

"I personally feel that the good doctor would be an asset to have on hand," Cameron stated.

There was complete silence around the table.

"Obviously, I am in no position to force you to do anything," Hartfield said. "I'll have one of the men escort you down to the lower basement."

"Thank you. May I also enquire where I will be spending the night? I'm not that fussy; however, at my age, I do need to get my eight hours."

Hartfield looked momentarily flummoxed. He had made no contingency plans for Wiseman remaining in Deal. The initial idea had been for the doctor to leave with him that same night.

"I find myself alone in a house with multiple adequate bedrooms," Cameron advised. "You are more than welcome to stay with me."

Both Wiseman and Cameron turned to Hartfield.

"Fine with me," the colonel replied haughtily.

"Where are you staying?" Cameron asked him.

"I am scheduled to fly back and report on the status of

the situation, which is what I still intend to do. I will return if and when I'm needed."

"With you gone, who is going to be in charge of the operation here on the ground?" Cameron asked.

"Or, in fact, under it," Jay added with a smirk.

Emma and Helena both rolled their eyes, surprised that he could still come up with one of his witty quips even under the current circumstances.

"Why, you are," Hartfield stated as he stared at Cameron who was clearly surprised at the news.

"That's not what I was contracted to do," Cameron pointed out.

"You were contracted to come down here with a team and clear up the mess."

"At the old cinema. Not take over the management of the entire operation."

"Congratulations. Your contract has been retroactively modified," Hartfield said with something akin to a sneer. "I will be taking my leave now. Cameron, you know how to get in touch."

Hartfield turned to one of the men milling around the entry area.

"Corporal Willis, would you please escort Doctor Wiseman down to the lower basement."

Before the officer could respond, Jay spoke. "We'd like to see the area as well, especially the tunnel access."

"We would?" Emma asked with a look of complete disgust.

Hartfield sighed, ignoring Emma's comment. "Fine.

Whatever. Cameron, would you mind seeing me to my ride?"

"Of course," he replied with zero enthusiasm.

*

Aware of the large number of humans that had arrived shortly after it had consumed the young human, and the resulting pain caused by fire and flesh-piercing projectiles, it had fled to a safe distance. It could still hear and smell the humans but felt it unlikely that any of them would attempt to pursue it in the dark tunnels – at least not yet anyway.

It found a small alcove where it could lay down and let its genetically customised system heal both the burns and the puncture wounds. Just as its dense black fur began to grow back over already healed flesh, it heard the distinct voice of the human that had launched the projectiles into its flesh.

Because of its heightened hearing and the echo-like properties of the tunnels, it could tell that the male had exited the building with another man. It managed to edge itself through a gap in the tunnel wall and emerge near a water run-off culvert that had been built at the base of one of the street's original structures. One in which it remembered accessing the basement and consuming the occupant. That had been before its last regeneration, and it seemed to recall the town back then as having been far less well tended yet with many more advantageously accessible premises in which to locate prey.

From behind the ancient metal bars that protected the run-off gutter, it could plainly see the two humans standing in the alleyway just beyond the structure in which its latest attack had taken place. The human that had caused it so much pain seemed subservient to the other; in fact, the other human did not even let him speak. Instead, its voice was raised as it verbally barraged the other; the one it recognised.

Around the corner and out of sight of the two humans was a large black conveyance, belching clear, yet acrid, fumes out into the night. It recognised it as being the type of thing humans use to get from one point to another when not wishing to use their own limbs. Another human stood leaning against the thing; his attention entirely focused on something in his hands that seemed to emit a bright glow. Every so often the human would touch the thing and the glow would suddenly diminish then brighten again.

It was not capable of what most would consider strategic thinking, but it could, through imparted reason, put two and two together and knew that the waiting conveyance was there to transport one or both of the men.

*

"You have your instructions," Hartfield said, his voice cold and officious. "I don't care whether you agree with them or not. It is your obligation to now carry them out. If after all this is over you wish to modify or even terminate your contract, that's fine. For now, just do your job."

The colonel turned and made for the waiting Range Rover parked around the corner on Middle Street while Cameron glared at the man's retreating back.

"That's right, you bloody coward," he hissed in little more than a whisper. "Slink back to Whitehall while everyone else does your job for you."

As he headed towards the vehicle, Hartfield heard the din coming from the High Street. The crowds had thinned slightly and those that remained appeared more interested in singing than fighting. He couldn't decide which was worse. Even if Cameron's voice had been audible over the revelry, Hartfield was too angry to notice anything but the fury that was swirling within him. While Cameron's concerns were annoying, they were not remotely the cause of his ire.

What upset him the most was that Wiseman had chosen to disregard the strict and specific orders to return with him that night. The fact that the decrepit old fool had, in front of everyone, announced he was staying was simply too much. Having to manage the country's most secret research projects and the boffins assigned to them was hard enough, but to have to kowtow to the whims of one who hadn't been active in decades was an embarrassment. For that same geriatric to blab away as well as ignore his instructions was galling to say the least. Once back in London, Hartfield would find some way to make the old man regret how he had treated him.

The colonel walked onto Middle Street and saw his car waiting and the driver who'd picked him up from the helicopter on Walmer Green sitting at the wheel.

Nearing the vehicle, he was slightly nonplussed that the man didn't get out to open the car door for him, but instead of making a fuss on the spot, he made a mental note to mention the act of laziness to his superior officer.

Hartfield climbed in and settled himself against the soft, cream-coloured leather and was about to give the driver instructions when he was overwhelmed by the smell of something feral mixed with the tang of something sweet and coppery.

"What is that disgusting odour?" he asked, retching.

When he noticed that the driver's head hadn't moved, he began to observe more anomalies about the man. Even from the back, the head wasn't quite the right shape. It seemed a tad too oval and the hair, while initially like the human variety, began to transform into the dark, matted pelt more usually seen on an animal.

Before the infamous penny dropped and he could react, the head turned to face him. For a brief second the features looked more or less human, if you discounted the bloody streamers of gore that hung from its mouth. Then, suddenly, the features began to elongate into an enormous, teeth-filled muzzle.

Before Hartfield could release the scream that was growing inside him, the creature twisted itself between the two front seats and sunk its fangs into the colonel's neck.

At some point during its manoeuvre, the Lusus inadvertently released the handbrake.

If anyone else had been present on Middle Street that night, they would have seen the expensive vehicle coasting very slowly southwards as it rocked from side to side while its windows became coated with an ebbing sheen of blood.

CHAPTER TWENTY-SEVEN

The narrow steps were steep and uneven. Wiseman had to be helped down to the sub-basement by one of the soldiers as Jay and Cameron followed closely behind. Emma and Helena had voted unanimously to stay upstairs, rather than having to see what was undoubtably a scene of complete carnage two floors below.

Another soldier was stationed at the base of the stairs on the lowest level. His expression foretold what the two civvies would encounter beyond him. As they reached the landing, the accompanying soldiers, not having the clearance to overhear what the two men had to say, retreated to the upper floor.

Jay stepped into the low-ceilinged space first. The lighting came from a single, low-wattage bulb that did little to illuminate the room. It was, however, bright enough for him to see what appeared to be a partially devoured thigh less than half a metre from where he was standing. After that, there was little that could be recognised as having come from a human being. Thick, congealing blood pooled on the unfinished floor all the way to what was left of a partially rotten wooden hatch that led, he presumed, into the tunnel network.

As Wiseman stepped into the space, he initially gasped, then became morbidly fascinated at the damage his creation had caused to a fellow human. With help from Jay, he crouched next to the remains of the limb and studied the bite marks and tearing patterns with growing respect and joy.

"It's better than we had hoped," Wiseman commented. "Though clearly savage and somewhat unrestrained, there is something clinically precise about where exactly it has chosen to focus its jaws."

"Didn't you test all this once you created the thing?" Jay asked. "I assume you must have observed it consuming numerous animals during the test phases?"

"Obviously there was endless testing; however, you must remember that the Lusus was programmed at the genetic level to attack and consume only humans. While it would – when there was no other target – hunt any living prey, the level of drive and blood lust that would be triggered by a human victim was never tested. Unfortunately, the powers that be deemed it inhuman to run trials using living people."

Jay could clearly hear the disappointment and regret in the other man's voice and involuntarily shivered.

"I won't ask what was used instead," he commented.

"Good," Wiseman said with a wink. "I wouldn't tell you anyway."

Jay left the doc prodding some remaining musculature with an old-fashioned rubber tipped pencil as he made his way to the tunnel access. Fully aware that the creature was doubtless somewhere in the inky blackness that lay beyond the shattered hatch, Jay had trouble calming his breathing as it fully dawned on him that he would, in the very near future, have to venture into that very same underground realm.

He activated his phone's light and shone it into the void. When Jay had been doing his study of the tunnel system and its relevance to Deal's dark past, he had only ventured into a select few of the tunnel access points. He remembered them as being relatively cramped and narrow but nothing like the one he was now facing which was clearly a small branch of a secondary tunnel. One that only ever needed to be big enough for a smuggler to crawl along with the illicit goods that required hiding or reselling.

On the right of the damaged hatchway, someone had mounted crude wine racks into the stone wall, presumably to benefit from the consistent cool temperature and low light. On the opposite side were the remains of discarded restaurant detritus, presumably deposited there over time to save having to lug the refuse to the dump.

Blood was smeared across some of the cracked and chipped crockery initially giving the impression that it was some sort of avant-garde pattern. To add to the macabre tableau, the stagnant damp air was infused with the smell of burned hair mingled with a musky animal scent.

Jay crab walked into the tunnel and shone his torch down the length of it. Though he could clearly see where it T-boned into the larger branch only metres away and there was no sign of the creature, a violent chill shimmied from his neck all the way down his spine.

He decided that any further exploration would have to wait until he had an armed escort with proper lighting – the type that would light up the tunnel network and give the creature a minimal supply of shadows in which to hide. In addition, he saw no good reason to venture forward without the benefit of sufficient manpower and weaponry to, even if only temporarily, put the beast out of action.

Once they had returned to the presumed safety of the dining room, Cameron announced that they had found sufficient acid to destroy the creature but that it would take at least twenty-four hours to ship it to Dover where it could then be transported to Deal.

"We can't let that thing run loose for that long. God knows how many more people will die in that time," Jay stated.

"I agree." Cameron replied. "That's why I just ordered the acid be collected by one of our helicopters and be brought directly here. That will still take some hours, but at least that will give us some time to trap the bloody thing somewhere where we can both confine it and douse it once the acid arrives."

"If I may offer one comment," Wiseman said. "If you start trying to corral the Lusus within the tunnel system, it has enough mental acuity to get above ground to avoid the imminent danger."

"That won't be a problem," Cameron advised. "There are enough soldiers and weaponry at the various roadblocks to cover every single street and alley in the grid area."

"That's all well and good," Helena said shaking her head. "But if it does decide to get above ground, wouldn't it do so via one of the access hatches in either a home or business within the old town? And if it did, wouldn't that endanger the occupants?"

Cameron looked momentarily stunned, clearly having not thought of such an obvious drawback to his plan.

"Evacuate the bloody lot of them," a voice said from the other side of the room.

Everyone turned and saw the mayor, glass of wine in hand, grinning back them.

"Forgot I was here, didn't you?" he said amiably and with a slight slur to his voice. "There's actually a council contingency plan to move all residents of old town inland in the event of a catastrophic tidal surge. The idea was to get everyone out of harm's way and house them in Sandown School on Golf Road until the all-clear was given."

"Is it big enough?" Jay asked.

"It won't be comfortable, but we estimated a max occupancy of around eight hundred people. It will be crowded, but they will at least be safe."

"Are there any tunnels under it?" Cameron asked.

"No. It's a block west of old town and was built long after the tunnels were dug out."

"There's going to be some very angry and very powerful people turfed out of their beds," Jay commented. "I don't relish being in your shoes."

The mayor laughed. "If I had a pound for every DFL that has grumbled to me about something that was wrong with the town, I would be wealthier than they are!"

"DFL?" Cameron asked.

"That's the somewhat derogatory term given to all the East End Londoners who descend on Deal throughout the year," Jay said, smiling. "It stands for *Down from London* or in some circles, *Dickheads from London.*"

"May I pipe up again?" Wiseman said almost apologetically. "Please understand that I am not disagreeing with your plan, in fact it's probably the only option at this point, but I must make one thing utterly clear."

"What's that?" Cameron asked as all eyes turned to the old man.

"By gathering everyone and cramming them together in one location, it may indeed be an optimal plan for a flood, but in this case, you are offering the creature a tantalising target."

"It will be too busy avoiding the soldiers to worry about a school full of angry residents and visitors," Cameron stated.

"No doubt. However, in its eyes, you will have created a veritable smorgasbord of human flesh all just waiting to be feasted upon."

The others couldn't help but notice the twinkle in the old man's eyes.

CHAPTER TWENTY-EIGHT

Because of the size of the house as well as its central location, Cameron chose his temporary residence to be the base of operations for the assault on the Lusus – at least until Jay pointed out that if the property had a basement, it had to be considered as a potential target.

Instead, the mayor suggested they use the New Century Nursery School located on Golf Road just a stone's throw from the temporary school shelter.

"Where do we go?" Emma asked. "Is the hotel safe?"

"Actually, it is," Jay advised. "It is the only remaining structure on the ocean side of the coast road from the smuggling and piracy days. It was remodelled at the same time as the road was torn up so that a smooth macadam could replace the old cobblestones, and the single tunnel that ran under it was blocked and never used again. It's doubtful the Lusus will want to come to the surface just to reach the hotel when there are so many other prime targets linked directly by the tunnels."

"Let's escort the ladies back to their digs," Cameron suggested, "and on the way, check out the rental I'm staying at. I don't remember the state of the basement, but to be fair, I was exhausted when I got there and didn't exactly give the place a serious once over. If it doesn't have access to the tunnels, I would like to stick with my original plan and use it as a base of operation. The nursery, while a very good suggestion, is too far from the area where the crucial tunnels will be explored. Plus, the fact that Doctor Wiseman would, I expect, like a lie down after such an exhausting day."

"Don't worry about me," he replied. "I may look as frail as a kitten but behind this wizened exterior beats the heart of a twenty-year-old."

The others all gave him a doubting look.

"Alright. Maybe that of a forty-year-old."

"Am I needed for the next hour?" the mayor asked. "Before we start evacuating the residents, I'd like to change into something a trifle more casual."

"Does your house have a basement?" Jay asked.

"It does not. From what I know of its history, when it was built, they found that there was a nasty mix of packed earth and loose sand. They were able to secure an above-ground row of houses but did not risk digging further down to add any basements."

After vetting that Cameron's house did have a basement, but that it had no access whatsoever to the tunnel system, they settled Wiseman into one of the guest rooms. Jay then escorted Helena and Emma back to the Regal Hotel. Having never changed from dinner at Victor's, he was still wearing beige trousers, a navy polo shirt and a pair of well-worn penny loafers. As his entire wardrobe was more casual than utilitarian, he hoped he could scrounge something more suitable to wear for what he knew would be a long night in the tunnels.

By 11:00, soldiers had begun knocking on doors. They started at Alfred Square and moved steadily south until, just after two in the morning, they were satisfied that all the residents and visitors had vacated each property and relocated either to friends, or in the case of the majority, to the school on Golf Road. In addition, each tenant had been asked whether there was a basement and if there was, did it contain an old access door to the tunnel system? In the properties where the occupants weren't sure, the soldiers did a quick inspection themselves. The data was logged and sent via a private satnet to Cameron and his team leaders.

While that operation was in progress, Jay had commandeered the flat screen TV in the hotel bar so he could share his old research on the tunnel system with the men who would be venturing below ground in only a few hours. He also ensured that they all had a digital version of his research, especially the detailed map and topographical charts of the entire tunnel network.

There would be eight teams – four starting from the south and four from the north. The plan was to force the creature into the tunnel branch that used to lead to the Regal Hotel but had since been sealed directly under the roadway.

Each team would, along with standard weaponry, be equipped with the L17A1 underslung grenade launcher. There had even been talk of bringing in a couple of flame throwers, but with the confined spaces and the possibility of there being pockets of trapped methane, it was deemed too great a risk.

As Jay made for the front door of the hotel, Emma appeared and grabbed his arm.

"Be careful, won't you."

"Trust me, I plan to hang as far back as possible."

"In that case, watch your back," she joked.

Despite her attempt at levity, Jay could see the real concern in her eyes. He was momentarily nonplussed at her show of caring. During the final year of their marriage and the years since, she had been nothing but cold and stoic.

As he tried to come up with the right thing to say, she suddenly stepped close and kissed him briefly on the lips. Before he could react, she turned and headed back towards the residential part of the hotel.

Two soldiers were waiting for him as he stepped out into the early morning chill. It was eerily silent, and Jay could almost feel the serenity that he'd come to know in the town as a younger man. A green Land Rover was idling in the parking lot, clearly waiting for him. As he climbed into the back, the driver handed him a sealed plastic bag.

"We found you a spare set of camos," the man said. "I think they're close to your size."

Jay ripped open the plastic and saw that they had found him a set of OCPs – the modern-day camouflage outfit that replaced the old military fatigues. As they drove down the coast road towards Alfred Square, Jay had to perform some serious contortionism in order to change into the provided clothing.

Once in the square, Jay met up with Cameron who

advised that he had decided on the initial three access points for the northern and southern ends of the system. The south teams would work their way north and the north teams, south. There were three main tunnels running under the old town. One ran just to the east of the High Street, another ran under Middle Street and the third ran to the west of the coast road. Three teams at either end would tackle those tunnels. The remaining two teams, one at the north and one at the south would split off and check on the tunnel branches.

The hope was that they could meet at the halfway point having forced the Lusus to flee ahead of them, thus driving it into the tunnel under Market Street and find itself trapped with the soldiers at one end and the blocked access to the Regal Hotel at the other.

The contingency plan, if they could manage to corner it somewhere else, was to use whatever weaponry was available to take it down. In addition, the soldiers were told that once the creature was presumed dead, to stay away from the corpse and contact Cameron immediately. To have informed them that the beast could not just reincarnate but morph into human form was considered too much information, which would ultimately cause hesitation or worse, panic – both of which could easily result in death.

Jay was assigned to be with the D group – the one that would start in the north and focus on the tunnel's confusing branches. It had been determined that the basement of the King James pub in Alfred Square would be the best access point for his team.

Once the two publicans had been convinced, reluctantly, to leave the premises, the team made its way through the lounge and dining area to a service hallway behind the bar. An extremely narrow stairway led down to the two lower floors. The main basement was used primarily for alcohol and food storage. To get to the lowest level they had to negotiate a steep stairway that to Jay seemed more a ladder than anything else.

The lower basement still had a rough stone floor and was only about three metres square. Because of the damp and size, the space had been deemed unfit to store much of anything.

On one wall was a cheap, modern interior door that looked out of place and had obviously been someone's idea of a quick and inexpensive way to cover something up.

One of the soldiers carefully opened it as two others aimed their assault rifles at the opening. Once it was swung aside, Jay could see what must have been the original doorway, at least what was left of it.

It appeared to have once been a solid piece of oak that had, over time, become warped and rotten from the bottom up. All that was holding it closed was an antique metal latch that rested on a reciprocal notched bar. By the look of it, Jay doubted anyone had opened it in a century or two. The soldier who had opened the outer door, did the same to the inner one.

As it swung outwards into the tunnel, the smell of rot and damp wafted into the small space. Jay couldn't be certain, but he thought he sensed some other scent lingering in background – one of feral staleness mixed with mould and rot.

The leader of team D looked to the others.

"You ready?"

Jay knew the question had been primarily aimed at him, but everyone answered as one.

"Yes, sir."

Without another word, the team entered the blackness of the tunnel system wondering what exactly they were going to encounter and whether all of them would make it out alive.

CHAPTER TWENTY-NINE

It knew instinctively that something had changed. It could tell, even underground, that the humans had all, almost at the same time, left the dwellings that interconnected with the tunnel system. In addition, the almost constant thrum of noise from inebriated humans along the central High Street had also ceased.

While that had been concerning enough, its extreme sense of hearing and smell began to detect younger, healthier humans entering the tunnels from both ends. Even worse, it could tell that these particular humans were carrying the tools they used to kill and maim.

It was huddled in a branch of the main tunnel almost equidistant, or so its senses were detecting, from the approaching danger. Due to its ingrained and heightened sense of self-preservation, it knew what the humans were looking for.

It knew that they were hunting much the same way it did, only this time, its prey was hunting for it. While it initially felt that it could find suitable concealment, it could now detect that the humans were approaching in multiple groups. What truly shocked it was that they had begun to explore the branch tunnels as well as the three main ones.

It realised that thoughts of concealment were a waste of time. It needed to find a place to hide, somewhere outside the main tunnel network – somewhere the humans would not consider searching.

*

Emma poured more brandy into the two provided bathroom glasses as Helena looked out from their hotel room balcony. With the pier lights shutting off automatically at 10:00, the night was so dark that she could only see a few dots of flickering yellow light on the other side of the Channel. Though the French coast could usually be seen quite clearly from Deal, a patchwork of low clouds was blocking out almost all illumination, both man-made and celestial.

"It's hard to believe that a couple of hundred years ago, there would have been countless men of war and support ships anchored just off the coast," Emma commented as she handed Helena her refilled glass.

"And the town would have been awash with their seamen," Helena replied.

Emma snorted before breaking out in raucous laughter.

"What did I say?" Helena asked, concerned.

"Sorry. It's my sick mind. You said seamen as in crew, I heard semen as in spunk!"

Helena looked at the older woman in momentary shock before she too cracked up. They both laughed till they cried. Clearly the level of stress they were having to endure required some form of release and the childish misunderstanding seemed to serve that purpose admirably.

Once their mirth had turned back into near-silent self-reflection, Helena chose to speak. "What happened between you and Jay?"

"We were probably too immature and too caught up in our own baggage to have ever stood much of a chance at a successful marriage."

Helena took a sip from her drink before responding. "Did you try?"

Emma's first reaction was annoyance that the young woman had chosen to dig that deeply somewhere she had no business exploring. It wasn't until she gazed into Helena's eyes that she could see no sign of malice or prying, only a look of concerned curiosity.

"I believe we did try. At least in our own way."

"Want to translate that?" Helena asked.

"We each came to the marriage with quite a bit of baggage. Mine from controlling parents and then a series of controlling men, which, in France is a redundant statement. Jay's came from losing his father when he was in his early teens and from a mother who, though apparently brilliant and funny, was distant as hell when it came to dealing with an adolescent son. He unconsciously felt abandoned by both parents and by the time I met him had nurtured some defining emotional issues."

"I would never have thought that about him. He seems so easy going," Helena said.

"That's the problem with baggage," Emma replied,

nodding. "It never looks that bad until it's opened. Most people never bother to properly unpack and when they finally do, everything's gone a bit messy."

"When did that manifest itself with Jay?"

"Whenever we had a fight – any fight," Emma replied. "It would trigger some sort of abandonment gene within him. It wasn't that he didn't or couldn't fight – oh no, he could go toe to toe with me every time. The issue was that, once the fight was over, I would just carry on as before, but some dormant cloud in his psyche made him believe that it was the end – that the raised voices and stupid sentiments meant that my love for him had magically gone and that angry words could only mean he would once again be abandoned. He had no concept that people do actually fight, get over it and then carry on."

"If you knew all that, couldn't you have talked and found some sort of work-around?"

"That's the problem. I didn't realise what was going on in his head back then. Even if I had, I was too busy fighting my own demons. When faced with his fury during an argument, I only saw a man trying to control me, just as my parents had done. The result... I fought back even harder. I only began to understand the dysfunctional ballet we were performing once I sought therapy and got a better understanding of not just my reaction but of his as well. Not that it's much consolation now, but my therapist told me that we were pretty much textbook examples of our specific neuroses."

"Probably something you didn't want to hear?" Helena suggested.

"If I was stuck with having mental issues," Emma replied, nodding, "I would have at least hoped for some originality. Textbook, indeed!"

"Have the two of you ever talked about this?" Helena asked.

"I've tried a few times over the years, but Jay has become very proficient at avoiding me. This is the first time we've shared more than a very brief hello."

"If it's any consolation, I've seen the way he looks at you when you are focused elsewhere. He still cares. To what degree, I don't know, but maybe us all being stuck here under these circumstances could be a good thing."

"I'm not sure that Jay's going to be having any thoughts of romance while that creature is trying to eat the population," Emma replied.

"I don't think romance is in the cards either. Raw, animal passion however..." Helena held up the palm of her hands. "You never know."

"You sound very wise for your years."

"I had to be."

"Care to expand on that?" Emma asked.

Helena studied her for a few moments.

"I don't usually talk about my early days, but considering how forthright you've just been, I guess a little quid pro quo would be acceptable."

Emma, without asking, topped up Helena's glass and watched silently as the other woman took a long pull at her drink.

"The first thing you should know is that I was an orphan.

I never knew my father or mother. I was apparently dropped off in front of the A & E entrance of the Royal Berkshire Hospital in Reading. Thankfully, I was fostered then adopted by husband-and-wife professors at the Reading University within weeks of my being abandoned."

"You poor thing," Emma said, taking Helena's hands in hers. "What a terrible start to your life."

"Actually, I think it was a very fortuitous beginning. As my birth parents clearly didn't want a child, think what my life could have been like if they had begrudgingly chosen to keep me. My adoptive parents, Julia and Wally, were the exact opposite. They were unable to have children the old-fashioned way and focused all of their love and attention on me from the first day they took me to their home in Sonning. The only wrinkle in the otherwise perfect scenario was that it became obvious relatively soon that I wasn't the brainiac they would have spawned had I sprung from their loins. Instead, I was initially – or so they told me when I was a little older – a bit slow when it came to early learning.

"Now I realise that my brain had not been genetically moulded by my intelligent and learned foster parents, rather by the coupling of two people I never knew. These people could have easily been in the lower IQ realm and passed such unwanted individuality on to me.

"Julia and Wally, of course, understood that possibility and chose to devote their time to expanding my mind and learning potential. Every day from the age of three, one or both would spend hours using flash cards and picture books, as well as reactive comprehension and recall techniques, to ensure that my young mind would adapt to something of a learning machine. I'm aware that sounds dry and almost cruel, but they actually made it fun. I know full well that without them, I could have remained a disinterested pupil lost within the antiquated and uninspired school system and come out with little more knowledge than I'd started with.

"Instead, Julia and Wally made me crave learning. A desire that has stuck with me ever since."

"Where are they now?" Emma asked.

"At this moment they are on a three-month academic tour of India studying learning techniques that incorporate yoga and meditation."

"They sound amazing."

"They are, and I hope you can now see why I may have come across as being wise for my years. They say that with wisdom comes knowledge, but I like to think that it's the other way around. At least it was for me."

"I imagine that dating must be tough for someone with your background and intellect. I know that I am always scaring off suitors who feel intimidated by smart women," Emma commented.

"Actually," Helena replied grinning, "I haven't encountered that, probably because I prefer men to be simple – not blithering idiots, but not brainiacs either. I have found that with greater intelligence comes greater complexity in the mind. Complexity that can too easily lead to over-analysis and anxiety. A bloke who is happy watching sports and Marvel movies is going to enjoy life unconditionally and without introspection and insecurity."

"You are very refreshing," Emma said, laughing.

"The dumb ones are also much better at taking instruction when it comes to sex."

That set Emma howling with laughter.

CHAPTER THIRTY

Despite a nagging inner voice shouting at him not to, Jay followed the soldiers into the most northern end of the central tunnel. Despite having written his thesis on the Deal tunnel system, he had, in fact, spent little time physically within them.

Jay had used the last twenty years of his life diving and investigating wrecks that lay strewn across the world's ocean floors. He was used to crawling into unlit, cavernous hulls with certain death only one mistake away, yet, ironically, he only suffered from extreme claustrophobia once on land. His colleagues were completely unaware of this quirk, and Jay made sure they never became any the wiser.

It wasn't that he believed any of his friends or workmates would think less of him, but he knew for a fact that his rivals would dine out on such a piece of tantalising knowledge and would take every opportunity to bring the subject up at the most inopportune moments.

He had secretly hoped that he would be able to fend off the nausea and anxiety that usually came with finding himself in confined spaces. By the time he had stepped into the tunnel proper, he knew that he was not going to be given such a break. Jay felt beads of sweat rolling down his neck as a migraine began to pulse behind his right eye and tinnitus filled his head with a cicada-like drone.

Jay did his best to mask his symptoms, but when the team leader looked back to make sure everyone was in place before they started their trek, he could see the concern on the soldier's face.

"You alright, sir?" he asked.

"Shouldn't have had that second sandwich for lunch," Jay replied with a forced smile.

"You let me know if you get to the point where you feel you can't continue."

"That won't happen," Jay declared, having no belief in his words whatsoever.

Jay knew the tunnel would be dark, but he had never imagined just how dark, dark could be. He was used to diving in situations where there was, at worst, some trickle of illumination either from the surface or from the bioluminescence that was plentiful in depths with low light. Yet, where he was currently standing, less than twenty feet underground, the blackness was so intense that even the peripheral light from their torches could only be seen while looking in the same direction they were pointing. If one dared to look back, the blackness was pure obsidian.

He had also never imagined the smell of the tunnels. On the few occasions when he had actually gone underground in his younger days, there had been the odour of wet soil and even mould. The one he was currently in was an entirely different class of odoriferousness. It was a mix of damp, root rot, sewage leaks, animal decomposition and something unpleasantly metallic that made him want to scratch his tongue. The odour was so strong Jay felt he could actually reach out and touch it.

The going was difficult from the first steps. The smugglers and thieves had laid down planks of wood or placed misshapen stones to create a makeshift path, but these had all either rotted or crumbled away with the passage of time. What was left was a thick, adhering mud that seemed intent on holding on to their boots with a strength that made Jay feel there had to be some cognitive matrix to empower such a determined force.

To make matters worse, the hand-hewn top of the tunnel had partially collapsed in places, requiring the team to either shimmy along the side of the muddy mound or crawl over the top. Either choice left the individual caked in a fresh layer of putrid mud that, no matter how hard they tried to prevent it, always seemed to find a way into a mouth or nose.

Oddly, the difficulty and sense of disgust during their slog south somehow made Jay forget about his claustrophobia and, instead, focus all his attention on not succumbing to the aggressively clinging black ooze.

Within two hours they had completed half their assigned patrol area without finding any trace of the Lusus. While this seemed to elevate the mood of the soldiers in the team, Jay felt that the milestone only meant they were closing in on the creature, ergo, a face-to-face confrontation was more imminent with each new quadrant searched.

As Jay dwelt on that fact, the team members in front of him came to a sudden stop. Within seconds, he could hear the sound of one of the soldiers being violently sick.

Taking a few steps forward towards where their lights were aimed, Jay felt his insides knot as an icy shiver made its way from his coccyx to the base of his skull.

Just inside the next tunnel branch it looked as if someone had covered the area with dark red paint. It took a moment for Jay to recognise that the mound at the base of the curved wall wasn't simply part of the tunnel that had given way.

The lower mandible of a human jaw was the big giveaway. Protruding from the gory mound, a row of perfect white teeth protruded from a blood-drenched jawbone. As the realisation came to him that he was looking at human remains, other objects became recognisable. A piece of the upper spine, a few ribs still attached, was partially submerged beneath the tunnel mud. Next to that was the top half of a skull, which appeared to be scarred with what had to be fang marks.

At first glance, there didn't appear to be any flesh left on any of the remains, with the exception of a pair of human eyes that were already clouded over yet seemed to be looking directly up at Jay. Behind the eyes, where the brain should have been, was an empty, blood-soaked cranium. Jay took a moment to marvel that the eyes had managed to stay in place considering there was nothing to hold them anymore, then he realised that, because of the position of the skull, it was just gravity doing its job.

The team leader approached Jay.

"Do we know who this could be?" he asked.

Jay shook his head. "We know for a fact that it's killed at least five people and that their remains have been found – at least as much as could be recognised – but there could be quite a few more who were taken without anyone knowing."

"Hopefully that lower jaw will help. There's visible dental work that should match with somebody's records."

"Should we take it with us?" Jay asked, mildly revolted by the thought of anyone having to actually pick up the remnants of a human being.

"No, sir. No matter who or what is doing these killings, we have to treat this as a crime scene. We leave everything as is until it's safe for the forensic team to come down here."

"Where do you think" – Jay gestured with his head at the grizzly remains – "he or she came from?"

"It's a he. The slope of that forehead is definitely male. As for the origin, I haven't a clue yet, but once we check out this tunnel branch, we'll know if any of the houses topside can be accessed from down here."

Jay looked past the mutilated corpse, or at least what was left of it, and saw that mud-drenched stalactites hung down almost as far as the boggy ground – some as wide as a man's torso. As if that wasn't bad enough, the smaller tunnel's roof seemed to slope downwards making the already difficult slog even worse.

"Lot of places for something to hide down there," Jay commented.

"That's why we're going to give it a good once over," the leader said before adjusting his torch and stepping further into the otherworldly landscape.

*

Richard Gallot slowly opened his secret wine cellar under a fake floor in his kitchen. When the soldiers had started rousting his neighbours, forcing them to vacate their homes, he had turned off all the lights, and using his phone torch, sneaked out of sight hoping that they would assume nobody was home and go on to the next house.

His cellar had originally been a small, low-ceilinged basement with a hatchway that led to the old smugglers' tunnels, but he'd had it converted to a wine cellar. One that could only be accessed from the kitchen via a hydraulic hatchway in the centre of the kitchen floor. The top of the panel was covered with a chef's kitchen mat and when the hatchway panel was closed, all anyone would see was the rubber surround and washable grey fibre of the mat. The seam was completely invisible.

Gallot's reasoning for the secret cellar was that, unbeknown to his neighbours and most of his friends, he was a collector of extraordinarily expensive and rare wines. His latest find was a bottle of 1869 Chateau Lafite Rothschild that he 'stole' at auction for just over £240,000.

Gallot had over fifty bottles hidden away under his kitchen where a very expensive system kept the temperature, humidity and air filtration at the optimum levels to preserve the bottles and their contents.

The wines were racked along one wall, while against the

opposite one sat a single leather armchair, a walnut side table and a brass floor lamp. This was where Gallot would sit for hours staring at the bottles as they lay in perpetual sleep.

Most people who had the wherewithal to own a collection of wine worth in excess of five million pounds would likely live in a multimillion-pound estate with a serious wine cellar and top security. Gallot, however, did not want the world to know his monetary worth – at least not until such time as paedophilia was no longer considered abhorrent and illegal.

Instead, he still lived in the terraced house his mother had left him and quietly ran his internet site located deep within the dark web, where he helped those who were willing to pay to find the boy or girl of their dreams. While the site had no actual name, he referred to it as 'Kiddie Tinder'.

His self-designed multi-layer firewall, triple bounce VPN and proprietary cloaking software managed to keep all prying eyes far away from his lucrative endeavour. Just to become a member required intense scrutiny and a ludicrously large 'security' deposit. What the site offered in return was protection from any fishing expedition by a government or policing agency, such was the complexity of its cyber concealment.

Once Gallot was back up in his kitchen, he listened by the back patio door for any sounds of searching soldiers. He could still hear them, but it was clear that they were moving away from his little blue house.

Knowing that he couldn't very well stay above ground and avoid detection while the militia was evicting the other residents, Gallot decided that he may as well get some work done where he knew he couldn't be detected. Using his phone's light angled directly at the floor, he made his way into the dining room that he used as his office and grabbed his laptop. As he disconnected the charger cable, there was a sound from the kitchen.

He knew he was alone in the house, but still, he had heard something. He crept back to where the secret hatchway lay open and listened intently.

There it was again. It sounded like something tapping on glass down in his sacred cellar.

Gallot felt relief. There was no way anyone could find their way down there without him knowing, so the sound was likely to have been a few drops of condensation falling onto one of the bottles.

Reassured that all was still hunky-dory, Gallot climbed down the narrow steps then shut the hatchway behind him.

CHAPTER THIRTY-ONE

Once Mayor Haley had been convinced by the soldiers at the restaurant that an escort would be provided to get him safely through the town, he knocked back one last snifter of brandy then staggered to his feet. As he stepped out into the narrow alley he was initially surprised at the silence. When he had first walked into the place only a few hours earlier, the inebriated townsfolk were singing and bellowing along the length of the High Street. He was only too aware that the revellers didn't live anywhere near the old town and had come from some of the less inviting areas of town, such as the north end or Mill Hill. He knew the military had forced them to all head home, but was mildly surprised that they had actually listened to anyone of authority.

Now all he could hear was the occasional sound of a seagull wailing somewhere in the distance.

"Once you have escorted me home, will I still have protection?" he asked.

"You're not going home," one of the men replied.

Haley came to an unsteady stop.

"What do you mean? Where else would I be going?"

"We have orders to escort you to the Golf Road school so

that you can help calm the evacuees."

"The last thing I want to do is to go anywhere near those people. They must be bloody livid. You know they'll blame me for all this don't you! I don't know what's happened to the world, but I seem to have to spend most of my days appeasing people who feel that I'm at fault for just about anything and everything that happens down here. This one bloke stopped me last week in the middle of the street and blamed me for his family having had a crap holiday. Apparently, they didn't know about the wind down here and felt we should put a warning on all our promotional material."

"I'm sorry to hear that, sir, but it was decided that your being there on the spot might just calm the people down."

"Calm them down?" he shrieked. "Who's going to bloody calm me down. Do you have any idea what this latest fiasco will do to the tourist business here. I can already imagine what the media in Ramsgate and Margate are going to come up with. 'Sure, Deal is a pretty place, but wouldn't you prefer a nice holiday where the chances of you getting eaten are zero?'"

In an effort to keep away from the High Street just in case there were pockets of drunk citizenry that had yet to be forced home, the soldiers chose to head north on Middle Street. Other than the mayor's slurred grouching about having to actually act mayoral, the entire road was strangely quiet. Once Haley had calmed down, the only sound came from their footsteps as they echoed off the quaint old houses. There was no sound of traffic and the only visible vehicle was a black Range Rover that seemed to have come to a stop half-on, half-off the low kerb.

After walking north for a few hundred metres, one of the soldiers held up his hand as a signal for them to stop. Up ahead, one exterior house light was on but was flickering badly. The men knew that all lights inside and outside the houses had been switched off so the only illumination sources other than the streetlights would be from the patrolling teams themselves.

One of the mayor's escorts radioed that there was an anomaly on Middle Street – a possible faulty light.

"It's just north of Exchange Street," the soldier stated. "It's on the west side. You can't miss it. It's bright blue and the light is flickering."

The three stayed put until they heard the sound of boots running from a side street. Within seconds, three soldiers, two men and one woman, appeared and slowly approached the little blue house. One of the men, Second Lieutenant Nigel Saunders, stepped up to the front door and used the oversized brass knocker to make his presence known.

Nigel couldn't help wondering, as he had for most of the day, what he and his squadron were doing in Deal. The pat answer from above, that there was a vicious canine on the loose, made zero sense. The army had spent a small fortune training him to become a front-line warrior. He was a specialist in munitions and strategic operations for desert warfare. He therefore couldn't for the life of him understand why his superiors were willing to waste his time hunting down some mangy dog. What made the whole situation even odder was that he and his team weren't even doing any of the actual hunting. Their orders were to patrol one specific sector of a residential area once all inhabitants had been relocated further inland.

There were rumours going around about there being an unexploded bomb somewhere in the centre of town, but if there was, Nigel questioned why the evacuated area was basically a mile-long rectangle rather than a large circle around the suspected bomb site.

Nigel knocked on the door again.

There was no response.

He leaned in and held his ear against the glossy wood door. Though distant and muffled, he could make out the sound of heavy breathing coming from inside the house. To Nigel, the raspy gasps had a strange animal-like edge to them, almost as if the person was panting.

"I can hear you," he shouted as he took a step backwards. "All residents have been instructed to shelter at the Golf Road school. Please exit the building immediately or we will be forced to open the door ourselves."

Dead silence filled Middle Street as the patrol stood in front of the door and the mayor and his escorts looked on from a block away.

The soldier stepped close to the door for a second time and repeated his words, this time adding, "You leave us no choice but to break the door in."

Just as the other members of his team moved closer to the house, the door slowly opened. At first it looked as if it had done so by itself, then the figure of a man could be seen just inside the entry hall.

The first thing the patrol noticed was that the man was extremely pale. The second, was that he appeared to be stark naked.

"Is everything alright, sir?" Nigel asked, trying not to see the humour in the situation. He couldn't help pondering why, with all his training, he was standing in the middle of the street in the wee hours of the morning, trying to start a conversation with some nude bloke who desperately needed time under a sun lamp.

The creature that Nigel assumed was a man, nodded.

"Would you mind coming out here with us, sir?"

The man shook his head.

From where they were standing, the mayor's group couldn't see who the soldier was speaking with.

"Must be some old geezer who decided to skip the evacuation," one of his escorts whispered.

"As mayor, maybe you could help persuade the man?" the other one suggested.

The open tack channel that the teams were using to communicate came to life.

"Lieutenant Saunders from surface team Tango. I have found an occupant in number 137 Middle Street. He has opened the door but appears unwilling to vacate."

"Approach and offer assistance to relocate him. If that doesn't work, let me know," came the response.

"Sir, there's something else. The man is extraordinarily pale and..."

"And what?"

"He's nude, sir."

Haley, who'd been listening to the exchange with little interest, suddenly felt as if he'd been hit by a bolt of lightning. Before his escorts knew what was happening, he ran, or at least came as close as his age, health and sobriety permitted, towards the little blue house.

His two minders watched him waddle and swerve up the narrow street.

"What's he bloody doing?" one asked.

"Fuck if I know," the other responded.

Haley had covered half the distance to the blue house, yet was already breathless and dizzy, which, considering that it was the first aerobic exercise he'd done in thirty years, was perfectly understandable.

"Don't go in there," Haley tried to warn the soldiers, but his voice came out as little more than a squeak.

Though Nigel couldn't make out the man's words, he could see the fear in his eyes and the fact that he looked about ready to drop dead of a coronary.

"See what he wants, will you?" the second lieutenant said to the soldier closest to him as he turned back to the open doorway.

"Don't go in there," the mayor managed to yell just as the soldier was about to step inside. "It's not human!"

Nigel stopped where he was, only inches from crossing the entry threshold, then backstepped down onto the pavement.

Haley felt a warm sense of relief wash over him at having stopped the man from entering.

Nigel looked over at the mayor, who was by that time still a good few metres from the blue house. He couldn't help being mildly amused at the sight of the overweight, sweaty man, stumbling towards him while his two 'minders' were keeping pace without any exertion whatsoever.

The mayor gave him a thumbs up and slowed down slightly believing that he had defused the situation.

"Care to explain that 'not human' comment?" Nigel called to him.

"Please step further away," the mayor insisted.

Before Nigel could ask why, he sensed rather than saw some movement within the house. By the time he turned to look, it was too late. The naked man seemed to step towards the front door, but in mid-stride began to change from the head down. The face became featureless then elongated at the same time as black fur started to appear across its entire body. By the time the Lusus passed through the door frame it had fully re-formed into its canine self.

Haley, ironically, had the best view of the attack. He saw the massive creature step out of the door while its hind quarters, for a millisecond, still appeared to be human. By the time it closed its jaws around the second lieutenant's neck, the transformation was complete. Only moments after Nigel had barked orders for his team to open fire, his quivering headless body somehow remained upright for a long few seconds before dropping to the ground like a bag of wet cement.

The Lusus shook Nigel's head out of its powerful jaws and, in one fluid motion, sank its teeth into the leg of the other male soldier. With an almighty snap of its head, the man's limb separated from his body sending yet more blood gushing into the Middle Street gutters.

The Lusus then turned and focused its eyes on Haley. It remembered the unhealthy male from the place where the humans had been feeding. Though it didn't feel vengeance – as that emotion had never been programmed into its brain – it did, however, feel a powerfully strong need to kill the overweight specimen that was backing away from it.

The remaining patrol soldier plus the two assigned to get the mayor back home drew their sidearms and opened fire at once.

Adrenaline and fear do not help when it comes to having a steady hand. Many of the shots went wild, some even clinking through windows of the surrounding houses. Others did hit their mark. With each impact the canine stumbled back, but then continued its slow steady pace towards the mayor. It wasn't until the patrol officer decided to ignore her training that things changed.

The woman reached for her pistol grip signal flare and, even with shaking hands, managed to load one of the flare cartridges into the breach. In a show of true bravery, instead of keeping her distance, she charged towards the animal until she was less than ten metres away. She then stopped, and as the Lusus turned to face her, she fired the flare.

The result was as terrifying as had been the earlier attacks. The strontium nitrate and magnesium burned as strongly as the sun and hit the Lusus in the centre of its forehead igniting bone, meat and hair.

To the onlooker's horror, the creature did not drop to the ground as expected. Instead, its head appeared to morph around the damage and, with its flesh rippling like ocean surf, the charred area relocated to a less critical part of the body. In the Lusas's case, the right hind quarter.

Even though its face had not fully re-formed, part of it managed to open wide as it let out a deafening scream of anger and pain, before it ran back into the little blue house. As the soldiers started towards the entrance, the door slammed with such force that it cracked from top to bottom.

The soldiers stopped in their tracks and turned to face the mayor, hoping that he might have some explanation for what had just occurred.

He gave them a shaky smile and asked, "So, what do you think of Deal so far?"

CHAPTER THIRTY-TWO

The creature was in pain and knew that this time its injuries were more serious. Though it was able to shift injured flesh to less crucial areas of its body, the heat from the fire stick that the human had wielded, had, it believed, actually damaged its brain – the one organ that couldn't metamorphise unless it underwent a full resurrection following catastrophic damage to its body as a whole.

Though not wired to have thoughts of guilt or regret, it couldn't help feeling both of these sentiments as it made for the small basement where it had devoured a male human less than an hour earlier. It knew that it needed to retreat into the tunnels once again and that it had to find a way of avoiding any more human contact until it felt stronger and more able to defend itself.

When the male had knocked on the main entry portal, it knew it should ignore the sound and enter the underground network immediately. Unfortunately, its own lust for killing overwhelmed what logic and cunning it may have had and drew it up to the ground floor where it morphed into a close replica of the male it had just feasted upon.

That same human had put up a surprisingly violent

struggle and at one point had even managed to climb up to the ground level and almost made it to the door. It had managed to stop the male and in doing so had inadvertently knocked him against a wall switch with such force that the human's head had shattered the plastic casing and torn wires free from their attachment points causing a short circuit of the exterior light.

It had finally dragged the human's body down to the small basement room filled with containers of pungent red liquid, much of which lay pooled on the rough flooring, their glass containers having been shattered during its initial attack.

It felt exhaustion after the wounding it had recently sustained and needed all its remaining strength to crawl into the narrow tunnel access. It knew that it didn't just need to hide, but also needed to rest and let its miraculous body heal itself as much as possible before the next inevitable human encounter.

An encounter that could well be its last, before it had to undergo a full renewal so it would again be able to fight on with the ferocity with which it was endowed.

*

It took only a few minutes for reinforcements to arrive at the little blue house. Before the second lieutenant's body could even be removed, charges were set against the door and, after the teams stepped far enough away, were detonated seconds later. Considering what had happened to the initial response team, nobody was taking any chances of a repeat performance.

Tear gas was shot into the house and thirty seconds later – the period within which the gas should have incapacitated the creature – five heavily armed soldiers with face masks and full battle gear stormed the property.

Thanks to the multiple trails of blood leading from the front room to the kitchen and then down into the custom wine cellar, it was clear which way the creature had gone. After more gas was fired into the basement, and after no apparent reaction, two soldiers descended into the smoke.

Before they realised that most of the fluid on the floor was unspeakably expensive vintage claret, they thought that the liquid lapping at their boots was blood. Their relief was short lived. As the smoke cleared, they saw an unrecognisable mound of flesh, bone and blood wedged within one of the custom wine racks. It took them both a few beats before they realised that what they were seeing were the remains of one Richard Gallot.

On the left side of the room, where once had stood an antique floor-to-ceiling mirror, there was now a jagged opening leading into the total blackness of the tunnel system. On the floor, around the roughly hewn access hole, the shards of the shattered mirror twinkled as they floated on a sea of 'Chateaux de Sang'.

*

The other tunnel teams heard tear gas canisters explode somewhere in the distance, but thought nothing of it until Major Whitehead, the company commander, advised them that the canine had attacked a house on Middle Street and had killed the occupant as well as two soldiers, both of whom were well known and liked within the unit.

The major stressed that the animal was wounded and couldn't have got farther than a few hundred metres since the attack. He ordered all teams to close ranks and move to within a quarter kilometre of the Middle Street location so that they could slowly tighten the cordon and hopefully force the creature into the sealed tunnel between the Regal Hotel and the centre of town.

The tunnel teams moved as quickly as they could considering the underground terrain, and Jay tried his best to keep up but found the going difficult at best.

"Please keep up with us," the leader called back to him.

"What the hell do you think I've been trying to do?" Jay shot back.

"We don't want you falling too far behind. You're going to make yourself an easy target if that thing somehow gets behind us."

With a spurt of energy that he hadn't known was even in his arsenal, Jay managed to half run, half crawl at a fast enough pace to catch up with the others.

*

Having polished off a good quantity of the brandy, Helena started craving a Diet Coke – something they hadn't thought to buy on the earlier expedition to Sainsbury's.

"If you stay put," Emma said, "I'll see if there's anyone downstairs who can get you a Coke. The bar's closed, but someone must have access."

Emma found the night manager reading a book about a haunted ocean liner while huddled in the hotel's tiny back office.

Sandra was in her forties and, despite the occasional disruptive guest, spent her nights in relative peace. That gave her the ability to read just about any book she could find that was set in the sixties.

Unable to understand the music, the television shows, the drab dress, or just about any other aspect of the present day, she chose to dwell in a time sixty years earlier. Sandra felt that the sixties must have been an era of hope and fun. A time of evolution and of people pushing boundaries rather than the modern-day ethos of secure, safe, narcissistic self-preservation.

She also believed that the sixties had, despite all the wonderful craziness, a sense of style about it. People dressed up to travel and to go to dinner. Now it was perfectly acceptable to turn up in sweatpants and a hoodie and sit glued to a smart phone so you could transport yourself to anywhere rather than where you were at that moment.

The book she was reading perfectly encapsulated the style, the grace and yes, even the romance of that time. Though she knew very well that the sixties were by no means perfect, and from a global perspective, the period was only magical for a tiny proportion of the population, she was happy to keep her rose-coloured glasses firmly in place and only see the positives.

Having been so deeply immersed in the book, she didn't hear or sense anyone's approach and looked up guiltily when Emma cleared her throat to get her attention.

"Sorry, love. I was miles away. What can I do for you?"

"Any chance of digging up a Diet Coke?" Emma asked.

"Easy-peasy. Just the one?"

"Maybe two would be safer."

The woman, who to Emma looked more like a stereotypical librarian than a seaside hotel manager, trotted off towards the bar. Emma took a moment to check out the vintage seaside photos and memorabilia that filled the walls. In one area, six photos, each taken twenty years apart, showed Deal's pictorial history through the years. The first shot taken in the late 1800s, showed well-dressed men and women strolling along the boardwalk, the former in top hats, the latter holding up parasols to fend of the harsh English sun. The last photo was taken in 2023. Though the buildings hadn't changed, traffic clogged the beach road and the crowds that were gathered at the entrance to the relatively new pier looked to be wearing overly bright, cheap clothing that Emma knew probably came either from online vendors or that powerhouse of disposable fashion, Primark.

"Here you go," Sandra said as she appeared suddenly by Emma's side, a can of Coke in each hand. "Should I charge these to Mr Salinger's room?"

"Yes, please," Emma replied taking hold of the frosty aluminium tins. "Thank you for this." She held up the Cokes as she turned to leave.

"Before you go, do you mind my asking you a question?" Sandra said.

"Of course."

"Is it true that Mr Sallinger is helping the military find some sort of stray dog?"

Emma was momentarily taken aback by the woman's grasp of the situation, considering that no announcement of such details had ever been made.

"Yes. He's something of an expert when it comes to the tunnels under the town. I don't know if you were even aware that they existed?"

"I wasn't," Sandra answered. "Until a few years ago."

"Why then?" Emma asked.

"That's when the owners paid to have the old hotel tunnel that led all the way to the High Street reopened as part of a smugglers tour they planned on offering to the tourists."

"Did those tours ever take place?" Emma asked.

"The tours never happened, but the tunnel was cleared just in case the council changed its mind about the tourist attraction at a later date."

"Have you been inside it?"

"Once, when the old manager took us on a quick tour one day when it was really quiet in the hotel."

"How was it?"

"A bit creepy, actually. Also, it is damp down there and smells frightful."

"I can imagine," Emma replied as she made for the stairs, her mild intoxication stopping her usually sharp mind from realising that what the night manager had just told her meant that everyone in the hotel was in imminent danger.

CHAPTER THIRTY-THREE

Doctor Wiseman had insisted he remain awake while the search and hoped-for capture of the Lusus was in progress. Despite all the best intentions, he found himself dozing in the front room while Cameron worked out of his makeshift office to coordinate not just the search but the delivery of the Fluoroantimonic acid, the equipment to safely pump it into the dead-end tunnel and the airtight container for the removal of the remains – if there were any.

Wiseman was dreaming about his mother – something that was happening more and more often as he neared life's finishing line. It was strange, as he hadn't consciously thought of her in over forty years, yet now she was very much alive in his subconscious psyche.

The dreams were very disquieting for a man who prided himself on having a steel trap of a mind – one in which he could control both the data intake and outflow as he so wished. These dreams, eerily similar from night to night, were of him working in the lab in present day and his mother casually walking up behind him and ruffling his hair as she had always done when he was a child. The odd part of the reverie was that, even in the dream, he knew her to be dead, yet he fully accepted her return as if the last forty years had never transpired. Wiseman even had a tinge of guilt at having moved into and remodelled what had been her house before her passing.

Cameron stood watching the old man as his eyelids fluttered in deep REM sleep and his mouth curved into what appeared to be a contented smile. For a brief moment, Cameron felt some pity for the old man and was about to let him get his rest, then he remembered that this same man was responsible for the creation of the Lusus.

The pity evaporated like sun-drenched morning mist.

"I've got an update," Cameron said in a loud enough voice to wake Wiseman, but not so loud as to startle him.

"Sorry, I must have closed my eyes for a moment," Wiseman uttered. "What's happened."

"The bad news is that it has struck again, killing numerous soldiers, and also appears to have devoured the resident of a house that we had thought to be empty."

"What's the good news?" Wiseman asked, not seeming the least bit perturbed at the update of yet more violent death.

"That acid you requested has been located and will be brought on a chopper. It should be here within the hour."

"Isn't that rather a lot of liquid for a helicopter to carry?"

"Yes, but not for the one we are using. It can lift a tank."

"Speaking of which, I assume you managed to find a suitable Teflon-lined storage container?"

Cameron smiled. "The same people who had the acid also had Fluoroantimonic-proof containers."

"Good. Now we just have to hope you can force the Lusus into the right area."

"That doesn't seem to be a problem. The last attack was just under an hour ago and occurred on Middle Street less than a quarter mile from the sealed tunnel."

"What about access for the transfer of the water and the acid?" Wiseman asked.

"There's a utility access shaft almost directly above the part of the tunnel we need."

"Why? There can't be any utility cables or piping down there, surely."

"There shouldn't be, and in fact there now aren't any, but back in the early 1900s when the Regal needed city power, water and sewerage, instead of creating a new conduit, decided to use the abandoned tunnel."

"How fortuitous," Wiseman commented.

"Now we just have to hope this acid of yours actually works."

"That's not the big caveat to this being a success. The Lusus is still the wild card. Though its sentient side is not that developed, its self-preservation genes are extraordinary. It cannot just sense a threat but can work out how to avoid it and in some cases use it to its own advantage."

"Worst case scenario is that we can't physically lure it into the right position. If that happens, we do things the old-fashioned way and track it and either shoot it or burn it to death. Even if that condition is only temporary, once it's incapacitated, we can still give it the acid treatment," Cameron stated.

"You make that sound so simple. Unfortunately, you are not dealing with a human mind or body. The Lusus is a killing machine and is able to self-repair on the fly. Don't get me wrong – I hope you are successful, but if not, there's always option B," Wiseman said almost reluctantly.

"No one mentioned there being any alternate options at this point."

"My dear boy" – Wiseman sat fully upright and tried to get a kink out of his neck muscles – "there's always other options in life. In this case, though, it's not one I would prescribe unless all else has gone severely pear-shaped. I must say, I am a little perplexed that Colonel Hartfield didn't bring up the subject, at least in passing."

"Well, he didn't, and I may as well tell you that he won't be involved in this endeavour any longer."

"Why? I mean the man's a complete philistine, but at least he had the good sense to get me involved."

"Sadly, it is believed that when he left the restaurant and made for his transport back to the helicopter, the Lusus was waiting for him in the vehicle. I say *believed*, because all the troops found was a mass of blood and what may have been his head, and identification involved a certain amount of deduction as it was devoid of all flesh."

Wiseman looked up at Cameron with clear piercing eyes.

"No great loss, really. The man was more interested in sucking up to the ministry than doing his job."

"This might be the right time for you to tell me about this backup plan," Cameron suggested, mildly surprised at the old man's callous disregard for the death of a colleague.

"Like so many scientific discoveries, the best way to destroy one subject is with another similar subject. It's fundamental mathematics. They will simply cancel each other out."

"I'm not sure I'm following you," Cameron replied as an icy chill ran down his neck.

"It's very simple, really." Wiseman grinned. "Knowing the difficulties of tracking and destroying the initial creature, we created the perfect antidote."

Wiseman leaned forward and gestured to Cameron to get closer so he could whisper conspiratorially.

"Before the project was formally shut down, we created a second Lusus."

Wiseman sat back and looked up at Cameron expecting to see some sort of elation or at least relief. What he saw instead was an expression of complete and utter shock.

"You seem troubled by my little piece of news," Wiseman commented.

"Troubled isn't the word for it. We are in the middle of trying to defuse a killing machine that you lot created over eighty years ago, and you now casually mention that there's a second one of these things."

"You needn't be so alarmed. The second creature is currently little more than a few pounds of what, to you, would appear to be fine sand. That material has been frozen in an underground, airless storage facility. It would have to somehow come into contact with oxygen for the reincarnation process to take place – something that would never happen, at least not unintentionally."

"Please explain why you think that having two of these things on the loose is, in any sane world, an option?"

Wiseman smiled.

"My dear boy, the second Lusus was genetically modified during the creation process. It was never intended as a weapon."

"What was its purpose if not to kill humans?" Cameron asked, wishing the other man would stop grinning. Whether it was the subject matter or something about the low lighting, the old man's smile seemed disingenuous, and with his yellowed and nicotine-stained teeth, it made him appear both creepy and insane.

"It was created for the sole purpose of destroying the original version. It was meant to be what the Yanks call a Hail Mary play in case we were unable to control the original Lusus."

"That sounds problematic at best. Once these two canine mutants meet, what's to stop them pairing up and going on a joint rampage?"

"The original Lusus would never accept a hunting partner and the LPO thinks of nothing but killing the other one. So, you see, it's the perfect solution."

Cameron gave him a questioning look. "LPO?"

"Last Possible Option."

"That was its name?" he asked.

"It was as close to one as it was ever going to get," Wiseman replied.

"Did you ever name the original Lusus?"

"We felt that Lusus was sufficient as a moniker. We didn't

see the need to come up with some endearing name for two such horrific creatures. So, any more questions or are you comfortable with our failsafe option?"

"Not quite. Let's say the second creature does indeed destroy the first one, how do we then contain *it*?"

"It's programmed to do nothing once the other one is fully destroyed. It will simply find the nearest human and surrender itself."

"If the first one is, for all intents and purposes, impossible to kill, how can a clone destroy it in such a way as to render it incapable of resurrection."

The old man laughed.

"It devours its rival... consuming the brain first. The dispersion of the creature's cells within the second Lusus makes it impossible for any revival whatsoever. The genetic matrix that permits the cells to bind in either the human or canine form is neutralised within the LPO's digestive system."

"Is there any chance of the two creatures mating?" Cameron asked bluntly.

"None whatsoever. The two will be filled with nothing but a raw, instinctual hatred of the other. There could be no thought or drive to mate. We made sure of that."

"If the original Lusus is such a perfect killing machine, why do you think the second one would overcome the first?"

"That, if I do say so myself, is the true beauty of their creation," Wiseman said with another unnerving grin. "The original Lusus is male; the second is female."

"What's the difference?"

Wiseman gave the other man a puzzled and slightly

concerned look.

"I know what the difference is between male and female, I don't know what the difference is between these two monsters."

"Very simple. The female is roughly twice as powerful as the one you are dealing with."

Cameron looked back at the grinning old man and felt an irrationally strong urge to throttle him on the spot.

CHAPTER THIRTY-FOUR

Once sufficient time had passed, it crept out of the narrow, concealed tunnel spur that at some point had been hewn from solid rock. Whatever its original purpose had been, it was the perfect hiding place while the humans continued to close in from all sides.

Its injuries had mostly healed, and the cell redistribution had rebuilt the more serious wounded areas. Even its thick coat had self-replenished. It knew from the proximity of the voices and their odour that humans had, at some point during its healing, moved much closer. While it didn't comprehend strategy, as such, it could tell that they were trying to cut off its means of escape. It understood that it always had the option of going above ground and most likely evading their hunt, but its pre-programmed craving to kill and devour couldn't allow it to flee from so many approaching bodies. Bodies rich with fresh meat and warm nutrient-rich blood.

During the hours it had spent in the tunnels it had been able to re-familiarise itself with the layout of the system. There were three tunnels that paralleled the seafront. Many more, smaller and far less traversable ones ran perpendicular, connecting buildings throughout the older part of the town.

The humans were approaching primarily from within the main tunnels, though the branches were examined to ensure that it wasn't hiding in any of them.

It could tell that if it remained where it was, they would reach its position in a very short time. It knew that there was no way it could double back in the hopes of letting the humans pass by, and from what it could gauge from the sounds and smells, there were too many for it to attempt to assault them.

The only option left was the one tunnel that ran under the paved road, separating a large seaside structure from the rest of the town. It had never ventured that far from the centre of the system, as it knew the tunnel had to end somewhere under that building, meaning there would be no means of escape underground should it somehow become cornered.

It knew, from the bygone time when it had last feasted in the same town, that the place was often filled with humans. The sound of their laughter, though muffled, could reach deep into the tunnel system.

While no such sounds were being produced on that night, it could still sense the likelihood of there being at least a few humans within the structure. Its reasoning had become clouded and the decision to head for that particular dead-end tunnel was made based on its craving for flesh, not self-preservation.

*

The Teflon-lined tank had been lowered onto the narrow bend in the road between the Regal Hotel and the rest of the old town. A team opened up the old access hatch in the asphalt and two men carefully lowered themselves down into the tunnel so they could help position the hoses for the fresh water and the acid. They knew that because the road sloped down towards the hotel, the tunnel would do the same. The plan was that the liquids would pool at the point where the sloping tunnel met the area where it had been sealed off, ensuring the creature, once lured there, would get a good drenching from the lethal cocktail.

As the men reached the tunnel floor, they turned east so they were facing what they believed would be a wall of rock and soil. Not only was there no wall, but they could feel a steady breeze coming from the direction where the tunnel was supposed to be sealed. They aimed their combat LED torches further down the tunnel, hoping that the obstruction was simply a little further east than expected.

Both men were stunned to see that there was no blockage whatsoever. If the tunnel had at one time been sealed, that had been reversed and, as far as they could tell, the tunnel ran all the way to the hotel.

Cameron was standing a few feet from the access hatch looking out at the vague twinkling of coastal lights across the Channel in France, when his in-ear monitor came to life.

"Sir," an anxious voice stammered over the radio. "The tunnel doesn't appear to be blocked anymore. If we release the water and chemicals from here, they will simply run off towards the Regal Hotel."

Cameron was not a man who froze during an operation, yet that's exactly what he did. Not for long, probably only for a few seconds, but it seemed like an eternity to the men below ground. He looked towards the open hatch, his head filled with half a dozen possible options, none of them great, all of them dangerous.

Those thoughts suddenly evaporated as it dawned on him that the search teams in the tunnels were still funnelling the creature towards the one that, rather than being blocked, was intact and led directly to the hotel where over fifty guests were sound asleep, unaware that they were now little more than a buffet waiting for one overly gluttonous diner to show up.

"Tell the search teams to hold in place."

"Yes, sir," a disembodied voice acknowledged through his headset.

The two men stood in the dank, low-ceilinged tunnel waiting for word back on what they should do. Both were members of the Corps of Royal Engineers, and neither could understand what all the fuss was about. To escort a giant container of acid all the way from a North Sea petrochemical distribution centre seemed like overkill just to get rid of some rabid bloody dog.

"Why don't we just climb out and wait for instructions," Neal, the taller of the two, suggested.

"I think that's called abandoning one's post, and that, my friend, could get you a nice two-year holiday at Shepton Mallet," Tim replied.

"Everyone up there seems to be wound up like a top. I

wouldn't put it past them to forget we're even down here."

"Do you smell something rank?" Tim asked as he wrinkled his nose and retched.

"It has smelled like shit ever since we got in this tunnel, you'll have to be more... wait. Oh blimey. It suddenly smells like a dead animal down here."

"That's it, lads." A voice came out of their headsets. "You can come up now. Your side of the mission has been put on hold."

Neal rolled his eyes. "What a load of muppets," he said as he stepped back to the metal ladder that they had used to climb down.

"I'll stay down while you retract the hoses from above. Don't want them snagging on anything," Tim offered.

"Sounds like a plan," Neal said as he climbed up into what was turning out to be a very windy morning. Though still dark, he could distinctly hear large waves breaking onto the pebbled shoreline.

Once Neal was out of sight, Tim adjusted the two hoses, one, little more than an oversized version of what he used regularly in his garden, the other, a Teflon coated custom job that weighed a ton and was of a type he'd never seen before.

"Clear," Tim said into his headset.

The hoses started to move along the uneven ground then stopped suddenly as if snagged on something. Puzzled, Tim aimed his torch towards where they were coiled a little further down the tunnel.

There was no obvious reason for them to have ceased

moving. Then he realised that, though he could see the hoses and the surrounding tunnel quite clearly by the light of his torch, in the middle of the coil was complete blackness.

Then, in the midst of the obsidian shadow, a pair of yellow eyes snapped open, and the tunnel filled with a guttural growl.

"I think I just found the bloody dog," he whispered into his mic.

"Get out of there," Neal shouted back.

Tim kept his eyes riveted on the dark shape as he slowly, moved towards the waiting ladder.

His hand reached the cold metal rail and he gently lifted one leg onto a lower rung.

Just as he thought that there was a chance the creature would let him go, it sprang towards him. By the light of his torch, Tim could see that the thing was no ordinary canine. It was huge and had jaws that seemed to widen to an impossible degree before latching on to his right leg.

The crew topside heard his scream as clearly as if he'd only been a few inches from them.

"Tim!" Neal screamed down the open hatchway, aiming his torch towards where he believed his colleague's cry had emanated from.

All he could see was a huge, black, heavily furred body ripping at something beneath it. He rolled away from the hole and stared up at the others in complete shock.

"It's taken Tim."

"Is he still alive?" Cameron asked.

"I don't see how."

Cameron turned to the engineer who was still standing at the pump controls for the water and acid.

"Turn them on," he barked.

"Which one?" the man asked.

"Both of them."

Though unsure of the operation director's reasoning, he knew when to obey a command.

The hoses shuddered as they filled with the two liquids.

"Tim?" Neal tried one last time, knowing it was pointless.

For a moment there was complete silence then, from the open hatchway, there came a weak, "Help me, please."

A millisecond later the water and acid combined beneath them in the tunnel sending an acrid stench up into the open air.

Cameron momentarily thought of turning the pumps up even higher, then realised that, if there was any way the man was alive down there, he had to give him some sort of chance.

"Turn the pumps off," he ordered.

Neal, shocked and confused at hearing his friend's voice only seconds earlier, hung his body halfway down into the tunnel, hoping against hope that there was some way Tim had survived.

The vapours from the brief chemical interaction made breathing almost impossible and Neal was about to give up when he thought he saw something move.

The others stood in a circle around him, unsure of what exactly to do. Cameron shook his head and gestured for two soldiers to force Neal away from the opening.

Before they could reach him, Neal's body suddenly convulsed then stopped moving. The soldiers grabbed him by the waist and lifted.

His body emerged from the hole, but his shoulders and head did not. The creature had literally ripped him in half.

CHAPTER THIRTY-FIVE

After waiting until its healing was as complete as possible without a full regeneration, it moved out of the narrow alcove and reached the tunnel that crossed under the roadway. It stopped immediately as it observed that two humans were already there just ahead of it. Above them, a hole in the earthen ceiling seemed to lead to the outside world. Strange man-made objects draped down from above and were coiled on the damp floor. It was these that the males seemed to be fixated upon, rendering them oblivious to their surroundings.

Such was their focus on the task, the humans seemed unaware of its proximity. It sensed that the two were not part of the groups that had been hunting it throughout the night and neither appeared to have the tools to harm it.

Fascinated, it observed the males as they stretched the objects this way and that, until they seemed satisfied that they had placed them in the optimum position for some purpose or another.

Suddenly, an electronic version of human speak seemed to reverberate from the two humans' head gear. Both looked surprised and even disappointed. The taller of the two said something then used a vertical walkway to climb up and out of the hole.

It continued to watch the remaining male as he again fiddled with the cylindrical objects. While the human's focus was drawn away from the coils on the ground, it took the opportunity to creep closer so that it could have a better idea of what the strange things were that so interested the male.

Without warning, the coils trembled as they appeared to be pulled from above. One of the loops suddenly tightened around its right leg and before it realised what was happening, a bright light shone directly in its face.

Even though partially blinded by the intense illumination, it could sense the human's panic and fear and could thus determine exactly where the human was located and that the male was moving ever so slowly towards the vertical walkway beneath the circular opening.

Suddenly, its curiosity was replaced with a craving for the taste of fresh human blood. It lunged directly at the light and clamped its massive jaws around the human's leg, ripping it away from the body. As the male shrieked in pain and fear, it dragged the body to the ground and began to feed.

While ripping into the male's stomach, the coils that had been laid on the tunnel floor started to vibrate and within moments began spewing vile liquids that burned its nasal passages and stung its eyes. Some instinctual reflex caused it to emulate the sound of an injured human's crying. Within less than a second, the liquid stopped flowing and it noticed the tunnel darken as the second human leaned his head into the opening in the ceiling.

Unable to see clearly through the caustic mist, the male

leaned still further down into the tunnel. It launched itself directly up at the dangling form and, with a forceful twist of its head, ripped the entire top half of the body from the rest without having to slow its momentum in the least.

Despite its effort to not do so, it landed in a narrow rill of liquid that was slowly trickling down the tunnel, inadvertently causing the fluid to splash up and douse its muzzle, searing away fur, bone and teeth as it tried to keep a firm hold on the bottom half of the human it had clasped within its jaws.

*

Jay, with his team told to stand and hold fast, saw no point in remaining underground until the situation changed. He found his way to the surface and joined Cameron by the open manhole. Before he could ask him if the plan had been effective or not, Jay saw Neal's remains being dragged away from the opening.

"I want that fucking tunnel flooded with acid," Cameron shouted towards the pump crew.

Jay stepped over to him and, keeping his voice low, asked, "Where's the creature at this moment?"

"We know it came up the Market Street tunnel, and from the look of Neal's body, it seems the thing must have torn him apart in mid-air. Worse still the creature seems to have been heading east."

"That's not possible," Jay advised. "The tunnel is blocked roughly below where I am standing."

Cameron turned to Jay intending to break the news to

him about the tunnel blockage when one of the men near the manhole called out, "Sir? You may wish to see this."

Jay and Cameron walked over to the group. A fibre-optic camera had been fed down below ground and with the aid of its incorporated LED light, showed the interior of the tunnel in crisp and clear detail as it moved through the remaining cloud of acidic haze. A large-screen tablet carried the live images.

The acid had done extensive damage to Tim's corpse. In places, it looked as if he had actually melted; in others, gaping, blackened wounds penetrated down to bare bones.

"How long until we can retrieve his body?" Cameron asked.

"Thankfully, the stuff seems to be running down the slope. So, hopefully, within the hour," a voice replied.

"Any sign of the remains of the other engineer?"

"Not yet, sir.

"Would you mind reversing the camera, so it is facing towards the sea?" Jay asked.

The camera operator looked to Cameron who gave him a brief nod.

They all watched as the image on the tablet panned almost one hundred and eighty degrees. For a moment the LED light flickered and went out, leaving those above ground facing a black screen. Then, suddenly, the light came back on.

Jay felt his blood run cold.

"Bloody hell," he whispered under his breath.

The tunnel was no longer sealed. Marks on the walls

clearly showed where the old brickwork had been, but at some point, the wall had been removed leaving the tunnel open and accessible.

"Oh yeah," Cameron said shaking his head. "Your valuable knowledge about the tunnel network wasn't quite as accurate as we had hoped. There is no blockage down there anymore."

"Then where's the Lusus?" Jay asked, panic evident in his voice.

"The team at the junction of this branch and Middle Street reported no sign of the thing retreating in their direction."

Jay looked across the street at the ghostly outline of the Regal Hotel and felt his innards turn to ice.

Cameron followed the other man's gaze then paled as it dawned on him that the creature might just find a way into the hotel.

Jay broke into a run as Cameron began to bark orders at the others.

*

Sandra had been fielding quite a number of complaints from guests whose rooms faced west. She wasn't sure what exactly was going on even after nipping outside to have a look. Two surly soldiers practically frogmarched her back inside and told her to make sure that nobody came out until they gave the go-ahead.

Though her sortie was fleetingly brief, she had managed to see that there was quite a gathering of people and vehicles directly behind the hotel. There was even some sort of giant pumping unit being run by a surprisingly loud generator. She completely understood why the guests were complaining and repeatedly gave each one the same response.

"I've just checked, and they should be finished with the emergency roadworks in a few minutes."

While her blatant lie did seem to calm some of the guests, she didn't have an answer for those that claimed to have heard screaming coming from the same area. Despite having offered her reassuring words, Sandra had no idea when things would actually quieten down, so when they suddenly did, she was mildly shocked. After a further five minutes of relative peace, she decided that the worst must be over and returned to her reading.

Within minutes she was back on board the doomed liner and could feel the fear of the passengers through the increasingly gripping pages. She reached a point in the story when the main characters came across a man who was slowly being consumed from his feet up by some sort of virulent flesh-eating fungus, when, back in the real world, a putrid odour suddenly filled the reception area.

Sandra knew that the most likely source of the smell was the basement toilets that were used by both the diners and staff. She placed a *BACK IN FIVE MINUTES* notice on the reception desk before going to investigate.

Maybe it was the result of her love of reading too many ghost stories, but every time she went down into the below-ground areas of the hotel, chills ran up her back and she half expected some demonic creature to sneak up behind her.

Sandra first checked the ladies' room, and apart from the usual mixture of air freshener and damp, nothing smelled unusual. Next, she tried the men's. Again, there were no unusual odours save for the fact that someone had, for whatever reason, thrown a half-eaten bag of chips in the waste bin giving the enclosed space a distinct whiff of frying oil and vinegar.

The last possible contender was the wet room where mops and buckets were dumped out and then cleaned. It was an area that never smelled particularly pleasant, but much to her disappointment, there was no trace of the odour that had found its way into the reception area.

Sandra was about to head back upstairs when something told her to check out the lower level where the access door to the tunnel was located. She doubted that anything down there could be responsible for the stink, but knew that if she didn't check, the day manager would want to know why.

The lower level was always slightly damp so was never used for much of anything. There was only one large room with a low ceiling and support pillars evenly spaced throughout. The only light came from four neon strips that Sandra guessed must have been installed before her parents were born. Not only did they constantly flicker, but their voltage ballasts incessantly buzzed like angry bees.

The original floorboards had at some point been covered with cheap brown-and-white patterned linoleum that did little to improve the look of the space. The walls were raw brick, most of them leaching lime and giving off a subtle acidic tang. Sandra tried to match that scent with the one she'd encountered upstairs, but they weren't even close.

The final option was to physically open the heavy metal and wood door that led to the tunnel. To Sandra, the door appeared way too substantial for the simple purpose of shutting the hotel off from a disused tunnel, but she assumed that back in the smuggling days it was probably put in to assist in the nefarious goings-on of the times. Then she noticed that thin tendrils of smoke were coming from the base of the door and that it seemed almost as if some of the wood and metalwork had been eaten away.

She removed a sizeable key ring from her brown jacket and found the oversized antique one from amidst the dozens of more modern Yale and Chubb counterparts.

The double lock turned easily, but it took all her strength just to pry the door open less than an inch. Despite the mere sliver of an opening, the almost overpowering stench from the other side caused Sandra to retch and stumble backwards.

Even with her head swimming and eyes watering, she felt she had to know the cause before notifying authorities. As these thoughts reverberated in her brain, she realised that, due to the roadblocks and non-working phones or computers, there was not going to be much chance of getting word to anyone. Still, Sandra wanted to know what was behind that door.

She grabbed a rag from a drying frame in the wet room, dampened it with water and tied it across her mouth and nose. Back at the door, she tried every which way to get it to open further, but to no avail. What frustrated her the most was that, had the slit been a fraction wider, she could have potentially found something to help jimmy it open.

Sandra tried one last thing. She removed the cloth from her head and fed it through the ancient metal handle. She then tied the ends together and after looping her left arm through the cloth, she placed her feet against the abutting brick wall then leaned backwards as far as the cloth would allow.

At first nothing happened, then without warning and with an almighty squeal from the rusted hinges, the door opened a fraction more.

Exhausted, and with her muscles aching from the exertion, Sandra stepped up to the widened crack and tried unsuccessfully to see into the tunnel while holding her breath. Though her gaze was met with utter darkness, she sensed that there was something alive just beyond the door. As she strained to listen, she thought she heard the sound of raspy breathing.

Just as she was about to try and fit her hand through the crack, a voice behind her said, "What are you doing?"

Sandra almost jumped out of her skin as she spun around and came face to face with the woman who ordered the two Cokes and a younger woman that she didn't recognise.

"Fucking hell, you scared me half to death," Sandra blurted out. "There was this godawful smell in the lobby area and after checking everywhere else I thought I'd better see if it was coming from the old tunnel."

"Judging by the stink down here, that's exactly where it's coming from," Helena stated.

Sandra nodded then had a thought. "Why are you both down here? This area is supposed to be off limits to guests."

"The mystery smell got as far as our room, so I thought it best to tell you," Emma said. "When you weren't back in the allotted five minutes, we tracked you here."

"Feel like giving me a hand at getting that door open?" Sandra asked with a smile.

"Is that a good idea?" Helena said.

"It's the only one I have." Sandra shrugged.

The three turned to face the door in question.

"What do you have that could be used as levers?"

At first Sandra's mind went blank, then, as an idea hit her, she started to smile.

"Follow me," she replied as she led the other two to the wet room.

Less than a minute later the three again stood facing the door; this time each of them was armed with a mop – the plan being to try and use the handles as levers.

"I think that the best course of action is for—" Emma started to say before the door swung violently open and smashed against the brick wall.

Out of the sheer blackness, the Lusus stepped into the light.

CHAPTER THIRTY-SIX

It was in pain. Whatever had flowed down, even momentarily, from the coiled tubes had somehow not just burned its coat and skin but had eaten away flesh at the same time. Though its body was able to self-heal in almost real time, the lingering liquid that had splashed upon it seemed to attack the replacement flesh as fast as it re-formed. In a crude sort of understanding, it knew that if it hadn't chosen to leap across the growing pool in the tunnel, it would not have survived. Even now, as some of its open sores had finally stabilised and crusted over, some of the deeper injuries were still unrepaired and, if anything, were becoming even more painful. Among the worst were on the right side of its face – the area that had received the full brunt of the initial soaking – damaging its eye, ear and part of its jaw.

Its tail, usually the first area to heal after an injury, was no more than a painful stub. It knew that if it could only find a place to rest so that its system could carry on with the regeneration, the healing would continue and most if not all of the damage would repair.

The problem was that its genetic predisposition to killing and consuming far outweighed its need to care for itself. The urge to rip into human flesh was as strong as ever, and as it neared the tunnel doorway, it could sense a veritable hive of humans spread out on multiple floors just the other side of the ancient portal. The idea of feasting on their fragile bodies as they slept, triggered its mouth to begin salivating, causing drizzles of drool to dampen its muzzle.

When a band of light appeared at the edge of the door, and then, minutes later, the gap widened still, it knew it was time to feed. It rushed headlong at the door, and once it had gained sufficient speed, lifted itself so that all four legs would make impact at the same time.

The door was no match for its weight and speed. It flew open with such force that it found itself momentarily off balance. Once it sprang to its feet, it immediately saw the three humans standing only a few body lengths away. For a microsecond, it felt a euphoric surge of adrenaline knowing that their blood would, in a few moments, be filling its gullet and stomach and would help provide the energy that it so desperately needed to self-heal.

Then the reality of its genetic programming came crashing down on its moment of joyous anticipation. The humans were female. Though it knew consciously that they would bleed and taste the same as any male, it could not attack or even wound any female. The same applied to young children of either sex. It was, after all, a weapon programmed to kill a specific enemy: males between puberty and infirmity.

*

The three women screamed at the same time and with equal intensity. The thing that stood before them was like nothing they had ever seen or even heard of. Though its entry was almost comical – the thing having basically fallen flat on its face – there was nothing funny now about the hideous beast eyeing them as it drooled what appeared to be blood from an open wound in its maw.

It was definitely a canine of sorts but was half as big again as the tallest Great Dane or Irish wolfhound. Its body was heavier and more muscled than any ordinary dog. Then there was its snout. It reminded Helena of a prehistoric raptor with its elongated muzzle packed full of what looked to be rows of razor-sharp teeth.

What made the creature even scarier were its injuries. Something had burned away a third of its face including the right eye and ear. Where the flesh had been removed, a mucus-like jelly seemed to be forming and attempting to fill the biological voids.

The three started to move towards the staircase with the intent of using their mops to stop the creature from getting to the stairs. Though terrified beyond belief, Emma still noticed their reflection in a cracked mirror on the far wall, while trying to keep her gaze fixed on the creature's eyes.

Despite their perilous position, she couldn't help but let out a strained and short-lived chuckle at seeing the three of them with mop handles at the ready and expressions of taut defiance on their faces.

Helena and Sandra both shot her a concerned glance thinking the poor woman had obviously lost the plot.

The brief laughter had an even stranger effect on the Lusus. It actually took a step backwards. The women, believing that the sound was, for some reason, abhorrent to the beast, began to laugh in discordant unison.

The canine did not retreat any further, but it also didn't try approaching either. It stared at the three females with a look of confusion on its damaged face. The three, believing that they were actually gaining the upper hand, took a step towards it, hoping to force the creature back into the tunnel.

With the craving for fresh meat blinding its senses, the Lusus suddenly lunged, but not at the women. Instead, it passed alongside them and charged upstairs towards the main part of the hotel.

*

Though it did not understand its own reasoning, it could no more feed on human females than on its own flesh. It vaguely recalled having the same issue when it had used the town as a feeding ground in a previous existence, yet it couldn't understand why. Surely their flesh would be as richly fulfilling and their blood as quenching as any of their male counterparts. It was as if its brain was not wired to even recognise the females to be part of the same species.

Frustrated and with an unabating drive to slake its need for human flesh, it charged up two flights of stairs until it arrived at the ground floor. It stopped for a moment to get its bearings, then followed its senses towards the strong odour of humans coming from the upper floors.

*

Still suffering from mild shock after their encounter, the three women were nevertheless emboldened by the creature's inexplicable refusal to attack them and instead brushing by them with astonishing speed.

"It might just have decided that the pickings were better on the upper floors. The hotel is full to the rafters," Sandra suggested.

"We can't just let it run loose. We need to try and stop it," Emma stated.

Helena did not seem anywhere near as optimistic about their chances.

"Is there a back way so we don't run right into it?" she asked.

"Yes," Sandra replied. "Though, I'm not sure what's more dangerous, the stairs or that wolf-thing, but if you feel brave enough, there is a staircase at the back of the building that used to be for the prostitutes to come and go without being seen. They'd come into the hotel via that tunnel, then go straight up to see their clients."

Sandra led them through the clean room to a dank hallway with a single electric bulb hanging from a stained and flaking ceiling. Beyond that was a low door that didn't look as if it had been used any time recently.

With a squeal of dismay from its rusty hinges, it opened revealing a horrifyingly steep, wooden, spiral staircase. Instead of a banister, a ship's rope had been bolted to the wall.

"Is that thing safe?" Helena asked as she looked up the central spiral all the way to the top floor of the hotel.

"I don't know anyone who uses it anymore, but, if you want to get above the creature and hopefully stop it from reaching the guests, this is the only option."

*

It began to climb the thickly carpeted stairs, aware just how dangerous it was to venture where there was unlikely to be an easy escape should the need arise. It had never, as far as it could recall, climbed above ground level at any point in its existence as it felt safest in subterranean environments where it could blend into the darkness.

Suddenly, it picked up a strong scent of a male human approaching unseen from above. As it moved up towards the first-floor landing, the sound of rushing water could be heard, followed moments later by a door opening. An oversized human male appeared on the landing above and for some reason chose to look down over the banister.

It could both see and smell the fear that blossomed within the human. It could also pick up the heavy fragrance of alcohol leaching from his pores. It didn't care. The meat would still taste just fine even if the blood was likely to carry a slightly bitter aftertaste.

The human seemed unable to move as it stared down at it. There seemed to be something wrong with the male's eyes, judging by the human's furious blinking and squinting, as if it was having trouble focussing.

"Good doggie," the human called down in a slurred voice.

It was about to leap up the final few steps when the human was suddenly grabbed and pushed aside. The three females it had encountered when it left the tunnel stood blocking its access to the landing.

They raised their wooden sticks and waved them threateningly at it while shouting unintelligible words. It could see that there was no way around the females without hurting or maybe even killing them. Every fibre in its body screamed for it to do just that, but again, it simply could not do them harm in any way.

It wondered if it could simply stay where it was until the females gave up their vigil and went away, but even as that notion swept across its pre-programmed brain, the three, in perfect unison, stepped down towards it.

*

Jay stealthily entered the Regal reception area with three heavily armed soldier at his side. He desperately wanted to call out and warn the guests of what might be loose somewhere within the hotel. It took all of his willpower to stay silent, but he knew that by screaming out a warning, panic could easily ensue. If the Lusus was, as suspected, already within the building, such chaos could easily lead to a feeding frenzy.

As the four stood stock-still and listened for any tell-tale sounds, Jay was shocked to realise that most of his concerns seemed to focus on Emma's well-being. Considering how they had left things and the coldness that they'd both displayed whenever they had run into each other, he was confused at his own emotional reaction to the situation.

His thoughts were interrupted as a loud roar echoed throughout the interior. The soldiers took a firmer grasp on their weapons and, as they took a step deeper into the hotel, a commotion drew their attention towards the main staircase.

Before they could get any closer, the Lusus appeared, seemingly running for its life. It was so focused on checking if it was being followed that, at first, it didn't notice the four men, three of which were bringing their semi-automatic weapons to bear.

What followed next was both terrifying and comedic in equal proportions. As the creature was about to reach the ground floor, three figures appeared on the staircase running at full tilt while waving what looked to be long-handled mops out in front of them.

"Don't fire," Jay yelled as he stepped between the soldiers and the staircase. While he trusted their training and thus their aim, he couldn't risk any stray shots impacting the mop wielders whom, he realised, were Helena, Emma and a woman he didn't know.

The beast reached the ground floor and finally became aware of the males only a short distance from it. Its genetics took over from its conscious thinking as it began to salivate at the thought of consuming some if not all of the four humans. It lowered its head and began to stalk them, and

Jay could see the damage that had been inflicted on the creature by the acid.

As it bent its hind legs in preparation to leap onto its prey, the three women reached it and began raining down blow after blow with their mop handles. Clearly confused, and if its facial expression was anything to go by, conflicted, it began snapping at the wooden handles while still glaring at Jay and the soldiers. Finally, in a move of exquisite bravery, Helena, Emma and Sandra positioned themselves between the Lusus and the men.

Jay expected no good to come from the showdown, but after less than a second, the creature let out a doleful cry before charging off towards the empty dining room and bar. The soldiers gave chase but, by the time they reached the seaside room, the creature had dived straight through a plate glass window and vanished into the dark and misty morning.

CHAPTER THIRTY-SEVEN

Jay and Emma were left startled by what had just occurred and even more so by the creature's dramatic escape. As if by some telepathic force, they moved together and without a word held each other in a tight embrace. For a full two minutes neither spoke, until finally, they separated and looked at each other with growing discomfort.

"Sorry," Emma mumbled.

Jay, never one to be comfortable in intimate situations, met her gaze. "Me too."

"What just happened?" she asked.

"I think we all just came close to a very nasty death," he replied.

"Not, what happened in the hotel. What just happened between us?"

"I think we were in shock," Jay replied.

"You sure that's all it was?"

"What else could it have been?"

Emma sighed and forced a weak smile. "Of course, you're right. What else could it have been?"

Jay wanted to say more but couldn't seem to find the right words.

"Maybe if we get through tonight, we could have a drink or something. I can't help feeling that we left a lot unsaid," Emma suggested.

"I seem to remember that you told me exactly what you thought about me during the divorce."

"That's my point. I don't think I meant most of what I said. I was just angry at the world."

"So was I," Jay agreed then laughed. "We're quite a pair."

"Are we?" Emma asked. "Are we a pair?"

"Let's see if we survive this little debacle, then maybe we should talk."

"Maybe?" Emma said smiling and shaking her head. "Oh my God, you can't even commit to a conversation."

"I meant to say that we will talk. We will definitely talk."

Before Emma could respond, Cameron approached the pair.

"You are a very brave woman," he said to Emma.

"I think it's fair to say that it took the three of us to appear brave. I couldn't have found the nerve to stand up to that thing on my own."

"You're being modest," Cameron said before turning to Jay. "I just spoke to Doctor Wiseman and brought him up to date on what occurred here."

"What did he say?" Jay asked.

"He laughed," Cameron replied with a sigh. "It seems the Lusus, though programmed to kill and devour humans, was only ever wired to attack adult males."

"Why?" Jay asked before grasping the inappropriateness of his question. "I don't mean why not kill women as well.

I meant... Oh fuck, you know perfectly well what I meant."

"Back in the 1940s, war was fought by men," Cameron explained, hiding his amusement at Jay's faux pas. "Women certainly helped whenever and wherever they could—"

Cameron stopped, sensing Emma's displeasure at his words.

"I'm not giving an opinion, that's simply the way things were," he offered. "The point I was making was that the boffins at Porton Down did not feel comfortable creating a killing machine that would slaughter any human it came into contact with, including women and children. The only way they agreed to proceed with the project was if they were allowed to reduce the scope of the target base and only have the beast focus on human males between puberty and geriatrics."

"Are you saying that the creature physically couldn't attack us?" Emma asked.

"More the case that it was a mental rather than physical block, but yes, it was apparently programmed to target males only."

"So, what happens now?" Jay asked. "Back to the tunnels?"

"I'm done trying to catch this thing in its own area of familiarity and comfort. I've sent for some help that just might tip the scales in our favour."

"More troops?" Emma asked.

"No."

"Some sort of specialised weaponry?" Jay asked.

Cameron shook his head.

"No. I've decided to use what Wiseman referred to as his doomsday weapon. Something called an LPO."

"Dare we ask?" Emma said, smiling.

"Let's just say that the time has come to fight fire with fire."

"Emma looked at him questioningly as Jay's expression darkened.

"You're not suggesting that there is another of these things somewhere?"

"Apparently there is," Cameron replied. "It's currently in an inactive state but could be brought back to life simply by exposing it to oxygen."

"That sounds like one hell of a risk."

"I don't want to lose any more human lives to this bloody monster. If what Wiseman says is true, the modified clone may just be the best solution."

Emma joined in. "You're bringing down another of these things? What if they choose to hunt as a pair? Think of the carnage two creatures could cause."

"Wiseman assures me that that will not be the case. The second one is genetically programmed to only attack one of its own kind, and as there is only one other in existence... Well, it should be able to solve our little problem with a minimum of fuss."

"Then what?" Emma asked. "What happens to the second one? Do we have to use yet another one to rid us of that mutant?"

"No. If it does as it says on the tin, once it has destroyed the original Lusus, it will locate the nearest human and, while in a docile state, surrender itself."

"Speaking of the original, any idea where it is?" Emma asked.

"Not exactly," he replied. "After it crashed through the dining room window, one of my men saw it leap off the promenade and head north on the beach."

"Are your people following it?" Jay asked.

"I have stationed a lookout on the promenade every twenty metres. I don't want to send any of the troops down onto the beach proper because of it being pebbled rather than sand. It's hard enough to bloody walk on. Running would be unthinkable, especially with a full kit. Once the sun comes up, we might look into a more detailed search. At the moment, with all the properties locked up, the lookouts in place and the population tucked away in the Golf Road school, there's no easy targets for the creature to go for. I have faith that things should stay relatively calm, at least for the next few hours."

"I hope the Lusus agrees with you."

Before the words were fully out of Jay's mouth, the old hotel shook as the sound of a low flying helicopter roared by.

"Ah," Cameron said as he listened to the craft continue on to Walmer Green – the only place to land anywhere near their position.

"I do believe that Lusus mark two has arrived."

*

Having had trouble enough sleeping since Cameron left him

alone in the old beach house, Wiseman finally managed to doze off. He was in a pleasant semi-dream state when a military helicopter tore past less than thirty metres above the ground. He woke up with a start and, momentarily confused, opened the front sash window to see what the blazes was going on. He cringed as the swollen window frame rubbed against its housing, emitting a godawful screech.

He craned his neck out into the fresh, early morning air and managed to see the craft's navigation lights as it headed south while slowing down.

Too startled to go back to sleep, Wiseman decided that the best course of action was to have a nice cup of tea and maybe even a biscuit or two if he could find any. The kitchen, like so many of the older homes in Deal, was located in the basement. He managed to navigate the narrow staircase and found it at the front end of the house. It too had been nicely restored, though, like many others in the area, the ceiling height was absurdly low. Even with its expensive counters and appliances, nothing could take away from the claustrophobic feeling of having the top of your head only a few centimetres from the ceiling.

Wiseman found the fixings for the tea as well an unopened pack of generic gingernut biscuits. As he waited for the kettle to boil, a thought hit him. He couldn't remember if he'd closed the front window or not. Just as he reassured himself that he must have done, he heard the distinct sound of someone, or something, walking on the floor above.

CHAPTER THIRTY-EIGHT

Wiseman stood stock-still as he listened to the upper-level floorboards creak as the footfalls neared the stairway to the basement. It was very rare that the man felt fear, but something about the pace of the steps and his concern about not having closed the upstairs window was causing his stomach to knot and chills to run rampant throughout his aged body.

As he looked about the counter for something to use as a weapon, a familiar voice called down from above.

"Are you down there?" Cameron asked. "Sorry to disturb, but I just needed to grab something from my briefcase."

Wiseman almost ran up the narrow stairs to greet his host.

As he reached the landing, Cameron was just putting his battered leather attaché case down at the bottom of the stairway that led to the upper floors.

"It is you!" Wiseman blurted out, immediately realising how stupid his statement must have sounded.

"Who were you expecting?" Cameron asked, mildly concerned at the old man's obvious anxiousness.

"I thought I'd left the window open and then I heard a

noise from upstairs, and I have to admit that I seem to have come down with a case of the willies."

"Well, you do appear to have left the window open, but apart from letting in some night air, I don't think you have too much to worry about."

He hoped that his words would go some way to calming the man, but as he studied Wiseman's face, he saw that he had had the opposite effect on him. Wiseman's eyes were open comedically wide as the colour drained from his face.

"What's the matter?" Cameron asked.

"Did you come in alone?"

"Yes. Why?"

"Then who's that?" Wiseman said as he pointed towards the front wall.

Puzzled, Cameron turned around and for a moment saw nothing amiss, then, to the right of the window, what he had initially perceived to be a shadow, moved away from the heavy curtains The figure of an extraordinarily pale, naked man stepped into the light.

"It's the Lusus," Wiseman whispered.

*

Once outside the old hotel, it considered running along the promenade until it saw armed humans take up evenly spaced positions on the walkway. It instinctively knew that trying to find a safe escape route through the narrow streets of the old town would be highly dangerous as the humans would have most certainly blocked all surface roads.

It took the only remaining option and ran down onto the beach. It immediately lost its footing on the loose pebbles, making way too much noise if it hoped to go unnoticed.

It moved cautiously back towards the promenade, but instead of climbing up onto it, it used the concrete overhang to shield itself from seeking eyes.

The going was slow. It had to both lean into the wall below the walkway while, at the same time, ensuring that each step was calculated and methodical so that the shifting pebbles moved as little as possible. It also came to understand that if it timed its steps with the crashing of the nearby waves, any sound it might make would be, for the most part, muffled.

It had travelled a couple of hundred metres along the beach when a high-pitched shrieking sound caused it to freeze in place as it tried to determine where the noise had come from.

Within seconds, the offshore breeze carried with it the smell of a human male. A moment later it shuddered as the scent grew in complexity and distant memories began flooding its head. None were detailed or even cohesive, yet it knew that the flitting mental images were detailing a time long ago and far away.

A time of its initial creation.

At first it found the snippets of long past remembrances to be oddly comforting. Then, as the scent strengthened and details began to fill in the grey areas, it recalled the horrors of its own conception. Though it couldn't quite weave a full tapestry of recollection, the bits that did fall into place provided a scant history of pain, torture and continuous mistreatment.

It could not place the particular male whose scent was causing such recollection, but it knew that the human had to have been deeply involved in every aspect of what had been done to it so very long ago.

Despite knowing, or at least sensing, the dangers of trying to cross both the promenade and abutting roadway to investigate the source of the scent, it had no choice but to follow instinct, and instinct was dictating that it seek out fresh kills. It did not have the cerebral capacity to understand the irony of its own genetic pre-programming inciting it to kill and devour what potentially was its own creator.

It simply needed to feast.

By the time it made it across the promenade and road, the scent of the human had greatly lessened. It was not sure how to proceed until it noticed that one structure, among the dozens that faced the sea, appeared to have one ground floor window open. Keeping away from the light cast by waning moon, it hugged the buildings until it lay directly below the window in question.

It raised itself on its haunches and sniffed deeply at the opening. The heady aroma of a human male was unmistakeable. What was even more exciting was that it was the exact same scent that it had picked up while on the beach. It was the scent of its tormentor and, even though the human did not appear to still be in close proximity, it could tell that the male was still somewhere inside the building.

Before it could evaluate the best plan of action it heard the sound of a vehicle approaching. Lights appeared on the road, and as the engine pitch increased, so did the illumination. It knew that if it stayed where it was, it would doubtless be spotted by the occupants of the vehicle.

Within seconds, it had transformed itself into human form and pulled itself up and through the open window. As is lay on the interior floor it heard the vehicle stop just outside the structure, and then footsteps rang on the stone steps leading up to the front door.

It slid itself noiselessly up onto two legs and eased its human form behind some heavy material that seemed to hang from the ceiling.

The moment the human stepped inside, it recognised the male's scent as well. While not having the same depth of memory, it knew this scent emanated from the human it had encountered in the restaurant. The human that had fired pieces of hot metal directly into its body.

It stood silently and waited as the human rummaged around, then seemed to speak out loud to nobody in particular. While it was trying to process what exactly was happening, a second human responded from somewhere below ground. Just the sound of the male's voice made it feel a sense of both euphoria and rage all bundled up in one gnawing urge to rip both males to shreds.

It managed to restrain itself until both males were in the same room at which point it slowly emerged from the shadows and stood silently waiting to see their reaction.

It could tell that its creator was the first to notice, as his eyes mirrored the fear that had enveloped him. Once the other male turned to face it, he too showed surprise but strangely not fear. Almost as a reflex, the younger male reached inside his coat for what it presumed would be the same weapon that had earlier been used against it.

It only took it a millisecond to transform back into its canine cloak and a further millisecond to bridge the gap between it and the human. It sank its massive fangs beneath the human's chin and bit down with all of its strength. The head separated from the torso and bounced down onto the thick carpeting. The body, as if unaware of its new circumstance, remained upright for a good few seconds before also dropping to the floor.

"You know me," the older male said in a shaky voice. "You know who I am, and you know that I am responsible for you being here."

It watched as the human spoke words it did not understand as it licked the rich, warm lifeblood from its snout.

"That's a good boy," the human cooed. "Why don't you and I sit down and—"

It managed to wrap its jaws around the old male's head before it could even finish whatever it was trying to say.

CHAPTER THIRTY-NINE

Jay, Helena and Emma were sitting in the empty hotel lounge, not sure of what they should be doing. The one thing the three were certain of was that they didn't want to head up to their room on the off chance that the creature might return and decide to check out the upper floors.

Jay checked his watch and couldn't help wondering why Cameron had yet to return. He was only supposed to go back to his rental to retrieve his heavily encrypted laptop.

Just as he was about to check outside, Douglas Osbourne, Cameron's number two for the entire operation, walked into the hotel. He was short, officious looking and was the most senior military officer currently in Deal and, judging from his and his aide's expressions, something was very wrong.

"Mr Sallinger, I need you to come with me."

"Why?" Jay asked, staring up at the man.

"If you come with me, I will explain," Osbourne replied as he gestured with his eyes towards the two women.

"Whatever you have to say you can say in front of Ms Tramis and Ms Malins. They know everything about what's going on down here. Check with Cameron. He'll vouch for them."

Osbourne looked uncomfortable and confused.

"Give us a moment," he said to his aide then sat amidst the three. Once he was satisfied that there was no one else within earshot, he took a deep sighing breath.

"Cameron's dead, so is Professor Wiseman."

"Was it the Lusus?" Emma asked.

"I'm afraid I don't know what a Lusus is, but it was the missing canine that appears to have killed both men."

"What do you mean, you don't know what a Lusus is? I assume that Cameron or your commanding officer, wherever they are, must have read you in on the specifics of the situation here?" Jay said, confused.

"Actually, that's why I need to talk to you. Because of the highly sensitive nature of this operation, nobody but a few people at the very top of the food chain know the specifics of what's going on here. Unfortunately, I am not one of those informed individuals, yet with Cameron dead, and my having been sent here with minimal information, I find myself in somewhat of a quandary. Even though he was a contractor, Cameron was in charge. My immediate superior is Colonel Alderton, who is based in Colchester and has also been kept in the dark. I just spoke to him via satellite phone, and he advised that he had no intention of coming down here to help catch some bloody dog."

"So, who is in charge?" Emma asked.

"That's the crux of the issue. I am, but there is no way that I can assume that level of responsibility without any of the background knowledge. I therefore have a request to make of you. I know that you have been involved in this situation from the start and that, after an initial period of sabre-rattling, became one of Cameron's trusted advisors."

"So, what is the request?" Jay asked as an icy chill began to creep up his spine.

"I would like to suggest that you assume overall control of this operation, with me as the military liaison."

"That's absurd," Jay shot back. "I know nothing about military operational procedures."

"But I do. That's my point. Because you know what it is that we are looking for, exactly what it is, and even ways to trap and destroy it."

"I know nothing of the kind."

"Actually, sir, you do. Cameron told me only a few hours ago that you, your colleagues and Professor Wiseman had discussed every detail of the canine, as well as methods to destroy it."

"Wouldn't it be easier for me to simply explain everything I know to you, then you can do what you've been trained for and take control of this mess?"

"The canine is loose and, judging by the damage to a wall in the basement of Cameron's lodgings, it may well have made it back underground. Unfortunately, all of the recon teams were pulled in from the tunnel network to force the creature into the one than led directly to this hotel, so there's no intel where exactly it might be headed. We don't have time for you to bring me up to speed. You are the closest thing we have to an expert on both the canine and the tunnel system. That makes you the prime candidate."

Jay looked to Emma and was surprised when she

shrugged and nodded.

"He's right," she stated. "We'll help as well if you need us."

Jay bent over and for a moment held his head in his hands. Before Osbourne could say anything else, Jay got to his feet and faced the officer.

"If the creature entered the system via Cameron's house, then it is already in the northern segment of the old town. What we have to do is figure out where exactly it might go so it can find some more prey. We know the homes have been evacuated and the tunnel system ends at Alfred Square, so let's check the map and see if anything jumps out."

*

Jay and Osbourne stood outside the King James pub in the murky fog. The day was dawning grey and cold despite it being midsummer. Troops were scattered around Alfred Square waiting as the tunnel teams emerged at what was the northern end of the network. Helena and Emma, in an attempt to stay relatively warm, were huddled inside the pub waiting for news.

Finally, each team emerged from underground – the leaders gave a thumbs-down gesture as they approached Jay and Osbourne.

"Well, where the fuck has it gone?" Jay asked.

"I have no idea. There's no way it could have used surface streets and the tunnel teams would have seen it if it was still down there."

"Then where is it?"

"I just hope it didn't somehow get past this point before we locked things down," Osbourne commented.

"I couldn't help but overhear you," a voice slurred from somewhere above them.

Both men looked upwards and saw an unshaven older man looking down at them from the top floor of the building on the north side of the square.

"I thought everyone had been evacuated?" Jay asked.

"Everyone in the areas above the tunnels were relocated. According to your charts, from here north to the end of Deal, there's nothing underground but utilities."

"That's correct. And I remember now that Cameron did say that they could only remove those directly within the danger zone. Beyond that there were simply too many people to deal with."

"What exactly are you lot looking for?" the old man asked.

"I don't suppose you've seen an oversized dog come this way, have you?" Osbourne asked.

"All this kerfuffle for a bloody dog?" the man replied.

"It's a very special animal," Jay advised leaving out the part where it could rip a man's head off in one second flat.

"I've not seen a dog yet this morning. It's a bit early, but if you lot wait another half hour or so, you'll have your pick of hundreds of the buggers; that's when the residents start walking their pets."

"Thank you," Jay said as he took a deep breath then sighed.

"In fact, I've only seen one living thing all morning before you lot showed up. Strange looking bloke in a right posh camel hair coat. Must have cost a few quid. I'll tell you that much."

Osbourne gave the man a nod and a thumbs up, hoping that would shut him up.

"One thing's for certain," the old man continued. "Whatever it had cost new, he's likely to get nought for the thing in its current condition. I don't know if the bloke had been in a fight or what, but the top of the coat was covered in blood."

Both Osbourne and Jay looked back up at the man.

"I almost didn't notice, as he was wearing an old-fashioned trilby, but once he passed under that streetlight on the corner, I saw the blood, clear as day, especially against the light tan of the coat."

Both knew of only one person in that day and age who wore a tan camel coat and a trilby, and that person had been decapitated only an hour earlier at the same time as Professor Wiseman's body had been ripped to shreds.

"Which way did he go?" Osbourne asked.

"Went right on College Road. You can't miss him what with the expensive coat, hat, all that blood, and of course there were those pale naked legs. Cor, what a fucking sight!"

Osbourne turned and glanced towards a dark green, newer model Land Rover that was parked in the central 'herringboned' parking area. The same vehicle that had earlier been loaded with a sealed lead-lined box that had only moments earlier been onboard an unmarked military helicopter.

"If it comes to it," Jay said in almost a whisper, "we just have to hope that the second one can do everything that Wiseman said it could."

"I feel like we're going be throwing one grenade at another grenade in the hopes that they cancel each other out."

"We have to trust that it will be able to not only destroy and devour the Lusus but will then give itself up to us when that's all done and dusted."

"You never told me if this second creature has ever actually been tested?" Osbourne asked.

"From what Wiseman insinuated, that would never have been possible as there was only ever one final working Lusus. Destroying it simply as a test would have been highly unproductive."

"So, we just have to hope that a secret experiment from eighty years ago will work."

"That's pretty much it," Jay replied with a shrug.

"While I'm grateful that you gave me an abridged version of what the hell is going on here, there's one thing I must have misunderstood. According to you, this Lusus thingy – no matter how many times you kill it – can reconstitute itself from its remains so long as there is oxygen to start the process. Is that right?"

"That's what I've be told and, to be fair, judging from what we saw in that old cinema, that really does appear to be the case."

"Why, once the thing is in its dried up powdery form

or whatever, don't they simply scatter the stuff over a big enough area so that the thing simply can't reconstitute itself."

"I asked the same question. Apparently, the boffins were never certain what that outcome would bring. Though it might stop the regeneration, their fear was that if even one fish or one rodent, for example, ingested even a microbic sized piece of the Lusus, it could well turn into some sort of hybrid mutant. One that they would have no control over whatsoever. There was even the concern that a particle could find its way from there to our water supply, creating human mutations."

"Maybe they shouldn't be allowed to invent shit they can't control," Osbourne said with a shake of his head.

The two crossed the square to be out of earshot of the old drunk. As they neared the pub, Emma and Helena emerged.

"What was that about?" Emma asked. "You both look a little shell-shocked."

Jay recounted what the old man had told them.

"So at least you know it's above ground," Helena observed. "Now we just have to work out where it's heading."

"If its past behaviour is any indication, I'd say it's looking for prey," Jay suggested.

"So far we're lucky that most everyone is still asleep and locked safely in their homes," Osbourne said.

"So where is it going to go?" Jay asked.

"Quick question," Helena said in a quiet voice. "How far away from the square is that school where all the residents have been housed? I mean, if the thing hunts by scent, that place must be putting out one hell of a tempting aroma."

Jay felt as if a pitcher of iced water had been poured directly into his stomach.

CHAPTER FORTY

After surfacing from the tunnel and breathing in the cool, damp morning air it immediately picked up the scent of humans. Not the usual trace of one or two enclosed within their dwellings, but countless males and females all, if its senses were correct, huddled in one place and within one structure.

After devouring his creator and the younger human, It had thought it prudent to don some of the clothing from the male it had recently beheaded. Once it emerged from the tunnels it picked up the scent of the gathered humans and realised that the streets were devoid of activity and that it was very much alone. When it exited the square and turned onto College Road it morphed back into its canine form as it followed the exquisite aroma of sweating humans. After a few moments, it stopped for a moment so it could calm its breathing and heartrate. Still weak from the acid attack, it didn't want to expend too much energy until such time as it was ready to lay siege to all that glorious fresh meat.

The scent was getting closer, and it could tell that it was coming from a spot directly west of where it was currently walking. It turned left onto Cannon Street and hugged the unkempt homes that lay on either side of the road.

As it neared the crossroads with Golf Road, it heard the rumbling of heavy vehicles and of heavy footwear running as raised voices drifted across the fog. It reached Golf Road and slowly glanced around the corner looking south. It appeared as if the armed humans were creating some sort of blockage around one long, single storey building. A building that was veritably oozing with the perfume of unwashed and anxious human males and females.

Just as it started to doubt its ability to reach the prize, it looked on in wonder as the armed humans, instead of forming a tight perimeter around the building, moved off in every direction, some directly towards where it was crouching.

It crept out of view and looked anxiously back down the depressing road. On the right side of the street was nothing but housing, but on the left, only a few metres away, was an open, paved area currently filled with tents and bunting surrounding one unusually tall, windowless structure that rose up into the fog.

It crept across the road and ran into the open space hoping to find somewhere to hide. Other than the characterless tower and various empty stalls that smelled of day-old food, it could see nowhere safe to conceal itself until, behind one particular stall, it found three huge metal tubes that had been cut in half, and judging by the scent, contained the remains of burned wood and coal as well as the grease from cooked meats. It had never before encountered a barbeque and had no clue as to its purpose, but it knew that these tubes were the perfect place to hide.

It crawled into the biggest one and nestled itself among the ashy residue until it was covered from head to paw in greyish-black powder. It lessened its breathing and heart rate until it could lay amidst the ash without any movement or sound.

As the fog began to lighten and the sun's illumination finally reached the cold ground, armed humans quickly inspected the area and appeared satisfied that there was nowhere for anything of its size to conceal itself.

Once they had gone and their sounds and odours were far enough away, it crept out of its hiding place and again snuck to the end of the road.

*

Emma and Helena were pleased that every effort was being made by the military to protect the townspeople, but they weren't one hundred percent happy with the building itself being left unprotected, in case the creature somehow slipped through their dragnet. They mentioned this to Jay, but he felt that the soldiers must know more about protecting assets than any of them so, maybe they should just let them get on with it.

The troops may have spread out in all directions, but the dark green Land Rover was parked just inside the school gates, its unliving cargo still safely encased in an oxygen-free canister. Only two soldiers, one female, one male, stood guard at the main entrance to the school.

Thankfully, most of the rehoused population were still inside helping themselves to the complimentary full English breakfast that was being provided by a number of restaurants in town. About two dozen early-risers were in the play area at the front of the school, oblivious to the danger. Though it had been discussed whether to tell the townspeople what exactly was happening, it was decided that the resulting panic could only make things exponentially worse.

Emma was about to go inside the 1950s structure when something caught her eye. One block from the school, at the intersection of Ark Lane and Golf Road, something was creeping towards them.

It was keeping to the shadows and moving at such a slow pace that, at first, Emma thought she was seeing things.

"Have a look towards that convenience store on the corner, one block north," Emma said in a lowered voice. "Tell me what you see?"

Helena nonchalantly glanced as instructed, but with the remains of the morning fog plus the orientation of the building, no direct light was as yet hitting the west facing wall.

"I see some items for sale. There's Calor gas, some cheap beach chairs, bottled water and bags of charcoal, what else am I supposed to be seei—"

Helena froze, as what she had assumed was a shadow cast by the one of the stacks of chairs started to move.

"Bloody hell," she whispered frantically. "It's the Lusus isn't it?"

"Looks like it."

"We need to get the troops back here," Helena stated.

"I think that would only lead to panic, confusion and, almost certainly, yet more deaths. I have a better idea."

*

Jay and Osbourne were being driven around the back streets within the cordoned-off area surrounding the school in an unmarked Ford SUV. There had been no sign of the creature except the camel hair coat and trilby, which had been found discarded on College Road. Both men agreed that it was highly likely that the Lusus had returned to its original form.

"Do you think it's gone to ground?" Osbourne asked.

"I doubt it. It needs to feed and, so far, has ignored just about any threat to do so. I don't see it being able to resist a building choc-a-block full of people. If it could somehow get inside, it could feast to its heart's content. I'm still worried that relocating the troops so they could form a wider perimeter was the wrong move."

"You agreed that I would make the operational decisions, and troop placement is very much part of that responsibility."

"I know." Jay nodded. "It's just that the creature has managed to outsmart us at every turn. I'm not saying that it's more intelligent than us, just that its hunting instincts are way more finely honed than ours."

Before Osbourne could respond, his headset was suddenly filled with a panicked voice.

"It's here!" a female soldier screamed. "It's right next to the school. We're opening fire now."

The sound of gun shots could be heard both outside the car and through the headset.

The shooting stopped abruptly. "I hit it," the male soldier shouted. "I think I... no! It's coming right—"

Static filled the vehicle.

"Floor it!" Osbourne shouted. The driver rammed the gear into second and accelerated down the narrow side street. They made the trip from Water Street to the school in under a minute.

Even from a distance, they could see the creature standing in the centre of the road staring at the fenced-in building.

"What's it doing?" Osbourne shouted.

*

It had used all of its cunning to stealthily approach the location where the humans were being hidden. The odours had strengthened and, as it got nearer, became almost intoxicating. It could virtually taste the coppery sweetness as it fantasised about ripping open throat, after throat, after throat.

After what seemed like an eternity, it found itself only two buildings away from the target premises. It had a clear view of the low brick building and was slightly surprised to find that the entire property was encircled with a tall and substantial metal fence.

Though it had no memory of having used the ability, it somehow knew that it could easily leap as high as the fence top and land safely on the other side. With the humans trapped within the barrier, feeding could then be undertaken at a leisurely pace, at least once its initial overpowering desire to feast had been partially sated.

It only saw two armed humans outside the fencing, one male, one female. As it debated how to rush the pair without harming the female, the two split. The male stayed in place while the female walked towards the far side of the property perimeter.

The male, though armed, did not seem that alert; in fact, it knew that he was slow-witted. The eyes were the giveaway. It could tell by the alertness of a prey's pupils whether a potential victim would be quick or blessedly slow to react. Considering that both types would taste almost as good, it naturally preferred the latter option.

It chose the most direct approach; the one that it had found in the past would freeze the prey in fear. It waited until the dullard turned away from the shadowy area where it lay in wait, then immediately charged while roaring at the same time.

The human spun around and shouted something into the air. The male managed to raise his weapon but was unable to steady his arms enough for the projectiles to have any accuracy.

In the microsecond before it bit into the man's throat, it smelled the strong odour of urine as the human's bladder involuntarily released. Once fully incapacitated, it desperately wanted to feed on the newly slaughtered carcass but knew that it had to focus on the bigger prize. Even though only a few of the humans who had been outside the building witnessed the attack, they were screaming loudly enough to wake the dead.

It knew that it had to act swiftly. Still a distance from the fencing, it mentally calculated which part it should scale to ensure the best landing area.

Its ponderings were suddenly halted as the front gate began moving aside. Its first thought was astonishment at its good fortune, then the school doors opened, and a line of humans began running out towards the opening in the fence.

The creature was forced to take a step backwards such was its shock to see that every single one of them was female. It could still detect countless males within the structure, but of those that were exiting, not one was male. Before it could regather its thoughts and adapt to the ever-changing situation, the women formed a cordon the entire way around the school. They cleverly stood a full three metres away from the fence making it almost impossible to scale it without harming some of the females.

It began to howl and cry out in frustration as it came to understand that, at least for the time being, the human feast would have to wait. Before it turned and ran to find some means of escape or at least concealment, it recognised two of the females. Standing with their arms linked with the others in the primitive barrier circle were two of the females from the oceanside structure. They had been part of the trio that had stopped it mounting the stairs so it could feed on the sleeping guests.

Its gaze met that of the older of the two females, and it

was shocked at the power and determination in her eyes, enough so that it shuddered briefly before turning away.

*

As Jay and Osbourne neared the school, neither could comprehend what they were seeing. The Lusus stood in the middle of the street facing the building but did not appear to be moving. Encircling the school grounds were at least a hundred or so women. All were holding hands and staring defiantly outwards, away from the school. He recognised two of them. Helena and Emma looked formidable as they faced off against the Lusus.

"Am I hallucinating?" Osbourne asked.

"If you are, then I am too," Jay replied.

They pulled up at the school entrance and Emma turned to face the other women. "Ready, ladies?" she shouted.

A chorus of 'we are' echoed off the surrounding homes and businesses.

As one, the ladies, their hands still joined, stepped away from the fence and as they formed a line, began approaching the Lusus. Startled and clearly conflicted, the creature backed away just as the sound of running boots and over-revving vehicles began to approach their position.

The Lusus let out an ear-shattering cry of frustration before it turned away and ran back towards the shadows that abutted Golf Road.

CHAPTER FORTY-ONE

Wes Gainer had a five-alarm hangover and wished to God that he were back in his bed instead of having to clean up the grounds and the tunnel area of the new mine ride. His father had always dinned it into him that hard work beat education every time, and that wasting years in college while pompous lecturers filled his head with useless information would do nothing to keep him employed later in life.

No, his father had instructed, he needed to get to work as soon as possible and harden up his soft hands and weak young muscles. At first Wes had liked the idea of working hard and getting paid for the effort. Like his father, and his father before him, life was about heading for the pub after a day's work, playing some darts, drinking some beer and, when they were playing at home, going to watch Folkestone Invicta FC play on a Saturday afternoon.

His father, though a functioning alcoholic, was, at least to Wes, the poster boy for that lifestyle. It didn't help that when he did meet up with some of his mates shortly after starting his first low-paid job, they did nothing but bitch and moan about the stresses and strains of higher education. More than once, they told him that they wished they'd chosen his path instead.

Wes followed his father's plan to the letter and for the next twenty years was perfectly happy with his lot. His weekdays were spent in Dover harbour as a general dock worker and in the evenings, when not in the pub, he'd go home to his wife of eighteen years. Though nobody would ever mistake Cindy for a supermodel, especially since she'd given birth to their two children, she was a kind woman with a handsome face.

Then things pretty much went to shit. One winter afternoon at work, as the light started to fade just after 3:30 in the afternoon, he'd somehow misjudged his footing as one of the ferries came into dock. He slipped off the quay and just managed to grab the heavy rope holding a dock fender in place. Unfortunately, nobody on the ferry or the dock saw him. The starboard hull of the Calais Princess nudged against that same buoy, in effect squashing his leg and smashing just about every bone within it.

It took eight operations and four years before he could walk and, even then, he was stuck with a pronounced limp that would not go away until he'd taken his last breath on this earth.

There were no jobs for a limping forty-year-old on the docks or anywhere else that could have provided Wes and his family anywhere near the income they had come to expect. Since the accident and his subsequent recovery, such as it was, Wes was forced to take menial work at menial pay.

Through a friend of a friend, he had been told about the new mine ride in Deal and had applied for the position of after-hours caretaker. There were astonishingly few applicants, not so much because of the work itself, but because half of each shift would be spent alone, hundreds of feet beneath the ground, picking up the detritus that visitors left behind within the mine itself.

The past four hours had been spent cleaning the mine cars after all the opening day celebration rides. Not only were the cars filled with discarded food and spilled drinks, but he also had to clean coal dust that had drifted down from the walls and ceiling, covering the cars and the locomotive with a thin black layer of what almost looked like soot. It was a thankless job that paid little and made Wes wish that he could go back in time and throttle his father before he'd brainwashed him into taking the easy route and settling for a very uninspired life.

Wes dragged the last bin bag to the elevator lobby where it joined the ten or so others. He looked back towards the tunnel as he unlocked the wall panel and switched off the overly bright maintenance lights. He could no longer see much farther than the first curve in the tracks and smiled as he remembered the ribbing he'd taken from his friends who all seemed to have stories about how the old Betteshanger Mine was haunted.

Apparently, after one particularly bad tunnel collapse, eighteen men died, and their bodies were never excavated. Their souls supposedly still roamed the mine. Wes had never seen a single ghost or anything else untoward while underground. In fact, he found the place somewhat calming. There was hardly any ambient sound, and because of the depth, the temperature remained consistently warm.

Even though the ride had only just opened, the tunnel had been functional for over six months. Instead of the future visitors who would end up littering the place, it was the mechanics and engineers who treated the tunnel like one great big waste bin. When he had first started work far below the surface of the planet, he had worn ear buds and played his music library as loud as he could, partially to ward off any errant spirits, but also to ward off the occasional sense of claustrophobia.

Within a matter of a few weeks, Wes had begun to like the solitude and otherworldly stillness and had ditched the tunes in favour of being able to hear the occasional motion of the earth and creaking of the old tunnel beams.

Once Wes realised that nothing was going to kill him down there, part of him – the part that his father had instilled in him – kind of enjoyed the solitude and stress-free nature of the gig.

He took one last look around then pressed the lift button. Considering that he was the only one to have used it all night, it was, as usual, already on the lower floor waiting for him.

During the slow but smooth rise up to the top, Wes wondered what the day would bring. Maybe there would be news about that old ship they took off the Goodwin Sands. Whatever the day had in store, he knew it couldn't faze him. Folkstone were playing at home in two days, and he had a pair of tickets to the game.

He shook his head at the fact that such a small token could somehow make life worth living.

The lift began to slow then came to a complete stop moments before the doors slid open.

*

It found itself back at the corner of Golf Road and Cannon Street. Armed humans were closing in and its brain just couldn't extrapolate the data needed to get out of the current predicament. All it could do was follow its instincts, which at that particular moment, were telling it to find a place to hide.

There was only one option, and that was to return to the open area with the strange tower where it had hidden amidst the ash in the halved barrel. As it had worked before, it hoped to stay concealed again in the same way.

By the time it reached the back of the food stands, the first of the troops appeared. It knew that they had seen it, and it knew that its only choice at that point was to go on the attack. At the back of its simple mind, a thread of innate memory reminded it that even if it was killed, it would simply return and carry on as before.

It stepped out from behind one of the stands, ready to rush the armed humans, when the strangest thing happened. A chime sounded from within the base of the tower. It turned towards the noise and could see, through the ground floor windows, a pair of interior doors slide magically open.

Without any conscious thought, it charged and crashed through the glass and rushed towards the opening, its simple mind believing that whatever lay beyond those doors, had to be better than any of the outside options.

As the doors fully opened a human male could be seen standing within what appeared to be a small square room. The male saw him and began jabbing at the inner wall. To the its horror, the doors began to close. Throwing all logic and instinct to the wind, it leapt the last few metres and slammed into the human just as they shut behind it and the room began to vibrate.

The human tried to back away, but the space was tight, and it was famished. Almost comically, the male held out his arms as if to ward off the attack.

As it feasted on the lean male flesh, the vibration continued as the lift headed back down, deep beneath the surface.

CHAPTER FORTY-TWO

Jay and Osbourne pulled into the above-ground section of the new 'Mine Experience', as the ride was called. They only just managed to see the Lusus barrelling towards the open lift door that carried visitors down to where the restored mine car ride took place.

A man they didn't know seemed about to emerge from within the lift when the creature knocked him back inside moments before the lift doors closed.

"That can't be good," Osbourne said as they stepped out of the vehicle, still not completely sure what he'd just witnessed.

"Where does that lift go?" Jay asked.

"Apparently some bright spark thought to reopen one particular tunnel within the old Betteshanger Mine and turn it into an amusement ride."

"How big was the mine?" Jay asked.

"I have no idea other than it was the biggest colliery in Kent," Osbourne replied.

"How do you know that?"

Osbourne pointed to one of the many banners that were strung above the welcome area. "It says so right there."

Jay read one to himself then shook his head. "Wonderful. The thing is now loose half a mile underground and has the biggest mine in Kent to hide in."

"I don't think it will like it down there for long. There's little to eat, I would imagine."

"We know it's having a meal on the way down, so that should tide it over for a while. The worst part is that we have absolutely no way of knowing what it's doing and where exactly it's going."

"Actually, that's not entirely the case," a voice said from behind them. Both men turned and looked at a well-dressed man in his late forties standing between two soldiers.

"Sorry sir," one of them said. "This gent claims to own this ride or whatever it is."

"Is that true?" Osbourne asked the man.

"Yes," he replied holding out his hand. "My name is Sasha Glenn. We only opened to the public the day before yesterday. May I ask what exactly is happening here and why you need to see what's down there?"

"We are trying to catch a missing dog," Osbourne replied.

Glenn looked around at the soldiers and their weapons then looked back, confused.

"It must be a very unusual dog."

Jay reached out and shook the man's hand. "Trust me, it is."

"Then you had better come with me to the operations room. It's pretty basic but it does have CCTV throughout the lift lobby and the tunnel."

They followed him to the back of the brick building

where a door led to a bland hallway. A unisex WC was at the far end while an opening led to a mini kitchenette on the right. Across the hall was the operations room and Glenn's description of it being basic was a blatant overstatement.

The room consisted of two workstations facing each other across what looked to be an inexpensive, laminate dining table. Both stations had a forty-two-inch monitor, and the proprietary software had split each screen into eight segments, each showing the status of some specific function within the ride.

"As you can see," Glenn said with a sense of pride, "each insert screen allows us to monitor everything from the temperature to the lighting, even the status of the locomotive. We had this designed—"

"You said something about us being able to see the tunnel from here," Osbourne interrupted.

"Sorry. Yes, of course," Glenn said as he sat down and pressed a couple of keys on a somewhat grubby keyboard.

The eight squares changed from status data to live video. Glenn touched the top right screen, which then expanded to fill the entire monitor. The image was clear, in colour, and showed the lift lobby at the lower level.

The lift doors seemed to be trying to open, but after only separating a few inches, they closed, and after a few more moments, tried again.

"What's going on down there?" Jay asked. "Why aren't those doors opening?"

"I don't know. Something is causing it to keep cycling through the opening and closing sequence for some reason."

Glenn reduced the image back to a smaller square then brought up the lift utility screen in another square. On it was a checklist of every function. All had green checks next to them except the third from the bottom. That one had a flashing red X.

"What's that mean?" Osbourne asked.

"That's the auto-opening solenoid. Something seems to have knocked it out of whack. It's stopped on the lower level, but the doors aren't opening. Give me a second."

He brought up a series of sub-menus and after a few tries at fixing the issue, opened the lift's master admin control page.

"I'm going to have to reboot the system," he announced.

"How long will that take?" Jay asked.

"Not very long at all."

The three watched as the screen went momentarily black then a stream of data swarmed across the monitor until it changed back to the checklist view. This time all the boxes were green.

Glenn enlarged the lift lobby camera feed.

"Can you zoom in on that?" Osbourne asked.

Glenn zoomed the camera so that the door filled the monitor screen. For a few seconds nothing happened then the doors slid open.

Glenn screamed.

Crouching down in the centre of the lift was the Lusus. It seemed oblivious to the door having opened as it tore at a particularly sinewy piece of leg meat from what remained of the night custodian. The rest of him was either splattered against the lift walls or had already been consumed.

Suddenly the creature stopped feeding and tilted its massive head to one side. Then, as if somehow sensing the others, it stared directly at the camera mounted on the lobby wall. Without taking his eyes off the camera, it rose to its feet. Maybe it was the lighting or maybe it was the quality of the camera, but its damaged face looked more grotesque than ever. It was obvious that the acid had continued to erode away flesh and bone since they had seen it in the hotel. Pieces of its muzzle had gone entirely revealing blackened bone and jagged fangs.

All three were too shocked to think clearly. It wasn't until the Lusus took a step towards the lift door that Jay shouted, "Shut the doors!! Don't let it out!"

Surprisingly, Glenn reacted fast and brought up the lift operation screen. He pressed the close button and the three stared, unblinking, at the monitor. The doors did start to shut, only by then the creature was half in, half out. The door briefly touched the Lusas's flanks, then, as required by safety regulation, opened back up again.

It stepped fully out of the lift and slowly walked to the far wall. The three men in the control centre got a very clear view as it suddenly reared up and clamped its massive jaws around the camera.

The screen went black.

Glenn had the wherewithal to immediately switch to a different camera feed – this one at the far end of the below ground lobby giving a view out into the tunnel proper. They watched in silence as the Lusus cautiously exited the lobby and walked towards the stationary mine cars that made up the Mine Experience.

Glenn was the first to speak, his voice little more than a croak.

"You weren't lying," he said. "That is one very unusual dog."

The others looked down at him but couldn't initially think of anything to say.

Finally, Jay broke the silence.

"What now?" he asked.

"Now we fight fire with fire," Osbourne replied.

"I assume that the fire you are referring to is the second Lusus?"

"I don't see that we have any other options at this point. That thing is now running free at the bottom of this mine. Do you know what that means? There must be dozens of tunnels and shafts running for countless miles right beneath us."

Jay turned to Glenn. "Apart from your operation here, is there any other access down to the tunnels?"

"No," he replied. "When it was decommissioned, every access was permanently sealed. This is the only way for it to get out."

"Could it find food down there?" Osbourne asked.

"I assume you mean animals it could feed on, and the answer is, yes. I wouldn't say that there are, what you'd call, rich pickings down there but there are rodents and bugs and insects that one would expect under the ground."

"Does it eat rodents and bugs?" Osbourne asked Jay.

"Who knows. The thing was created to only eat human males. I have no idea if it will switch its diet to what's at hand."

"Did you say it was created to eat humans?" Glenn asked as he looked up at the two visitors.

"I'm not sure what that means for us," Osbourne said, ignoring the question. "It's trapped down there. That means that as things stand, we are safe up here. Maybe we should just leave it there to die."

"From what I was told, it can never fully die unless its remains are completely destroyed, like with that acid, or if it is consumed by the second creature. Leaving it down there would just be putting off the inevitable."

"Why? There's nothing for it to feed upon, and if we shut off the air intake, it can't possibly survive."

"I agree. It will die and seemingly decompose, then at the first sign of oxygen, it will come right back to life again. Don't forget, we brought it up from a shipwreck that had been submerged for almost eighty years, and I don't have to remind you of the carnage that thing has wrought upon this town since then."

"Excuse me," Glenn interrupted their conversation. "We may have a small problem."

"What sort of problem?" Osbourne asked. "The elevator's out of action, right?"

"Yes. It can't possibly come up that way."

"Good, then what's the problem?"

Glenn, his hand shaking, enlarged one of the CCTV feeds so that it filled the monitor. The image was of a section of a stark looking concrete stairwell. The camera angle was looking down at the lower landing. On the far right of the image, a metal security door was slowly opening, seemingly by itself.

The three looked on in complete horror as the Lusus used its snout to push the emergency exit door open.

"Where is this?" Osbourne asked.

"The emergency exit staircase adjacent to the lift lobby."

"How many stairs are there?" Jay asked.

"Two thousand one hundred and sixty-seven," Glenn responded with a mix of pride and dread.

The other two gave him a puzzled look.

"I designed and built this place. I know these things."

"How long do you think it will take it to get up here?" Osbourne asked.

"Not long enough," Jay replied watching as the Lusus began walking up the stairs.

"If it does make it up to the top, please tell me that the door is locked?" Osbourne said.

"From the outside, yes."

The other two turned and glared at him.

"It's an emergency exit. It has to open from the inside. That's kind of the point."

The three stared at the screen for another few moments.

"Now do you think it's the right time to release the kraken?" Osbourne asked sarcastically.

Jay turned to him and slowly nodded.

CHAPTER FORTY-THREE

To ensure some degree of secrecy regarding the goings-on at the Mine Experience, soldiers were busy nailing plywood over the hole the Lusus had made as it smashed through the front window. Meanwhile, a team of soldiers was carefully removing the polished chrome cylinder that had, until very recently, been warehoused deep underground in one of Porton Down's most secure storage areas. Looking on was a circle of well-armed soldiers standing three-deep about ten metres from the Mine Experience tower.

The container was just over one and a half metres long and three-quarters of a metre wide. A steel, notched band encircled the centre of the cylinder. At one end was a simple swivel key that, when turned, would free the band's locking mechanism. A small steel plate was affixed to outside. On it were the letters LPO.

"What does that mean?" Osbourne asked.

"Last possible option," Jay replied. "At least that's what the doctor told me after his third bucket of brandy."

"I never imagined the boffins at Porton Down to have a sense of humour."

"I don't think that acronym was meant to be funny."

The men placed the container on a small handcart then turned to Jay and Osbourne for further instructions.

"You sure this is going to work?" Osbourne asked.

"I have as much idea as you do. The only thing I can tell you is that if the LPO works as well as the original Lusus, you don't want to be anywhere near that thing when it rises from the dead."

"I thought you said that this one was programmed to not attack humans?" Osbourne asked.

"That's what Wiseman told me right about the same time he mentioned that this version had never gone through the full testing regime. I'd say that we should all take that promise with a very large grain of salt."

Osbourne sighed then looked back at the two waiting soldiers.

"Where is it now?" he asked glancing over at Glenn who was staring at an iPad he was holding out in front of him."

"It's only come up nine levels. At this rate it will take it hours to get up here."

"Can you guarantee that?" Osbourne said before turning back to the soldiers. "You're safe to position the weapon now. Once you unlock the exit, place it on the landing just inside the door. One of you then has to turn that old locking mechanism, then exit the building immediately. You both clear on that?"

The men acknowledged that they were, even though they had no idea what was in the cylinder.

"There's a maintenance light directly above the centre of the landing," Glenn advised. "Place it there and the camera will get a better shot."

Both men turned to Osbourne to get approval to act on the civilian's suggestion.

"Do what he says."

As they wheeled the chrome cylinder through the exit door, Glenn suggested that they all regroup inside the operations room so they could have a better view of what was about to transpire on the staircase and below.

*

It stepped out of the lift while still chewing on a morsel from the disembowelled human it had consumed on the ride down to the bottom level.

The moment it walked into the lift lobby its senses immediately began reporting that there was something acutely wrong with where it currently found itself. The air smelled unnatural even compared to what existed within the tunnel system just below the town. There was a staleness and acidity that was like nothing it had ever encountered.

As it peered beyond the lobby to the main tunnel, the hair on its back involuntarily rose into full defensive posture. There was no scent of anything living within that tunnel. There was a vague trace of past human presence, but not enough to warrant a search any deeper within the machine-hewn chamber. It observed that unnatural light illuminated the first half of the tunnel, but after that, it rapidly darkened to pitch black.

It could tell that the only air that was reaching where

it currently stood was coming from one large, grated vent in the ceiling. Even though that same air carried hints of the outside world, by the time it was forced down into the darkening cavern, it took on the lifeless taste and smell of a dead place. A place that neither it nor humans could ever survive without scientific and mechanical intervention.

As it retreated into the lobby, it first explored the closed lift door. Though unable to reason at anything close to human level, it knew that the chamber beyond that door had somehow transported it down to where it now was. It tried pawing at the doors but couldn't get enough of a purchase to open them beyond a few centimetres. After several minutes it began exploring other parts of the lobby and was drawn to a smaller closed door. As it sniffed around the edges of the portal, it sensed fresher air than existed in the tunnel. It then quieted its breathing and held its good ear against the faux-wood veneer and thought it could almost make out the sound of human voices somewhere far, far away.

The door had a metal bar that ran horizontally across its middle and after nudging it with its snout to no effect, it raised its forepaws and leaned hard on the bar. Much to its surprise, the bar suddenly swivelled, and the door opened.

Driven by nothing more than genetically modified instincts, it tipped over a metal waste bin that had been placed there for the use of visitors, thereby jamming the door open, then began climbing the stairs.

*

Jay, Helena and Emma joined Glenn in the control room as Osbourne stood at the open exit door watching the two soldiers as they removed the canister from the handcart.

"You're doing fine," Osbourne encouraged them. "Lay it on the floor then turn the key."

The men did just that. Once the binding lock was released, the cylinder opened in two halves with a slight hiss. One half appeared empty, while the other was filled with a fine grey powder.

"What do we do now?" one asked.

"Get out of there."

The men again did as instructed. Once they were clear, Osbourne signalled to the driver of a military transport lorry to pull up tight against the door. Being as how it was designed to open outwards with great ease, it was the only quick solution he had come up with to stop either creature simply opening the exit door and scarpering.

Once the lorry was in place, Osbourne joined the others in the control room.

"Anything happening?" he asked.

"The Lusus looked as if it was speeding up, but as soon as your men opened that canister... let me show you," Glenn said as he high-speeded back to an earlier spot on the video. The Lusus was indeed making better time as it charged up the steps, three at a time. Then it froze and its ears dropped flat as it began slowly shaking its head from side to side.

"It's almost as if it knows what's going on," Helena observed.

"Maybe it does," Jay suggested.

Before anyone else could speak, Emma gasped and pointed at one of the small images on the screen. Glenn enlarged it, at which point they could all see what had startled her. The canister was still where it had been deposited, but the silt-like contents had shifted to one end. As they watched, pockets of the powdery material started to solidify, slowly at first, but then, after a few minutes, the process sped up exponentially.

Nobody said a word. They couldn't. Their minds were too awestruck. The pockets of powder soon became recognisable as the reincarnation speed continued to increase. Soon the scattering of bones became the skeletal outline of some sort of animal. At the same time as the bones were re-forming, a green ooze began to seep from them and form into musculature and a cardiovascular system.

Within less than fifteen minutes, the creature rose to its feet and cautiously stepped out of the bottom half of the canister.

"I was expecting something a little more vicious looking," Jay commented.

"That's our doomsday weapon?" Osbourne asked, the frustration evident in his voice.

"It looks like a golden retriever," Emma offered.

The others couldn't find fault with her comparison.

"And Wiseman said that that was going to kill and consume our Lusus?" Osbourne asked the room.

"I don't somehow see that happe—" Jay didn't finish his sentence as the newly formed creature suddenly bounded down the stairs towards its prey.

CHAPTER FORTY-FOUR

It sensed the activity at the top of the stairs as soon as the canister was placed on the landing. At first it felt only curiosity, then adrenaline began to flood its sensory system as its genetic instincts relayed warnings of high-level, impending danger.

It froze on the staircase and focused all its attention on the sounds, smells and even the taste of the air. It couldn't be certain what exactly was above it, but it knew that whatever it was would soon be fully regenerated and looking to find and kill a very specific prey.

Even with its limited capacity to undertake deep reasoning, it knew that it had become that prey and it had best find a better site for what it was sure would be a substantial battle.

While trying to work out where to go to either hide or make a stand, it sensed the entity complete its regeneration and begin the descent towards where it was currently standing.

The Lusas turned and ran as fast as its damaged body would allow.

*

"It's reached the bottom," Glenn remarked as the original Lusus stepped out of the stairwell and began to lope deeper into the tunnel.

"Where's the other one?" Emma asked.

"As I mentioned before, we didn't have the budget to install a camera at every one of the stair returns. We know it passed the halfway mark, but the next camera is between that and the bottom."

"So how long will it take it to—" Jay didn't need to finish his question as they all saw the LPO tear past the three-quarter mark.

"It's got about five hundred steps to go," Glenn advised solemnly.

"I assume that we can follow both creatures via your camera network?" Jay asked.

"Only for the length of the ride, which is just under half a mile. The tracks do go further, but that was just so we could use them to transport equipment from the dumping area out to the section we reclaimed for the ride. After that, we didn't do any restoration or install cameras or anything. There's a third of a mile of abandoned equipment and minor tunnel collapses. We didn't see the point. The lighting and cameras stop a good quarter mile before that, but the track, as I mentioned earlier, carries on right up to the dumping ground."

"The original Lusus better get a move on or the other one's going to catch up pretty soon," Emma commented.

Jay turned and gave her a puzzled look. "You do know

that we want it to catch up, right?"

"Of course. My concern is that the LPO is half the size of the first one, and I don't see how it could possibly kill it even if does reach it."

"I can't say I disagree with you, but Wiseman said the thing was created specifically to destroy the original. So, considering how well Lusus 1 has been functioning according to its genetic directive, we have to hope that the LPO will do as good a job."

"Speaking of which," Emma continued. "What happens to the second one when it's finished its business, considering it must be just as indestructible?"

"Supposedly, it bears no malice towards humans whatsoever," Jay commented. "It's currently hunting its one and only prey and when it has destroyed and consumed the Lusus, will simply approach the nearest human as would any well-trained dog."

"Let's not forget that it is not a dog," Osbourne reminded them. "If it's capable of destroying the original Lusus, then it is a highly dangerous weapon just like the original. The only difference between the two is the programming, and while I concur with the adage of not being able to teach an old dog new tricks, I'm not sure I would want to gamble my life on the assumption that it couldn't somehow be reprogrammed into something far more dangerous."

"May I suggest we focus on what is about to happen in that tunnel rather than getting bogged down with the ramifications of what may or may not be the outcome of our little gladiatorial event down in the mine."

"Which just got more interesting," Glenn stated as he pointed to the bottom right of the monitor.

The LPO had reached the bottom level and was easing itself through the door that the Lusas had left wedged open.

"It still looks like any other golden retriever. It's even got a smile on its face," Emma commented.

The five sat in absolute silence as they observed the LPO trot up to the end mine car. After sniffing the air, it moved under one of the overhead spotlights, then sat back onto its haunches.

"It's waiting," Jay said in a whisper. "I was expecting something a little more aggressively proactive than for it to just sit around until its prey makes the first move – and speaking of which, where did it go?"

"Last I saw, the Lusus was checking out the locomotive," Glenn replied.

They were all so fixated on trying to spot the original Lusus in or around the locomotive that when it did suddenly jump down from the driver's compartment, all five of them were completely startled.

"Sneaky little fucker," Helena said once she'd caught her breath.

They watched as the larger canine, its coat bristling and its fangs in full view, stepped out into the light and, settling on its haunches, stared down its adversary.

"It's like an old western gun fight," Jay said.

"Except with teeth and claws instead of bullets," Emma answered, matter-of-factly.

The LPO seemed almost bored as she sat looking over at

her sibling (scientifically speaking). The Lusus was nowhere near as composed and was visibly becoming more and more agitated by the minute.

Just as the observers were starting to think that nothing was going to happen, the golden retriever clone placed one paw out in front then drew it back across the bare earth.

That was it.

"What was that about?" Osbourne asked.

"Probably nothing," Jay started to say just as the Lusus rose on all fours and stepped forward. With its coat still bristling and its teeth bared, it slowly moved towards the other canine. It wasn't until it neared the LPO that its demeanour suddenly changed completely. It dropped its head and lowered itself to the floor, at which point it basically dragged itself forward until it was only centimetres from the female.

Osbourne looked as if he was about to speak, but instead screamed as the LPO's head and upper body expanded in less than a second. Though the back half still looked like a golden retriever, the front half looked like a cross between a grizzly bear and a hyena.

In one blindingly fast move, it raked a claw that only seconds before had been a furry looking front paw across the original Lusas's throat, ripping away everything but its spine.

Before any of the observers could fully react, the LPO grabbed the Lusas's seemingly lifeless body within its jaws then sprang to its feet and trotted deeper into the tunnel.

"What the fuck!" Jay said as the others stared, shocked,

at the video screen.

*

Even before it stepped out of the locomotive, it somehow knew that what it was about to face was not something it could destroy. In fact, in a strange way, as it approached the harmless looking canine, it understood that its time was over.

Instead of fear or anger, it felt a sense of calm, knowing that for the first time in its life, it would not be able to regenerate and live again. Somewhere in its genetically butchered brain, that thought gave it comfort, knowing that it would never again have to feel the craving to kill, nor the sense of dread at being constantly hunted down.

When the front of the creature changed into a monstrous mutant and tore away its throat, it did not immediately die. Instead, almost as if drugged as it had often been when first created, it felt as if it was floating above the ground rather than being clenched in another's jaws.

It was carried deep into the tunnel. At first there were lights that humans had strung along the walls, but after a while all illumination ended, and yet its destroyer continued, only able to see its way because of its genetically modified vision.

Finally, they reached a section of the tunnel that seemed to be filled with old and unworking human machines. It felt the jaws relax and sensed itself fall to the ground. It managed to look up into the eyes of the other monster, hoping to see some sort of compassion or at least regret.

All it saw was lustful hunger.

The blood loss, coupled with the injuries it had sustained after its dousing with acid, had drained all of its strength. It desperately wanted to stay conscious so it could comprehend what was happening, but the moment it hit the ground, its eyes closed, and it drifted into a dark oblivion.

For a fleeting second, it felt that just maybe, it had already died and that it would never again feel any more pain. Then the other creature used its jaws to pull away a sizeable piece of flesh from its left thigh and it understood that it was being eaten alive.

Oddly there was little pain. Instead, it sensed its own flesh melding with the other beast's body and, just before taking its last breath, it knew that they were somehow combining and creating something very special.

Something both enduring and indestructible.

*

As the LPO consumed the creature as it had been programmed to do, it sensed a feeling of inner peace and fulfilment. After all, its entire purpose was to achieve one goal – one simple goal then it too could rest. Now that was complete it somehow knew that it had to find the closest human and allow him or her to take charge of its destiny, whatever that might be.

The strange thing was that as it consumed the creature, it could actually feel the meat and blood somehow combine with its own. It knew, though in a very basic way, that its own chemistry was being altered and that something within it was already starting to form.

As it turned to head back towards the humans that it could sense would soon locate it, the LPO stopped as a wave of extreme nausea and severe cramping consumed it.

It moved closer to one of the dark outlines of an abandoned piece of machinery and found a spot that could not be seen from any direction without knowing exactly where to look.

It suddenly began retching. As the pain grew, the retching intensified to the point that it felt something rising within its gullet.

CHAPTER FORTY-FIVE

The five stared at the screen without speaking as the LPO dragged the incapacitated male deeper into the tunnel. Not a word was said until the pair reached a bend and disappeared from view.

"Up until two days ago," Helena commented, breaking the silence. "I was thinking of getting a puppy."

Jay turned to her and with a straight face said, "What's changed?"

"Do you mind if we take this a little more seriously? We need to stay rational at this point," Osbourne snapped at the pair.

"That's not possible," Jay replied. "We left rational the moment we went back into that old cinema. What we're living through now can't be taken seriously or your mind will explode."

"Be that as it may, what has just happened was real and we need to get down there and make sure that the original has been destroyed as advertised."

"How do you plan on doing that?" Emma asked. "Why don't we just wait and see if the LPO reappears?"

"I don't believe that Whitehall would approve of my

troops simply waiting to see what happens. I need to speak with my munitions team and see if we have the capability of sealing that entire tunnel once and for all."

"Excuse me for interrupting," Glenn said sarcastically. "But I just spent the past five years and every penny I have creating this ride, and you have no right whatsoever to—"

"Actually, I have every right," Osbourne fired back. "As officer in charge, I have the authority to do whatever it takes to ensure that this fiasco ends right now."

"I thought I was in charge?" Jay pointed out.

"You were only in charge when your knowledge of the tunnels under the town was valuable to us. Unless you have some insight as to the layout of the mine tunnels below us, you are, to put it in simple words, of no more use to me."

Osbourne stood and stormed out of the control room.

"What a lovely man," Emma commented as she rolled her eyes. "Isn't there something that we can do?"

"I don't see what," Jay replied.

"What if *we* brought the goldie out," Helena offered.

"Are you suggesting that we go wandering, unarmed into that tunnel and just hope that the cute little doggie doesn't rip us to shreds? We don't have the manpower, the lighting or the equipment to try and get all the way into that tunnel."

"That's not entirely true," Glenn said as he grinned at the other three.

After explaining his idea, the others looked at one another to gauge each of their reactions.

"Won't they see us going for the lift?" Emma asked.

"They would have, but with the shattered window now

covered with plywood we won't be seen."

"How's that possible?" Jay asked. "The window might be boarded, but the main door was left wide open. We'd have to walk right in front of the entire British army just to get into the lift lobby."

"No, we wouldn't," Glenn replied as he slid his desk chair backwards so that he could lean into the hallway. "See that door with the hi-voltage warning? That just happens to lead to the equipment room, which just happens to lead into—"

"The lobby!" Emma finished his sentence for him.

"So, the four of us are supposed to sneak into the lobby, take the lift down to the tunnel, then take a mine car ride deep into a place where we know that a pair of mutant killing machines are waiting."

"Pretty much, yes," Glenn replied.

"Just so I have all the facts, your reasoning for us to risk our lives is so that your amusement ride doesn't get nuked out of existence. Is that about it or did I miss something in the subtlety of the situation?"

Glenn grinned again. "No, you pretty much summed it up quite well."

Jay turned to the two women and saw the eager expressions that both were sporting.

"Oh fuck!"

*

Unarmed and, in the case of everyone except Jay, not dressed suitably for the occasion, the four entered the lobby unseen and stepped into the lift that Glenn had summoned with his iPad. All knew that the Lusus had slaughtered the night custodian in that very same claustrophobic space, but none had imagined quite the degree of gore that they would encounter. When seen on a TV monitor, the carnage had been bad enough, but a flat screen image cannot fully do justice to what happens when a human body is literally torn into shreds then partially consumed. The smell alone was enough to cause all of them to gag. There was something about the stench of raw meat, excrement and coppery blood that could not be captured and reproduced on a monitor, no matter how many lines of resolution the screen might have.

As they descended, Glenn continued to study the multiple camera feeds on his iPad both from the lower lobby and from the tunnel itself.

"How can you still be getting a signal for that thing?" Jay asked. "You can't have Wi-Fi way down here."

"Of course I can. The lift is hard wired as a hub. There's even Wi-Fi in the tunnel. I knew that though the visitors might like the authenticity of the ride, they would still want to share their experience on social media in real time."

"Any sign of our furry little friend?"

"Unfortunately, no. I don't think there's much doubt that it ventured past the restored section and is most likely hiding among the old, abandoned machinery."

The mood in the lift grew darker and more tense the farther they descended into the earth. Finally, with a gentle deceleration, they reached the bottom and the doors opened. The four practically burst out of the lift all gasping for air that wasn't tainted by the tang of a disembowelled human.

Staring intently at the bend in the tunnel just in case the canine monster chose to make an appearance, they made their way to the front mine car. Jay, Emma and Helena sat themselves in the cramped interior as Glenn powered up the locomotive. Thankfully, since its electrification, it made very little sound other than a high-pitched whine.

"You ready?" Glenn whispered over his shoulder.

"Not remotely," Jay replied with a false, toothy grin.

The mine cars began to move. At first, the passengers thought that the near-silent running would continue, but as the locomotive picked up speed, the noise of the old steel cars rattling against each other and friction of the metal wheels against the rails filled the tunnel with a cacophony of unwanted sound.

"It's making too much noise," Jay shouted at Glenn.

"So are you," came the reply from the engineer's platform of the locomotive.

No more was said as they rounded the first bend and headed deeper into the mine proper. As Glenn had advised, the walls were strung with low voltage light that, while hardly bright enough to allay their fears, gave enough illumination for them to at least see that nothing was waiting in the shadows.

The journey, though only a half mile in length, became almost monotonous. The rattling and grinding coupled with the low lighting started to lull the passengers into a false sense of normality.

Then, without warning, the mine cars began to shake seconds before an overhead support beam gave way sending blackened dirt skittering down the tunnel walls. To make matters worse, the lights began to flicker and for a horrid few seconds went off entirely.

"Get us the fuck out of here," Jay shouted. "It's caving in."

Glenn slowed their progress and turned to face them.

"Sorry about that. I should have warned you. That's just part of the ride. We thought it needed a little more excitement."

Emma, in a stern but still shaky voice asked, "Will there be any more little surprises?"

"No. Absolutely not. I could only afford one effect like that."

"What a shame," Helena said under her breath.

The sense of calm never returned to the passengers, so, when they reached the end of the reinforced and restored section of the tunnel, they were not emotionally prepared for the sudden darkness.

"This might help," Glenn called from the front.

The locomotive's high-powered headlight snapped on illuminating everything in front of it. The three leaned forward so they could get the same view as Glenn, but found the sight unnerving, if not downright scary. Not only was the light showing the true condition of a mine tunnel untouched in many decades, but it brought to the forefront the fact that they really were heading into a very inhospitable environment.

The fact that somewhere out in the cavernous blackness,

the LPO was waiting, didn't help the mood at all.

"I should warn you," Glenn shouted back to the others. "This part of the track hasn't been restored either, so the trip is likely to get a bit bumpy."

"Physically or mentally," Helena asked sarcastically.

"I would expect both," Jay suggested.

Glenn slowed the locomotive to little more than walking speed, which, though perhaps safer, did nothing to improve the ride.

"Not much longer till we reach the end of the—" he started to say just before a huge chunk of rock dropped from the tunnel ceiling and fell onto the engine housing causing the headlight to go off.

As Glenn stopped the mine car dead in its tracks, Jay leaned into the cab.

"For Christ's sake. I thought you said that there were no more special effect surprises?"

"I did, and I meant it. That was not an effect. The vibration from the locomotive must have loosened that rock from the ceiling."

"Then get us out of here," Emma said in little more than a whisper.

"I can't until I check that the engine's not damaged."

Glenn's cell phone screen snapped on and once he'd pressed the right icon, its flashlight suddenly illuminated the cab.

"You all stay seated while I have a quick look," he said as he stepped down onto the bare earth and moved to the front of the locomotive.

By the light of his phone, he could see that the rock wasn't as big as he had feared and that it had only put a slight dent into the engine cover. After managing to push the rock to the ground as the others looked on nervously, he opened both sides of the engine cowling and poked and prodded until he was satisfied that nothing catastrophic had happened.

"It all looks good," he called back to the others. "I think the headlight only went out because the impact caused one of the connectors to come loose. Let me just…"

There were some tinkering sounds then the light snapped back on illuminating the tunnel ahead.

Helena was the first to scream. Jay was a close second with Emma just managing to hold hers back.

Glenn looked at them in complete confusion, then following their line of sight turned and faced away from the engine.

Sitting casually in the middle of the tunnel, the headlight framing it perfectly, was the LPO. It looked as harmless as any other golden retriever but for the fresh smear of blood that ran down its left side from muzzle to midsection.

CHAPTER FORTY-SIX

For the longest time, neither the humans nor the creature made any sort of movement, then, before anyone could stop him, Jay stepped towards it as he slowly removed his belt.

"Get back here," Emma said in as calm a voice as possible, not wanting to startle the animal.

Jay ignored her words and covered half the distance to where the LPO was standing.

"Are you a good girl?" he asked in that babytalk way that humans speak to their pets.

The LPO tilted its head as if confused by Jay's question. Jay had seen what the canine could turn into, yet as he looked at the animal, it seemed just like any other well-groomed (apart from the blood) and well-trained golden retriever. Even as he studied it, the creature got to its feet and approached him, its tongue lolling out the left side of its mouth as it formed into what appeared to be a contented smile.

Something in Jay told him that there was no malice coming out of the animal and that they were perfectly safe.

As the others looked on in abject horror, Jay held out his hand. The LPO stepped up close to him and leaned its weight against Jay's thigh.

Jay slowly showed the animal his belt that he had formed into a loop. Without any prodding, it gently placed its head within the makeshift collar and smiled up at Jay who then slowly tightened it. Jay looked to the others with an expression of surprise and pride. He was about to walk the animal back to the mine car when it calmly turned and pulled against the leather, letting Jay know that it wanted to go somewhere else.

Jay gave the onlookers a quick look of dismay as the LPO led him away from them, deeper into the tunnel. Emma was about to run over to them, but Glenn held her back.

"I think it's best we leave them do whatever that thing intends. So far, it's been as docile as a newborn lamb. I don't think we should try and change that."

The three watched as Jay was led beyond the reach of the headlight into the part of the tunnel that was littered with abandoned equipment.

Jay used his phone for light as the LPO led him past piles of unrecognisable steel hulks that had once been part of the mine's operation but were now just rotting metal carcasses. After passing one exceptionally large piece of equipment, the canine turned right and led Jay to a clear area close to the tunnel wall where the hulk of an old mine car lay abandoned. There were signs of a recent tussle where the ground had been disturbed as the LPO destroyed the Lusus.

Even with the disturbed earth, there was nothing left that would help confirm the destruction of the creature, or so Jay initially thought. With its tail wagging and with a joyfulness to its gait, the LPO nudged him to the end of an upturned and rusty mine car. There, positioned between the wheels, almost like a trophy, was the oversized skull of something canine. A large portion of its muzzle had been eaten away by something corrosive.

The goldie lookalike smiled up at Jay the way a family dog does after retrieving a ball.

"Good girl," Jay said as he gently patted its head. Then, with far more bravery than he thought he had, he reached down and picked up the trophy.

*

"We've had enough," Mayor Haley said, his voice raised. "We've been shut in that bloody school building for too long. The toilets have overflowed, the food is a disgrace, and the people are about to walk out if something isn't done, danger or not."

Osbourne took a deep breath and forced something close to a smile. "I understand. We all understand," he said as he gestured to the troops who were preparing some serious looking explosive devices as well as a mobile version of the acid tank. "The entire reason for you and the other residents having been kept in the school was for your own safety. You, more than just about anyone else within the school grounds, must see the reason for this. You saw the creature at the restaurant."

"I did, and I also know for a fact that the beast is now somewhere below ground inside what's left of the old

Betteshanger Mine. Having been down on that godawful ride myself, I know full well that there is no way that thing is going to make its way back up here unless it knows how to operate a lift. Considering the residents were removed from their homes because of the threat of something coming up through their basements, and that threat is no longer valid, why can't we all be let go home?"

Osbourne, not wanting to divulge the fact that the creature had been carried off by yet another monster, was about to spin a tapestry of military bollocks explaining why the people were safer in the school when he noticed everyone in front of him staring at something over his shoulder. A wave of freezing ice cascaded down his spine as he imagined that the beast had not only escaped but was stalking him at that very moment.

With his hand dropping to his sidearm, he spun around as Emma, Helena and Glenn emerged from the lift lobby of the mine ride. Just behind them was Jay leading the LPO by what looked to be a modified leash made from a belt. As Jay neared him, he held up the skull of the original Lusus.

"This should go into the acid immediately," he said as he held it out for Osbourne to take.

"You went down there?"

"We had to. You were so eager to blow the whole thing up that we decided to pre-empt such unnecessary destruction and see if we couldn't find proof of the Lusus having been destroyed."

"Did you find proof?" Osbourne asked.

Jay, puzzled, nodded to the skull he was still holding."

"How are we to know that that isn't just some old skull you happened to find down there?"

"First of all, it's not exactly teaming with life down in that mine, secondly, you should be able to recognise the area where the acid destroyed its mouth and thirdly, if you look closely at the underside of the skull, you will see that there are a few minute bits of flesh still attached, and if you keep watching them, you will see that they seem to be trying to replicate and grow."

Osbourne took a step backwards as he shouted for one of the nearby soldiers to take the thing and drop it into the acid bath. There was dead silence as a young man took hold of the skull and marched it at arm's length to the waiting acid tank that was tucked away behind one of the vendor stands.

Jay and the others watched, albeit from an oblique angle, the man hand the skull to a fellow soldier who was clad from head to toe in a dense rubberised material. The woman took the remains in her gloved hand, then used a pair of industrial tongs to hold it between the eye sockets before slowly lowering it into the liquid.

The skull began to fizzle. Within less than a minute it had become a shapeless lump and by the five-minute mark had vanished altogether.

"That stuff really seems to work," Jay commented. "What happens to it now? You can hardly dump it down the loo."

"It will be disposed of by the original manufacturer as soon as we have finished with it here."

"I thought you were finished," Emma stated. "There's nothing left to use it on."

"Oh, but there is," Osbourne replied as he looked down at the LPO. "It's time for this little doggie to have a nice bath."

"You can't do that," Jay pulled the animal closer to him. "That would be like torture."

"You're absolutely right. What was I thinking?" Osbourne drew his sidearm and, without warning, shot the creature in the head. "Get this thing into the acid before it starts to regenerate," he ordered the waiting troops.

"You are as big of a monster as the Lusus was," Emma shouted at the man. "That dog was as placid as they come."

"That dog was also owned by the Ministry of Defence, and they gave me very specific instructions of what to do once it had outlived its usefulness."

"And you are one hundred percent certain that that day has come?" Jay asked as a team loaded the carcass on a handcart and wheeled it over to the acid tank.

There was a moment of silence as the body was lowered into the acid.

"There was only one original Lusus and that thing," he pointed to the retriever's inert body. "Was created for the specific purpose of destroying it should the need arise. That need did arise, and it did exactly what it said on the tin. Ipso facto, with the job done, its entire purpose came to an end."

"How do you know that there aren't others just like the original?" Emma asked. "We only know of the one that ended up here because it escaped. Who's to say they didn't create a bunch more?"

"I am willing to run that risk," Osbourne declared. "Now, if I may suggest, you lot are supposed to be working on that wreck that is currently being housed in Dover. Perhaps you should focus your concerns on that piece of history instead of this one."

"Does that mean you are lifting the quarantine?" Jay asked.

"What quarantine? The fact that there were a few troops scattered around this lovely town was simply part of a military exercise."

"What a load of bollocks," the mayor growled as he stepped into the fray. "You evicted a half mile of residents and kept them and me shut away in the old school building."

"That was only because, while we were carrying on the exercise, we learned of there being a rabid dog on the loose and thought it best to keep those of you near where it had been spotted, safe for the night."

"I will not permit such—" the mayor started.

"Before you formally tell me what you will and will not do," Osbourne interrupted, "I should advise you that the rest of the townsfolk who were inconvenienced overnight have, as we speak, been informed that as of this moment, they are all bound by the Official Secrets Act. You should be aware that you too are now bound by the same law." He then turned to face Emma. "This includes you, as well as Mr Glenn."

"What about us?" Jay asked gesturing to Helena.

"You both signed such a declaration when you joined the Marine Archaeology Trust. As a government support entity, it's standard practice."

"What about all the media that's been in town during all

this?" Helena asked.

"We've already spoken to them and apologised if our little training exercise inconvenienced them in any way. Besides, if there is one consistent trait among reporters it's their love of the demon rum. You'd be amazed just how many of them managed to stay inebriated for the past twenty-four hours. Most never even knew that anything was out of the ordinary."

"This drinking they were all coincidentally doing at the same time," Helena continued. "Was it voluntary?"

Osbourne shook his head as if he'd just heard gibberish from a young child.

"This isn't a police state, young lady."

As Helena levelled a near-lethal stare at the officer, the mayor spoke. "What about me? What if I simply refuse to accept something as archaic as the Secrets Act?"

"That's your right," Osbourne replied. "However, such an action will doubtless result in some very keen interest from MI6. They always get a tad suspicious when people refuse to protect their country's best interests. But, if you are not concerned about them poking into every dark corner of your life from taxes to sexual proclivities, then feel free to refuse."

"So, all of this just disappears?" Jay asked.

"All of what?" Osbourne replied with a wink and a lopsided grin.

CHAPTER FORTY-SEVEN

Jay and Emma were alone as they walked to the hotel along the seaside promenade. Helena didn't join them as she was still so furious about the killing of the dog that she went in search of the unhealthiest breakfast she could find.

The early fog had cleared, and the day was sparklingly blue, and with the tide low, they could see the clear outline of France just across the Channel. There were surprisingly few people out and about despite it being mid-morning on a workday.

"I suppose you will be wanting to get back over there as soon as you can after all you've been through?" Jay asked.

"I am on assignment here if you recall," she replied with a cheek-dimpling smile. "We have a wreck to evaluate and that will almost certainly lead to some extensive research. I could be here for months."

Jay nodded.

"That's all you have to say?" she asked. "If you would prefer me to go back, I will. I just thought that, maybe..."

"I've often wondered what would have happened if we'd been less reactive and actually tried to weather those storms we seemed to concoct for no good reason," Jay said as he stopped and stared across the white-capped water. "I've always had this gnawing idea that, just as you said earlier, there might still be some unfinished business between us."

"Business? That's a rather cold word for what we had."

"I need to tell you something." Jay turned to face her. "I've never stopped loving you for a minute."

"Then why the cold shoulder whenever we've run into each other?"

"Call it self-protection."

"Protection from what, being together – being happy?"

"Protection from our trying again and failing again. This may sound a bit pathetic, but it's been the possibility that we could have made things work that has kept me going. If we had tried again and just repeated the same old cycle, I would have been left with nothing."

"Are you saying that you would prefer to not even try just in case we fail? That *is* pathetic. I'll have you know that I love you too and am willing to try again even if we fuck things up even worse than the first time. At least that way I will know that we tried."

"That sounds like a stoically French response," Jay said before turning back towards the hotel."

"That's because I am stoically French, you soppy Englishman."

Jay smiled to himself as he started walking.

"That's it?" she called after him. "You just walk off?"

"Not at all. I would like you to walk with me on this fine morning while I try to get my thoughts into some sort of order."

"When you say get your thoughts in order, are you

including thoughts about us?"

"Number one on my checklist."

Emma shook her head and caught up to him.

*

The moment they walked into the hotel, they knew that things had again changed. The reception desk phones were ringing off the hook and everyone they could see seemed to be either texting or talking on their mobile phones.

"Things seem to be getting back to normal," Emma observed as they made for the main staircase.

Jay didn't say a word as they climbed to the top floor and Emma started to feel a knot tightening in her belly. She had always known that he was a stubborn man and only felt comfortable when things were organised and appropriately sorted.

Once they reached the landing, Emma wasn't sure what to say. She was about to head off towards the room she had shared with Helena when Jay gently took her by the hand, and without a word or even a glance, led her towards his room.

"What are you doing?" Emma asked, her heart fluttering in her chest.

"Something I should have done a long time ago," he said as he opened the door and let her pass. Before focussing all his attention on the woman he was terrified of losing all over again, he placed the *DO NOT DISTURB* sign on the door handle and closed the door.

EPILOGUE

Half a mile beneath the earth, deep within Tunnel 57 of the long defunct Betteshanger Mine, a lone rat crept out of its lair within one of the discarded mechanical hulks that populated the dark cavern. It was drawn by the scent of blood, but also by a sense of movement in a place where, before that day, there had been none.

There was no shortage of food in the mine even if it had required the rodent population to adapt their diet from fruits and vegetation to insects and fungi. Despite feeling relatively sated, its instinct forced it to investigate any possibility of a new food source.

Born in total darkness, the rodent could see almost as well in utter blackness as its relatives above that had the benefit of light.

Its tiny brain led it through the maze of discarded equipment to one particularly large metallic object. As soon as it rounded the base of the man-made monstrosity, it saw the source of what had triggered its senses. Lodged against one side of the machine were a batch of what first appeared to be some sort of fungus, but as it got closer, it instead saw, not a member of the mushroom family, but a row of incandescent orbs, each roughly the size of a large male tunnel rat.

Inside each one, a small dark mass was thrashing about amidst a red-coloured liquid. The rat's senses could, even through the orb's protective outer membrane, tell that the liquid was a mix of blood and some unfamiliar fluid that seemed to radiate a low level of ultraviolet light.

The rat approached the nearest orb and sniffed it from top to bottom. It had hoped that by doing so, it could learn more information about the find, but disappointedly picked up nothing new at all.

What it did notice was that as it neared the object, the black mass within became even more agitated. The rat looked down the row of identical orbs and saw that the squirming mass within every single one was reacting the same way.

Curious, it stepped even closer to the first one and gently stretched its nose out until it actually touched the membrane. The last thing it saw was the dark mass suddenly grow to the point that it filled out the entire orb. Before the rat could back away, a black claw protruded from the gooey outer membrane and grabbed the rat by the head. Faster than any eye could see, the rodent was dragged into the orb where its flesh and genetics melded with those already within the protective housing.

Even as little more than a struggling embryo, it had sensed the interloper and reacted completely by instinct alone.

Though its brain was far from sentient, it still felt pleasure at consuming living flesh.

Despite the fact that the other orbs had not partaken directly in the kill, every embryo felt the same sense of satisfaction as well as the first hint of the insatiable craving that would exist within them for the rest of their lives.

THE END